THE PATIENT

While working as a GP, Jane Shemilt completed a post-graduate diploma in Creative Writing at Bristol University and went on to study for the MA in Creative Writing at Bath Spa, gaining both with distinction. Her first novel, *Daughter*, was selected for the Richard & Judy Book Club, shortlisted for the Edgar Award and the Lucy Cavendish Fiction Prize, and went on to become the bestselling debut novel of 2014. Since then Jane has published three more bestselling thrillers: *Little Friends*, *The Drowning Lesson*, and *How Far We Fall*. Her books have sold more than 700,000 copies and been published in multiple languages. *The Patient* is her first novel with HarperCollins, and will be out in April 2022.

She and her husband, a professor of neurosurgery, have five children and live in Bristol.

janeshemilt.com
🐦 @Janeshemilt
📷 @jane.shemilt

JANE SHEMILT

The Patient

HarperCollins*Publishers*

HarperCollins*Publishers*
1 London Bridge Street
London, SE1 9GF

www.harpercollins.co.uk

HarperCollins*Publishers*
1st Floor, Watermarque Building, Ringsend Road
Dublin 4, Ireland

Published by HarperCollins*Publishers* 2022
1

A catalogue record for this book is available from the British Library

ISBN: 978-0-00-847591-8

This novel is entirely a work of fiction.
The names, characters and incidents portrayed in it are
the work of the author's imagination. Any resemblance to
actual persons, living or dead, events or localities is
entirely coincidental.

Set in Sabon LT Std 10.5/13.5 pt
by Palimpsest Book Production Limited, Falkirk, Stirlingshire

Printed and bound in the UK using 100% Renewable Electricity
at CPI Group (UK) Ltd

MIX
Paper from
responsible sources
FSC
www.fsc.org   FSC™ C007454

This book is produced from independently certified FSC™ paper
to ensure responsible forest management.

For more information visit: www.harpercollins.co.uk/green

For my family.

Prologue

June 2017

The footsteps were buried inside other sounds to start with: rain pattering on leaves, branches sighing in the wind, a lorry in the distance on the Blandford road. I thought I was hearing things again, things that Nathan had told me weren't really there.

There were few streetlights along this path, the floodlit cathedral behind the trees cast shadows on the gravel. A woman had been murdered here at night a hundred years ago; on cloudy nights like this one, walking here felt dangerous.

Sometimes the constable who policed the Close walked his German Shepherd here, or the laughter of women up ahead going home from the pub would echo back. I'd feel included, or maybe just safer.

I was out of luck tonight.

I began to hurry. The footsteps were louder now, closer. They sounded real. My skin crawled as if a swarm of ants were making their way from my collar up into my hair.

I wanted to put my hand to the back of my neck, but I was afraid of other fingers reaching to touch mine.

I wish I'd turned round, I should have done; I was forty-nine, a doctor, a wife and a mother, used to facing trouble.

I skirted a puddle and a few seconds later there was a little splash as a foot landed in the water. I began to run.

Chapter 1

My lawyer advised me to write everything down from the beginning, but it didn't have a beginning, not like that. I'd been walking towards this for years. If I had to pick a time, I'd go back to the moment I parked my car in the almost-empty car park five months ago. I needn't have done that. I could have gone straight home, I nearly did. Up to that point, the gods could have swerved me from my path, and I'd be at home with my husband now, instead of sitting in a brightly lit custody cell on my own.

The lights in the health centre reception were still on, which was strange at eight in the evening. Carol must be working late, waiting for me to return the medical notes after my weekly visit to Sarum Nursing Home. I had several bundles, lifetimes of problems and investigations, letters and results squashed untidily into pale brown cardboard envelopes. We kept those bundles for visits because they were portable and we were used to them. A link with the past when doctors had more time. Roger Morris, the senior partner, liked them. The writing itself was a clue for

3

other doctors, he said, a scrawled exclamation mark spoke volumes.

I almost didn't return them. Nathan would be at home; he might have started supper. We'd agreed to make an effort, I'd promised to play my part, but the notes belonged in the practice and if I took them home I'd be breaking a rule. Back then I was still a good girl, as Nathan would say, or at least I went by the rules. It would take just a few minutes to dump them in the tray. I indicated right into the car park and drove through the gates. I'd leave straight afterwards, drive home through Salisbury's quiet streets and then the quieter ones of the Cathedral Close and still be back in time for supper. We'd watch the ten o'clock news and one of us would take the dog for a last walk. Nathan would check the doors were locked and then we'd go to bed.

We wouldn't have sex. Sex was rare these days, Nathan was preoccupied and the truth was I didn't want to make love. I couldn't remember when we last had but I remembered the soreness, hormones or the lack of them, lack of desire too. Sweating could overtake me at night. Headaches as well, piercing sometimes. Tiredness, mine and Nathan's. It was both our busy lives, and no one's fault. We were close, close enough, or so I thought; sex didn't really matter, it didn't have to affect anything, though I see now that it did, it affected everything. Our bedside lights fell separately on the pillows; the room was quiet apart from the rustling as we turned the pages of our books. It was a measured life, safe, calm, enviable. After ten minutes Nathan would put his book down, switch off his light, turn away and fall asleep.

I'd lie awake, sometimes for hours as the cathedral bells tolled each quarter hour. I'd think about Lizzie and my patients and the lists of things I had to do the next day, results and visits, letters and meetings, patients to contact, until my heart was beating fast and the lists became muddled. I'd get up to make a cup of tea and then back to bed again. I'd listen to the cars that passed and watch the watery lozenges of light slide across the ceiling and disappear, soothing mysterious, companionable.

Carol's Kia was in the surgery car park next to Debbie's Ford, there was a red Mercedes too, parked across two spaces, the roof down, in February. Someone who had tickets to whatever was showing at Salisbury Playhouse probably, out to impress a date and too late to find parking.

Had there been another car, parked at the far corner where the overhanging trees make the tarmac slimy with rotten leaves? There might have been, I didn't notice; it was dark by then, darker under the branches. I glanced at my reflection in the gleaming metal of the Mercedes, lit by the lights from the surgery, a small forward-slanting figure with wind-blown hair. It was lucky it was too late to encounter patients, my escape would be swift.

I was wrong. The tension was clear from the door. Carol was leaning over the reception counter, her fingers clutching a temporary resident's card. Debbie was the other side, head bowed, listening. She was on call. One hand cupped her bump, her eyes were dark with fatigue, myself twenty-four years ago. I caught Carol's sentence mid-hiss.

'. . . suicide risk. I put him in Rachel's room. I know it's late, but I couldn't say no.'

Nathan might be uncorking the wine in the kitchen, it would be Chardonnay, chilled, his favourite. I preferred red especially in the winter – after a day at work, I needed the warmth. He might be glancing at the clock, but the mention of suicide swung the balance. Liam's face came to me, the rings under his eyes, the clenched fists, the despair that I'd missed.

'I'll get this, Debbie.'

She jolted and her hands tightened on her abdomen. I

hadn't meant to scare her, but the door opened silently and the carpet in the practice had been replaced last year. It was new and thick; you couldn't hear footsteps.

'It makes sense.' I put my armful of notes in Carol's in-tray. 'Seeing he's in my room already.'

'You'd left it unlocked.' Carol's hand went to her glittering bob of hair. 'He seemed upset.'

'Don't worry.' I smiled at her. 'I'm glad you chose it.'

Debbie's room was as functional as the reception area. A pregnant mother with a toddler doesn't have time to make her office a home, she doesn't need to. Her life beyond the surgery teems with colour and noise, children, friends calling in, laughter and chat.

Our home life was very quiet nowadays. Nathan liked pastels for the walls, he found them restful. I chose the colours I wanted for my office instead: turquoise for the walls, a framed poster of the Mediterranean, red boats against the blue, and one of Victoria's photographs, a volcano with lava erupting in a spray of gold and scarlet. There was a photo of Nathan with Lizzie on my desk, boxes of toys under the couch, and red bean bags for children to lie on. The room was scented with bunches of dried lavender from Victoria's garden; things that provided comfort – well, they comforted me.

'I'm on call.' Debbie bent awkwardly to retrieve her bag. She didn't want pity or allowances. I understood, I'd been the same; glancing down I could see her ankles were swollen, which happens in the third trimester when you've been on your feet all day.

'Owe me if it makes you feel better.' I was tired, but late-forties weariness is different from pregnancy. The fatigue has been present for a while, you get used to it, used to pushing on through.

Debbie straightened and stared at me, a complicated look: relief, guilt, resentment, pride, everything I recognized. I wanted to hug her, she was only twenty-six, just two years older than Lizzie though I couldn't remember the last time I'd put my arms round my daughter. She evaded hugs. She needed her space, she was used to it, she said. I'd been busy in her childhood, she told me recently, it was too late to make up for that now. She had laughed but it wasn't a joke.

Carol was talking to me, leaning forward earnestly.

'. . . name is Luc Lefevre.' She folded her lips between sentences, as neatly as sealing an envelope; it made her look disapproving. 'Half French, I believe. He lives in London, he was going home but, as it turned out, he—'

'Thanks Carol, I'll get back to you if I need to.' I preferred to have the story from the patient, unfiltered. It was often hidden in the silences or the way the patient was sitting, in the clenched hands or the quick sideways glance.

She handed me the temporary resident's card the patient had filled in while waiting, and started to sort through the files I'd brought back, thumping them down in turn on the counter. The pretty white jersey with embroidered lambs round the neck was at odds with her flushed cheeks. I'd offended her, again. It was no secret she preferred Roger. I loved him too, everybody did. Tall, kindly, disorganized Roger, grey-haired and soft-spoken. He would have stopped in his tracks, bent his head attentively and listened to everything Carol told him. He might have nodded and smiled, apparently grateful. I was more impatient, not just with her but with friends and family. I've always been impatient but Nathan thought it was worse nowadays. Time of life, he'd said, but I hadn't replied.

I should have listened to Carol as Roger would have done. She was quite right as it turned out. I needed a lot more information, though it's too late now to ask about the things Luc Lefevre might have told her before I met him. Months and months too late.

I would have been kinder to Carol if only I'd known; much, much kinder. That's one of the things that haunts me still. I should have tried harder. She sang in a choir, I've found out since, went ballroom dancing on Friday evenings and worked in the Oxfam shop on her afternoons off. I knew so little about her.

I sent a text to Nathan as I walked down the corridor towards my room. I'd be late, he should eat without waiting for me. Our health centre is large, it houses another practice as well as visiting physiotherapists and the nurses' clinics. The corridors are lengthy. Carol had forgotten to switch on the lights down here, and, as I walked away from the reception and towards my room, I seemed to be progressing deeper and deeper into shadow.

I remember stumbling so I put my hand to the wall to steady myself as I groped my way forward.

Chapter 2

'Oh. I'm sorry. Are you all right? . . . I mean, I can see you're not, but . . .'

I don't usually apologize or trip over my words when I meet patients, but he'd been crying, and it felt as though I was intruding. Women sob openly but men often hide their grief. Luc was different, tears had soaked his stubble; even his collar was wet.

He began to get up when I came in, but that was breaking an unwritten rule. Patients don't get up for doctors. I put my hand on his shoulder, another broken rule. Doctors don't touch patients unless it's part of an examination, in which case we ask their permission and, these days, offer a chaperone. He was upset, the excuse I gave myself at the time, but the truth was I was drawn to him despite myself, which was strange; good-looking men don't usually interest me. I imagine arrogance or entitlement.

My husband's looks were average, his face calm, the expression controlled. His smile was friendly enough. Luc Lefevre's face was the opposite, handsome yes, but expressive and

9

emotional. Open. I had the impression of wildness, not as in unkempt but undefended, as wild animals are. It was as if some veneer had gone and his soul was showing through his eyes.

I passed him the flowery box of tissues that Carol puts on my desk and he pulled out a handful, wiped his face and blew his nose. I eased my shoes off under the desk, he wouldn't notice. My feet were swollen, like Debbie's, a recent thing which was rapidly becoming a normal thing, along with the grey streaks in my hair, the arthritis in my thumb joints and having to wear glasses for reading.

I avoided his face for his sake, but clues were everywhere. His fingers were knotted together but his hands were tanned, the nails neatly trimmed. A Rolex watch, feet in expensive loafers. Whatever the problem, it wasn't money. I waited, which is the very least you can do for someone who is suffering.

'It's okay,' I told him. 'There's no hurry.'

The practice was quiet; the phones would have been switched over to the on-call centre by now. Carol wouldn't be knocking at the door to request my signature on prescriptions, no one was waiting. I could listen for as long as he liked. I would give him the time that I hadn't given Liam.

Liam Chambers had been slotted in at short notice during a busy morning surgery two weeks before. He was seventeen, with a blank gaze and bones in his wrists that protruded like marbles. He had a problem, he'd muttered, but wouldn't answer my questions and we ran out of time. I asked him to make an appointment with me the next morning but that evening he was found in his room, hanging from a beam by his dressing gown cord. His mother didn't let me in when I went round but agreed to see me in a fortnight on the 10th of February which was, I saw on the calendar, tomorrow.

10

The calendar hung on the corkboard above my desk, a gift from a drug company. Van Gogh's sunflowers for February jammed between the on-call rota and the protocol for treatment of kidney disease. I'd never looked properly at that picture, one of those familiar images your glance slides past. Today I saw that the flowers weren't young, I hadn't noticed that before. It's hard to see what's in front of you when you're busy – if you look again, you notice things you missed, obvious things. Some of the flowers had gone to seed, though the remaining petals flickered like little flames: saffron, ochre and burnt sienna, colours baked in the south of France. 'Arles' was scrawled at the bottom. I imagined how rich that name would sound when spoken in French, the 'r' warm in the mouth like something delicious to eat.

'There was a tree on a bend along the road towards Stonehenge; it seemed to be waiting for me.'

His words gave me a jolt, a small one, easy to disguise. It was the French accent; it was as though he had seen into my very thoughts.

'I decided to drive straight into it. I was going to call the police first, so they could clear up the mess before anyone else came by.'

I nodded, disguising shock. He was telling the truth and the matter-of-fact language made it worse. I said nothing; if you jump in too fast with words it can close someone up. It was quite possible I had closed Liam up. The silence stretched until he broke it again.

'Everything is grey and quiet, it's like I'm walking on ash. There's ash in the air, as if the world's gone up in flames.'

Ash. I've always loved the sound of that word, it feels soft in your mouth, which is fanciful – real ash would grate between the teeth, it would taste unbearably bitter.

'I can't remember a bloody thing. I don't want to do things I normally like doing, I can't be bothered.' He sounded

11

resentful, as if a stranger had come to his door in the night and shouldered his way in. 'I don't want sex any more.'

I glanced at his body, I couldn't help it. He was muscled though I couldn't see him in a gym somehow. His skin had a weathered look. I imagined him in some remote place with nothing but birds in the sky. The card in my hand put him at forty, the brown hair that reached to his collar was already going grey, dishevelled. He had large hands and wide shoulders, a long nose, dark brown eyes and a small scar by his mouth on the right side. It was the kind of face that would have caught my attention in a crowd. Doctors aren't supposed to think of patients like that but it's automatic; a way of gauging health, like registering weight or height. It's surprising what you can take in at a glance, decisions being made before the conscious mind becomes aware of them. Given the age, the sex and the name you can guess with surprising accuracy what the problem will be before a word has been spoken.

'Have you felt like this before?'

'Not as bad.'

'But you've been depressed?'

'Yes.'

'Enough to have had treatment?'

He nodded but his eyes clouded, some secret was being shifted to a deeper place. No one shares everything the first time. It's a matter of waiting, Roger says, of walking in your patient's shoes for as long as it takes. That's all very well, if you have time.

'Okay, helpful to know.'

The hands on his lap unfolded a little, he was wearing a thick gold wedding ring, gold cufflinks.

'I've everything you're supposed to want: a beautiful wife, an adorable son, well, stepson. No money troubles, not yet anyway. Work's fine.' He sounded angry, which was good, you can work with anger. Apathy is the danger.

12

'What work is that?'

'Architecture.' He looked down then and his voice became quieter as though admitting something private. 'I much prefer painting. I paint when I can.'

Some jobs make you more susceptible to suicide; anaesthetists and farmers are at risk. Vets too. It seemed unlikely an architect would have weapons to hand, nor would an artist.

'General health?'

'Good.'

'Does depression run in the family?'

'My father; always at this time of year.' A smile glimmered. 'Genetics and weather. Fatal combination.' His teeth were good, another reassuring sign, like the trimmed nails. The depression hadn't been going on for very long.

'What treatment are you taking?'

'Tablets. Can't remember their name, memory's shot. I ran out of them anyway.'

He'd known this was coming, it had roared from a distance like a tidal wave he thought he could outrun. He'd been too busy to renew his medication. He had a practice in London and was restoring a house in Wiltshire as well as a place he'd inherited in France.

'Near Arles, my great-great-grandfather's house, mine now.'

'Arles?' My glance went to the calendar and his followed.

'There are fields of those near the house.' He nodded at the picture. 'Van Gogh country. They're a blaze of colour in the summer.'

'He must have been captivated by sunflowers. He painted them with such passion, despite their age . . .' What was I saying? I never shared my feelings in a consultation. It must have to do with the warmth of his voice and the way he was looking at me, the openness that seemed to call for the same

13

in return. My guard had been lowered, but he didn't seem to notice.

'He chose them precisely for their age, that's when they are most beautiful.' He turned his gaze on me, his eyes were very deep. 'Their colours are subtler, the petals softer, the seeds have ripened.'

The words were sensual, they felt personal somehow, which was crazy, he was describing flowers, not women. I had to pull myself together. I glanced at the clock, we'd had forty-five minutes already. Carol would be furious.

'Okay. What bought this episode on today?'

'There's been no time for the things that keep me sane, like painting,' he said slowly. 'Work dominates everything. I've been feeling down for months but I ignored it, too busy. I'd come to Salisbury to meet builders, but I felt worse than ever. I tried to drive home but got lost. I found myself on the A360 to Stonehenge, which is when I saw that oak tree. I stopped to phone the police and a flock of birds flew up from the field next to me, glinting in the last of the light. God knows what they're called, you know, those little brown birds you see in the countryside that feed on fields of stubble.'

The image of that low yellow light coming through the bare trees was as clear to me as if I'd been there with him. I could hear the whirring flight of those birds, smell the scent of wet earth and damp straw. I leant forward to listen.

'I got out of the car and watched them fly into the trees. I heard them settling down for the night. They saved me. I'm not sure how much time passed, but I knew I needed someone to talk to, so I got into the car and came back.'

He passed his hand rapidly over his face as wiping something off. 'I saw the sign outside the health centre, so I parked the car, came in and registered. They put me in your room, and I felt safe immediately.'

'I'm glad you found your way to me.' But that sounded

too heartfelt, as if I'd been waiting specially for him. I sat back. He was a patient, we needed a plan. According to his card there had been no previous admissions or suicide attempts, though as he'd filled out the form himself he could have left things out, important things.

'If patients are suicidal, I often ask for an emergency review by a psychiatrist.' I was doing what a doctor should, what I would have done for Liam, if only I'd known.

'That moment has gone, truly. I don't want to kill myself any more.'

'All the same, I should make sure you're safe.'

'I came here because I needed someone to talk to.'

There was green in his eyes as well as brown, dark green lines radiating to the edge of the irises against a deep umber background.

'You've listened and it's made all the difference.' He continued, 'Besides, I have to go home. I won't commit suicide, I promise you.'

He was making this personal, a contract between us.

'Your GP will need to review you tomorrow then. I'll drop him an email. Meanwhile it might be an idea to restart those tablets.' I glanced at the card, but he hadn't written down the name. 'Which ones are they?'

'God knows.' His forehead furrowed. 'When I'm like this, I forget everything.'

'Serotonin reuptake inhibitors are often the first choice; citalopram—'

'Citalopram.' His face cleared. 'That sounds familiar.'

'They can make you feel worse before you feel better; there's a range of side effects.'

I ran through them, along with the contraindications. I always make myself do that, they're so easy to forget: the warning signs that mean you should stop taking them like increased suicidal thoughts or the opposite, latent mania. I

15

mentioned counselling, exercise and sleep. I reminded him to see his GP and then printed the script.

'If you need to talk to someone in the meantime, here's my number.' I scribbled it down and handed it over with his prescription. Roger would shake his head at me, he'd warn me not to give out my contact details, he'd say I was lowering boundaries. I'd have replied that I was putting a safety net under my patient; the truth was, after Liam, I wasn't taking any chances.

Luc pocketed the scrap of paper along with his prescription. His eyes lingered on my face as if wondering why I had chosen to be here so late on a Thursday evening instead of at home with the husband who must be waiting. When he got to his feet I stood too. He was taller than I'd thought but then I'd forgotten to put my shoes on.

'I expect people often say they're grateful to you, but I really mean it; you've been . . .' he paused as if searching for the right word and looked down at me '. . . lovely.'

It sounded truthful rather than inappropriate, though I had done nothing more than let him talk. He was at that stripped-away point when you say the truth as you see it, and in that moment, I, Rachel Goodchild, a middle-aged doctor with a grown daughter and a marriage of twenty-five years, appeared lovely to him. I even felt lovely.

He enfolded my hand in both his, his grip was warm. He smiled and his eyes became very bright, he looked different, younger. The transformation was extraordinary. 'Thank you.' He paused. 'For everything.'

I looked at my watch when he'd gone; an hour had passed. A whole hour. Normally I kept to time though there were any number of patients who'd benefit from talking as long as they wanted. It seemed unfair to have spent so long with just one patient but then tonight had been a one-off, a lucky break, that's all. It wouldn't happen again.

Nathan must have had his supper by now, he'd be asleep on the sofa or checking his lesson plans for tomorrow. My office felt cold, the heating switched itself off at night, I hadn't noticed the chill until now. I tidied up and scribbled a reminder to myself to email Luc Lefevre's GP in the morning, then went to apologize to Carol who was filing notes; her heels clicking angrily back and forth between the shelves. The list of tomorrow's jobs on her jotter had already been crossed off with deeply scored red Biro marks. She nodded without looking at me. I'm glad I said sorry, not that it made any difference but it makes me feel better now.

Outside the Mercedes had gone, though the small car in the shadows might still have been there. Looking back, I have the impression it was.

The Close was quiet and I drove through slowly. The cathedral still astonished me though I've lived here all my life; the sheer size of the walls, the shape of the windows and vaulted doors, the soaring spire seemed held in place as if by magic. The floodlights threw its shadow across the sky, a shaft of darkness against the paler clouds.

I passed other familiar shapes: the wooden sentry box for the Close constable, the letter box on the corner, Elizabeth Frink's statue of the Madonna on the Green, a thin form, pacing out her grief. Ted Heath's old house with its sharp black railings and Georgian frontage. Everything as it always was, an ordered world in which Nathan and I had our place, a teacher and a doctor; respected folk with reputations to keep up.

The North Canonry looked different tonight, the scaffolding that had surrounded it for months had gone. I stopped the car. I used to spend hours in this house as a child, my best friend, Cathy had lived here. We'd played in the garden all summer. I loved her family of four siblings; I had no brothers or sisters and I went for the adventure, the freedom, the chaos. The house had changed hands many times since, but it had been empty for a while now. Tonight, the stone looked cleaner, the crumbling windowsills had been repaired. The dark house must be waiting for new inhabitants. I imagined the ghosts of the family I'd known, myself among them, standing inside, looking out at the world from the shadows as if waiting for the chance to start our lives again, all those choices still in front of us, adventure and freedom beckoning.

A car went by, driving very close to mine, jolting me back to myself. The turning points of my life had passed a long time ago: the first job, the first house, the first love, the first child. I'd made my choices; you don't get them again at forty-nine. My day had been spent seeing people who were ill or struggling with loss or need; bad luck landing with unlucky people, that cruel postcode lottery of health that operated even in this privileged little town. I had a husband, a daughter, health. A fantastic job, enough money. How could I wish to start again, even for a moment?

I switched on the engine and the car slipped quietly past the Cathedral School playing field on my right; on my left stretched the shadowy line of trees and bushes running by the wall of the school. I'd hurried past them as a child. There had always been a haunted feel about those trees – a murder leaves a trace in the air, an invisible stain that lasts through time.

I manoeuvred the car through the thirteenth-century gate to De Vaux Place, and stopped outside the row of terraced houses. I heaved my bag from the boot. The windows of the house that joined ours on the left were dark, apart from a tiny light at the top which Abby, Victoria's cleaner, left on when she wasn't there. I should be used to the little plunge of disappointment by now, Victoria was often away. Our outside door opened to a cobbled courtyard like all the others in the row; ours was brick-lined and empty apart from our two bikes, the wheelie bins and a magnolia tree in a pot. In summer Victoria's was full of clematis clambering over white-washed walls, pots of lemon trees, deep red geraniums and troughs of lavender. The Denshams' courtyard on our other side housed Colin's mobility scooter and tricycles for their grandchildren.

In the kitchen Pepper, Lizzie's blue roan spaniel, lifted his head. His tail thumped a few times but he was too sleepy to come and greet me. My supper was in the fridge, covered with cling film, pale heaps of chicken and rice. I left it untouched and took a bottle of red wine from the rack instead, pouring myself a large glass. Nathan had tidied everything away. The units were painted a shade called smoke and the walls gunmetal, or perhaps I had the names the wrong way around, the units were gunmetal and the walls smoke. It was what Nathan had chosen but, as I looked around at the different shades of grey, I could taste ashes in my mouth.

Chapter 3

February 2017

'How can I help?'

I never like asking that question, the one I use when time is short. Shopkeepers or waiters always ask the same thing but that's all right, they can usually provide what's needed. In my case it seems spurious, dishonest even; you shouldn't offer to help when you can't address the real problem, the one hiding beneath the surface, the wretched inequality of it all. Health is apportioned at birth, it depends on where a patient comes from and goes back to his parents' lives and their income and further back than that. It's unfair and complicated and there is almost nothing we can do about it. We work at the far end, picking up the pieces.

The morning had started well. There'd been a run of straightforward problems: a sore throat, conjunctivitis, a painful knee, irregular bleeding. The kind of morning that made me feel I knew the answers, until Brian came in, bowed and shuffling.

It was his second visit that week, sometimes he came in more often than that. With his round face, pebble glasses and greasy slab of fringe, he looked like an aged school boy, apart from a knowing little smile. He talked in a whisper so I had to lean close. His eyelids were lowered but the occasional glance at my face seemed furtive. There was something about him that made me shiver.

'It's my back,' he told me in his whispery little voice. 'It came on before Mother died last year. I had to lift her, change the sheets, all those sorts of things. There was no one to help me. The pain keeps me awake now, I think it's getting worse.'

I could find nothing wrong with his back on examination, but he wasn't disconcerted. He moved his chair closer and licked his lips, the rapid movements of his tongue reminded me of a lizard. I resisted the impulse to move my seat back.

'I still miss her; days can go by without seeing anyone.'

I felt sorry for him in spite of the way he made me feel. He'd lost his job taking time off to look after his mother; he was lonely, still grieving.

'Have you been getting out more?'

'I fed the ducks in the park yesterday but there were some mothers looking at me. I heard them tell their kids to keep away from me – you know, that weirdo in a mac, that's what they said, I heard them. It's either that or the pub.' He spread his hands in a gesture of helplessness; the fingers were long and pale, the nails lined with dirt.

'What about your neighbours?'

'They don't say hello though I deliver their papers every day. It's as though I don't exist.'

Brian talked on and I let him, the grievances pouring out. When he left, shuffling to the door, he gave a little wave as though we were old friends. I lifted the slats of my blind and watched him walking across the car park. He was clutching a prescription for exercise at the gym and the telephone number of a grief counsellor but his gait was now brisk. He

22

could have been lying about the back pain. I trod down unease; he was a lonely man and there's no easy cure for loneliness.

Carol glared at me, her mouth pursed tight. I'd taken too long and kept her waiting as usual. Roger hurried by with a packet of notes under his arm, his gangly figure bent forward. He winked as he passed and I felt better.

'I'm visiting Laura Chambers, Carol. Can I have Liam's notes?'

She handed them over silently; this was a visit I was dreading. I'd met Liam's mother a year ago, a small woman with grey hair pulled into a scarf, underweight, a little shy. She had arthritis in her lumbar spine. I'd sent her for a scan, which came back as normal, and we'd discussed exercise, supplements and analgesics. I hadn't seen her after that.

It was cold, one of those dull days where the pavements seep damp and the sky is the colour of milk. Laura Chambers lived across town but I walked. I needed to think. I felt deeply guilty, wretchedly responsible. If she told me I'd failed her son, I could defend my actions legally but that wasn't the point, I couldn't bat my own accusations away. What about insight? Intuition? If I'd guessed Liam was suicidal, I would have referred him to a psychiatrist at the hospital and driven him there myself. I could have rung him at home or called in to see him. I might have phoned his mother – although that would have been breaking confidentiality, it's defensible in matters of life and death. But I didn't guess, I'd had no idea at all. My thoughts circled in a bitter loop as I walked down back streets, past women waiting at bus stops, children riding on scooters and a house where a tan and white terrier barked from a window at everyone who passed.

Laura Chambers' house looked like all the others in her street, a bow-fronted window, a paved space for a car, empty milk bottles on the top step; nothing to reveal the tragedy of a fortnight ago. Liam must have climbed on a chair, his upper lip beaded with sweat, those thin hands trembling as he knotted the cord over a beam, pulling it tight to make sure. Had he understood, in the way I imagine few people do, that this was forever? That there would be no more friends, partners, music or books? No more mornings, no sun and no flowers. He would never go to university, have a job or hold a child, his future would be obliterated in less than a minute.

The bubbled glass above the door was dark. I rang the bell and waited, rang again. I could feel the sweat on my palms, my heart was racing. The door was unbolted, a chain slid back, a slice of face appeared, a puffy eye, part of a thin mouth.

'Yes?'

'It's Dr Goodchild, Mrs Chambers. We made an appointment for today.'

She slid the chain off the door and walked slowly away from me down the dark hall. Her hair was matted at the back of her head as though she lacked the energy to reach that far. In the kitchen a bottle of Irish whiskey stood on the table, a half-filled glass beside it. She indicated a chair and took one herself.

'I'm sorrier than I can say—'

'There are things you should know.' Her mouth trembled, but she held herself erect as if determined. 'Liam came to see you but he might not have said why. I found this in his jeans pocket.' Her voice was hoarse. She unfolded a scrap of paper on the table. Test results from The London Clinic: *HIV positive*.

'You're right, he didn't mention it.' I felt sick. I could have reassured him if I'd known, referred him and monitored treatment, checking up on him from time to time. He would have had a normal life but I couldn't tell her that, not now.

'He didn't want anyone to know.' She folded up the paper. 'He felt guilty. He hadn't been careful.' She lifted her whiskey and drank, her head thrown back, tendons exposed, throat working. She put down the empty glass with a force that could have broken it. 'He never told me he was gay, not in so many words, but I knew. He was bullied at school for years, but he didn't say anything about that either. I wanted to protect him and he wanted to protect me back. That was the trouble.'

'The trouble?'

'Too much protecting, not enough truth. I didn't mind about his sexuality, I minded about the disease.' Her pale eyes filled with tears. 'I didn't know how to talk to him, so I told him to see you, though I guessed he might not tell you. It's my fault.'

I'd been braced for blame, but she was blaming herself. I put my hand on her cold one.

'It's not your fault or it's mine as well. I couldn't get him to talk, we only had seven minutes that day.'

She looked up and nodded, something gave a little in her face. 'It wasn't anything to do with you. He only came to see you in order to please me. I think he'd made up his mind a while back.'

In the silence, the radio came on, the two o'clock news; she looked round the kitchen slowly, as if surprised there was still news, that there was a world.

'Is there anything I can do to help you? Anything at all? It won't feel like that now but, in time, you might want to talk to someone.'

'No, thank you.'

The chair scraped as she stood up and then she led the way back to the front door. I can usually suggest something to help but that day I was at a loss – we both knew I could do nothing. When the door closed, I heard her footsteps slowly retreating down the hall.

There was no surgery that afternoon, so I walked home through the streets, sorrow and regret raging. A headache had started, the street seemed out of focus, the cars blurred. At the entrance to the Close where the pavement narrowed, I found myself among crowds of teenagers spilling from the pavement and into the road. Any one of them could get hit by a car, but they were young, they believed themselves immortal. They didn't understand how fragile they were, but then, I hadn't understood Liam's fragility either.

I didn't notice there was a car beside me at first, being driven so closely that the bumper was brushing my coat. I moved onto the pavement and the car went by. Five minutes later when I was walking along the path by the trees, the last stretch before the gates at the other end of the Close, I heard the quiet purr of an engine behind me again. Cars in the Close are driven slowly but this one was going more slowly than most, a medium-sized grey sedan with dark windows. I couldn't see the driver. Had he parked up ahead and waited for me to go by again? The car pulled past me then went through the gate in front of me. I didn't think to look at the number plate. I let myself into the house and slammed the door behind me, more irritated than afraid.

The fear hadn't started by then.

Chapter 4

March 2017

'It's your fault.'

My daughter's eyes were blue like her father's but, whereas Nathan's were a soft grey-blue, hers were darker and, today, harder. Her psychotherapist boyfriend Mike had walked out that morning. He had packed his bags and left her flat where he'd been living for the last six months. The relationship was at an end. She was upset, anyone would be.

'You must be feeling wretched, darling, but seriously, why is it my fault?'

'Everything went wrong after you talked to him at our party.'

I put down the serving dish with the remains of the beef and pulled out a chair. I wasn't up to this. I'd been up late checking appraisals and now I'd let myself drink in the middle of the day because it was Sunday. The empty bottle of wine stood in the middle of the table, my glass and Nathan's were empty too. Nathan thought wine took the edge off things, but Lizzie's anger sliced through the day like a finely honed sword.

'You really upset him.' She stared at me angrily.

'Remind me what I said, I honestly can't remember.'

Mike had been pouring drinks at her birthday party three weeks ago. I'd come straight to her flat from the practice and downed two glasses in quick succession on an empty stomach. He'd begun talking fast but then Nathan gave a speech about Lizzie and now I could only remember thinking how pretty she'd looked.

'You told him that psychotherapy wasn't a first-line treatment at the practice.'

It began to come back. 'Well, that happens to be true, but why should he end things because of that? It was my tactlessness, not yours.'

'You paid the deposit on my flat, which means I collude in your judgement.'

'That's ridiculous.'

'Exactly what you said about psychotherapy.'

'Oh, Lizzie, I didn't say that.' I looked at her flushed face; this went further back. I had to tread carefully. 'I don't even think that. I'd love to offer psychotherapy, but we have a limited budget. He can't have been listening.'

'That's what he said about you, you didn't seem to hear him at all.'

'I know it's tough now, but there'll be someone lovely who—'

'Don't even say it. I'll make my own choices even if you think they're mistakes.' She glanced at her watch and got up. 'I have to go, early start tomorrow, stuff to do for my job.' A little smile. 'Though it doesn't compare to yours.'

'You know I think your job is great.'

She pulled on her coat without answering and left the room. Seconds later the front door banged. We hadn't said goodbye.

These were old wounds. Lizzie thought I minded about

her choices because they were different to mine. Medicine had taken me away when she was small – in her eyes, that meant I rated it above everything, including her career as a librarian. Her convictions had been forged in childhood and I understood why. I'd missed things for work, important things: bath times, birthday parties, parents' evenings. No matter what I said now, she felt second best. The wounds might be old, but they went deep and my conversation with Mike had made it all worse. If wounds fester after surgery, the tissues should be opened up again, drained, allowed to heal from the base. That's what we needed to do but I wasn't sure how.

I lay awake sometimes, awash with regret, wishing I could do it all again. I shaped imaginary conversations in my head in which I explained how busy I'd been, how tired at the end of each day, that I was sorry I fell asleep when reading bedtime stories. I took work on holiday and spent the first days finishing it. I never hung around the playground at drop-off or baked cakes for her to take in; instead I'd feel guilty relief as I drove to the surgery, the emotional burden slipping away. The truth was it was easier at work. People were polite. Roger was interested in what I thought, even Carol made me a cup of tea sometimes. I was kinder to my patients, they had the attention that should have been my family's. I knew I'd messed up but somehow the opportunity for apology never came. Lizzie didn't want to talk about the past, at least not to me.

The beef sat in a pool of congealed blood, the delicately carved slices had folded over and were going grey. I began to clear the table, stacking plates in the dishwasher, running hot water into the cooking tray; distraction therapy, Mike could have said. I was sorting out the kitchen instead of sorting out the problem.

The garden door opened and I heard the thud of boots

as they were dropped on the mat, then Nathan padded through to the kitchen holding a bunch of white narcissi. He looked triumphant. 'For Lizzie.'

'Lizzie's gone.'

'She didn't say goodbye.' He sounded as disappointed as a child. He pulled down a vase from the dresser, an old one Lizzie had made when she was little, one of my treasures. The baked clay coils were lopsided and unevenly stained with pink and green.

'She was upset. Mike walked out today, their relationship's over.' I began washing glasses. I wouldn't tell him everything she'd said; it was too raw, too real.

'Ah. The psychotherapist.'

'What's wrong with psychotherapy?' I was immediately, perversely, on my daughter's side. 'Perhaps our practice should have a psychotherapist on the team.' I pushed away the thought that if Liam had gone to a psychotherapist, he might still be alive.

'Mike was a bit unrealistic though, wasn't he? A little immature?'

'She loved him.'

'Oh well. Love.' He was nudging the flowers into place in the vase, head to one side, absorbed. 'I think she's after adventure. She might be glad he's gone; my guess is she'd rather have her freedom.'

He made love sound so flimsy, so unimportant. I glanced out of the window to the courtyard where our bikes leant together, old-fashioned bikes with wide saddles and wicker baskets, a little rusty but they'd lasted us for years. I wouldn't rise to the bait; this wasn't worth a row. His remarks weren't personal. He wanted the best for his daughter, he'd just picked her some of his precious white narcissi. All the flowers Nathan grew were white. There were silvery crocuses under the cherry tree, ivory hellebores, pale snowdrops either side

30

of the path, but in Victoria's garden next door orange pansies glowed alongside daffodils and crimson-striped tulips, colours that exuded warmth, like Victoria herself.

An image came then, rich in detail as if it had been shaping itself in my mind all this time: my French patient at an easel, early daffodils on the table in a bright green vase. The beautiful wife humming as she cleared the remains of the meal in a room that was painted that orange-pink of the roofs in Provence. Her scent would be lemon or lavender, the expensive kind she always wore – he gave it to her for each birthday, it reminded them of Arles. She might put a slim hand on his shoulder. He'd look up and smile that warm smile, covering her hand with his and she'd bend down for a kiss while the adorable boy played outside on a swing.

I put the glasses upside down on the draining board and dried my hands. It was that dull stretch after Sunday lunch when thoughts tend to wander. It was only natural to think about patients you'll never see again. The encounters are intense, secrets are shared, deep fears laid bare. You are trusted; closer, for those minutes, than most friends are. And then it all ends. The bond is snapped. You are no longer needed, your part is done and you hear nothing more. I put the meat in the fridge and shut the door. That was good of course; if patients stay away it means they're better, which is the point after all. It's the ones who come back time after time who make your heart sink, the ones you can't seem to help, no matter how hard you try. We call them that among ourselves: heart-sink patients, like Brian, the ones who have an endless list of problems and an agenda you never really understand. I should put Luc Lefevre from my mind, he wasn't my patient any more. He'd be better by now. I wouldn't see him again.

I began polishing the glasses and replacing them on the dresser one by one.

'She'll forget him soon enough.' Nathan snipped the stem of a bud and forced it in with the others; there were too many for the vase, they needed more space.

'Would you forget me if I disappeared?'

'Lizzie's young, and the young are tough.' He hadn't answered my question, he probably thought he didn't need to. 'She's a survivor, try not to worry.'

He knew her better than me though it hurt to admit that. Teachers' holidays are generous; he'd been around more than I had in her childhood. He'd been in charge of treats and outings, the fun parent who devised treasure hunts, the one she'd told her secrets to, the good cop to my bad. When I came home from work, the only things left to do were the corrective ones, like checking homework or sorting through the kit bag. I caught up with her at weekends or attempted to. There was a silver-framed photo on his desk in the sitting room, Nathan shouldering a spade and smiling at the camera, Lizzie aged seven, a few paces away, muddy bulbs in her hands, frowning. Her own girl, even then. Perhaps he was right, she might be craving adventure and freedom. How could I blame her when the truth was I craved those things myself?

Nathan put the vase in the middle of the table and stepped back to admire his work. There was a sharp yelp from Pepper as he trod on his paw.

'Damn dog, always underfoot.' Nathan hadn't grown up with dogs, to him they were an extra job, a nuisance. 'I thought we'd agreed to give him back to Lizzie, did you forget?'

I bent to Pepper and stroked his head. I loved him. I loved the way he came to find me in the mornings, I loved his silky ears and even his obstinate streak, but Nathan had guessed right, I had forgotten to give him back. I was forgetting so many things, there were times I felt I was losing my mind.

Women came to see me all the time, busy women like me, approaching the menopause who'd become forgetful or anxious. I told them the menopause wasn't an illness, more of a condition that needed attention. We discussed diet, evening primrose oil and vitamins and whether or not they wanted hormone replacement therapy. The importance of friends and exercise.

I reached the lead down from its hook on the dresser. 'I'll take him out for a walk, there's cake in the tin.'

Nathan handed me my coat and kissed me goodbye. 'Don't worry about Lizzie, Mike wasn't her type.'

Do we have types? I glimpsed Nathan's relieved expression as he turned to shut the door after me. Was he still mine? Outside the air was cool; there was a sliver of moon in the sky already. There was a gap between us, like the hairline fracture on a china plate, one you didn't notice most of the time. Maybe that's what happened in all long marriages, tiny cracks opening up; who could tell? You could hardly ask around. Some couples seemed to grow closer over the years rather than further apart; our neighbours, Helen and Colin Densham, walked hand in hand at eighty, apparently content. We might appear like that too. Nathan was cheerful enough and we didn't argue, at least not in public. My restlessness wouldn't be apparent to anyone, it might simply be a symptom of middle age, of life sliding by so fast that I wanted to slow it down, do something quite different before it was too late.

I walked round the Choristers Green, past eighteenth-century Mompesson House and the gates of other houses, ancient places kept with care. The great wooden gates of the North Canonry were open for once. I glimpsed a red car inside. It was getting dark, one of those afternoons in the first weeks of spring when evening comes early. A light was shining in an upstairs window, ready for folk to move in, newcomers who wouldn't sense the echoes from the past as I did. I was attuned to this place, to the Close, to Salisbury itself. I'd come back after training, taking a GP job here in order to look after my father before he died. Nathan and I stayed on in the family house when we married; unadventurous, I saw that now, but Nathan loved it and I was busy, grateful for the familiarity. I coped with everything: working full time, running the house, organizing the family. I didn't mind, it had never occurred to me to mind, but according to Lizzie that was part of the problem. I should have minded. I had tried to do too many things and as a consequence did none of them well. She was going to manage very differently.

As we approached the shrubbery, where the trees clustered close besides the path, Pepper began to whine. I let him off the lead to root among the leaves. I walked ahead, lost in my memories of those years, the compromises and guilt, the love and the exhaustion. I hadn't wondered then if I was missing out, if there might be something else, some dimension of life which escaped me in the daily routine. I was too tired, too busy. My feet crunched on the gravel and that's when I heard them, those quiet footsteps behind me, like an echo of mine.

It didn't worry me much, that first time, any more than the car had worried me. It was still early and there were people about. Across the Close couples were making their way home from evensong.

I wasn't frightened. I felt uneasy, that's all.

'Pepper, come here, you stupid dog. Hurry.'

There was a violent rustling movement of the little branches in the undergrowth, then Pepper burst out between the bushes and ran towards me, his tail wagging. Behind him the branches became still again. I glanced around. There was no one behind me, there had never been anyone. The footsteps were imaginary. I had made the whole thing up; my mind was playing tricks. I clipped on Pepper's lead and hurried to the Close gate, the dog scampering at my heels. I didn't look round again.

The wood burner must have gone out, the house felt cool. Lizzie's coil pot made a splash of colour on the table, a bright note in the grey surroundings. Nathan wandered in, reading from an exercise book, a red pen in his hand, Sunday afternoon homework correction. He switched on the kettle.

'You're out of breath.' He glanced at me over his half-moon glasses.

'I ran the last few yards. I thought I heard footsteps behind me.'

'Did you see who it was?'

'There was no one there, I was imagining things.'

I didn't tell him I could still hear those quiet footsteps, still feel the menace that had accompanied them. Nathan made tea and handed me a mug.

'Easy to do when you're tired and the light's going.' He was being kind. I shouldn't feel patronized. 'You've pink cheeks,' he continued, smiling with approval. 'You look years younger.'

I wrapped my chilly hands around the mug. I didn't want to be younger. I'd thought middle age would be the start of something new. I'd imagined I'd be different from the women in my clinic. I'd expected to feel liberated, but instead I was becoming fearful. Lizzie's ex-boyfriend might have told me the footsteps represented my past catching up with me, things I hadn't done or wished I'd done better, the different choices I might have made.

The scent of narcissi filled the kitchen, I touched a pale petal. 'Lizzie loved helping you plant those bulbs.'

'She's outgrown that now. I doubt she's touched a spade for years.' He took a handful of logs from the stack by the dresser for the wood burner. 'I'll light a fire, you're shivering.'

'Thanks.' I smiled at him; he picked up the matches and went out of the door whistling.

Do you outgrow the things you loved when you were young? You can bury them deep like Nathan's bulbs, waiting in the dark for the warmth to return. I loved travel once, the journeys, the excitement of exploration. I loved drawing, my old sketch books were in the bottom of my desk. I hadn't outgrown those things, I'd just buried them, I hadn't had time.

I was drifting into sleep in bed later when Nathan murmured, 'I put the date for the housewarming on the calendar, sometime in April.'

'Housewarming?' What had I forgotten now?

'New people moving into the North Canonry; the invitation was on the mat this morning. A thick white card, I thought you'd seen.'

Hence the lights in the window this evening – the new occupants must have moved in already.

'What did it say?'

'Double-barrelled name, Ophelia Forbes-something, requests the pleasure, that sort of thing. Canapés and champagne.'

Ophelia, a pale body and tilted head, Millais' Ophelia, with her open hands and open mouth, the water soaking her clothes, starry flowers in her hair. Death by drowning. Her countenance threaded through my sleep, taking on Lizzie's pale face, half covered by water, her eyes staring at me, still furious. I woke horrified, gasping with terror, but Nathan's breathing calmed me down. I put my hand on the small of his back. Types weren't important; solidarity, presence, those were the things that mattered in a long marriage. Fidelity.

'Lucky,' I whispered. 'I'm lucky.'

Chapter 5

April 2017

The open hands and the flowers were prescient. Ophelia was standing inside the oak door flung wide to welcome guests. The great hall behind her was blazing with light, white flowers were banked against the wall. Warmth and chatter billowed out on a perfumed wave of air; Nathan lifted his face as if sipping at the scent.

'Welcome to our home.'

She took it for granted we'd know who she was, which, of course, we did. Her eyes moved swiftly over our faces, she was trying to place us. Her beauty was as cool and polished as a fifties film star, Grace Kelly or Tippi Hedren; old-style Hitchcock glamour. Her blonde hair was piled, a loose arrangement threaded with flowers that on me would have been laughable but on her looked fabulous. She wore a column of plum-coloured velvet, shot through with gold; in my brown dress I felt like a sparrow next to a bird of paradise.

Nathan had persuaded Lizzie to come, she met us outside the door, having texted to say she was held up. She was in jeans and a black jersey, metal chains looped round her neck; with her scarlet lipstick and slanting fringe she looked spectacular. The hostility in her gaze would be evident only to me.

'Rachel and Nathan Goodchild and Lizzie,' Nathan announced as he took Ophelia's proffered hand, his blue-grey eyes gleaming like pebbles the waves have just licked. 'We live just outside the North Gate in De Vaux Place.'

'Ah, that cute little row of houses, lucky you.' Having placed us at least geographically, she kissed Nathan and then me. I caught the scent of freesias.

Lizzie stepped back. 'I live on Milford Hill, the other side of town,' she said. 'Not with my parents.'

'We asked everyone we could think of,' Ophelia smiled, her gaze flickering over Lizzie. 'The least we could do after months of builders and scaffolders, how you must have hated us.' The American accent was faint but charming. Nathan was clearly charmed.

'Not at all,' he murmured. 'Everyone's been longing to meet our new neighbours.'

'So, you're a vicar?'

The bishop of Salisbury was standing in the hall chatting with the dean and the canon, it was a fair guess.

'I'm a teacher in the school over the way.' Nathan put his arm around my shoulders, but his eyes were on Ophelia. 'Rachel's a GP, Lizzie's a librarian in the city library.'

Ophelia moved closer to him, her smile deepened. She looked as pleased as if it was her birthday and she'd just been given the very gift she'd asked for.

'I thought I recognized the name. You teach at the Cathedral School, I remember the website. History, isn't it?'

Nathan nodded with a gratified smile.

'Such a coincidence. Our son, Oscar, starts next week.' A little laugh, her hand on his arm, she wasn't about to waste

38

this opportunity. 'History is his favourite subject. I must introduce you. He starts on Monday. So naughty of me to take him out of school in London, but we just had to start living in this house.'

Her shapely nails pressed into Nathan's sleeve. Despite her youth, there was something flinty about the smooth face, a hardness in the eyes behind the sparkle, one of those women unafraid to advance her plans. At that moment someone called her name.

'Drinks are in the library,' she murmured. 'My husband's around somewhere, you can't miss him, the untidy one who talks too much. Let's catch up later.'

She turned from us to welcome the guest who had just arrived, a tall man with a waistcoat, a bow tie and crinkly red hair.

'Henry!' The smile was back on her lovely face again.

In the library a fire blazed in the deep hearth, tiny flames were dancing in all the mullioned windows. There were rows of leather-bound books in polished shelves that stretched to the ceiling, red silk on the walls, thick Persian carpet underfoot. A bust of a child stood on a round table, an old globe on another. An exquisite grandfather clock ticked from the corner. I glimpsed Abby through the crowd, carrying a tray and wearing a uniform with a cap. A few tendrils of hair had escaped and were sticking to her flushed cheeks. She looked focused if harried. Ophelia had found her way to Victoria's cleaner then; she must have a knack for acquiring what she wanted. I waved at her but she was picking up empty glasses and didn't notice me.

'This is all froth.' Nathan whispered. 'Let's have a drink and then leave.'

He had been charmed by Ophelia, but this wasn't his milieu. It wasn't mine either, but I didn't feel panicked or bored. I liked the warmth and sparkle, I was hungry for it.

Nathan began to edge through the crowds just as Simon Holmes, head of the Cathedral School, hove into view. Top marks Ophelia, for homework properly done; with his blunt face and sharp teeth, Simon reminded me of an otter. He moved swiftly to our side through the throng as though breasting a stream.

'A familiar visage,' he said, sounding relieved and clapping a hand on Nathan's shoulder.

His wife smiled at me. If Simon was an otter, Sarah was a horse; a pretty one, in red jersey with a Peter Pan collar. 'I'm so glad you're here, Rachel. We were feeling a bit over-whelmed. I'd no idea it was black tie.'

Nor had I until that moment. I looked round, most of the men were dressed formally and the women in silks or velvet. My gaze was snagged by Lizzie, her face lit up and laughing. Laughing! She was with a tall man who was leaning against the wall, his back towards us, fair hair curling to his collar. As I watched, he turned to gesticulate at something in the room, in profile I could see a smoothly handsome face. American, like our hostess, I guessed, from the height, the tan, the relaxed stance.

He glanced around in the way people do when they sense someone is staring at them and then, spotting me, he smiled. His teeth were very white, like an advertisement for toothpaste. He murmured something to Lizzie, picked up a bottle of champagne from the table and walked towards our group.

'Hi there.' He grinned. I was right, American. 'I'm Blake, poor relation and hanger-on.'

'Welcome to the Close.' I raised my glass, wondering how to manoeuvre him back towards Lizzie, she'd looked so happy. Over his shoulder I saw her take a step in our direc-tion, but she was forestalled by the bishop. His voice boomed questions: what did it feel like living back in her hometown?

Had she a job? Lots of friends? A boyfriend? Her happy expression faded. The impudence of the old, how they blunder in with heavy feet. She would have to explain that she hadn't succeeded in finding a publishing job in London, that she had retrained as a librarian and was working in the town where she'd grown up. She wouldn't tell him she was lonely, that her school friends had scattered and her boyfriend had recently walked out, or that she lived alone and, according to her father, dreamt of escape.

Blake filled my glass with champagne. 'I'm Ophelia's brother. I restore properties for my sins, though sadly not this house.' He shook his head, sounding regretful. 'It was strictly hands off, the dean and chapter keep a tight grip.'

'What would you have done?' Nathan appeared at my shoulder; he was a historian, the thought of any modernization would have been intolerable. Honouring the past was his passion.

'Nothing at all. It's perfect already.' Dimples appeared on both Blake's cheeks. 'I'm here to help my sister settle in and I work with her husband.' He filled Nathan's glass so quickly it overflowed, then topped up his own. 'And you are?'

Americans can get away with questions that the average English person would baulk at.

'Local teacher,' Nathan replied stiffly as he shook the champagne from his fingers.

'My sister would love to meet you.'

'She already has.'

'Then you'll know how lucky we feel that Oscar is going to grow up in this amazing place.' Blake's dimples deepened.

Nathan nodded, beginning to thaw.

Gold shimmered at the edge of my vision: Victoria. She was wearing the metallic kaftan she had bought in a Moroccan bazaar, her tallest heels. She had obviously read the invitation.

41

'Finally!' She leant to kiss me – she smelt glorious, a mixture of roses and spice. 'You're always sodding out these days.'

'I've missed you too.' I hugged her. 'Thank God you're back, I'm sick of looking at your empty windows.'

'Come and see me tomorrow.'

'I've a full clinic; I'm second on the roster. I'm not sure when—'

'After that I'm away again.' Her eyes narrowed, daring me to offer another excuse.

'A holiday?' She travelled often. Her photographic images found their way into *National Geographic*, *Condé Nast* and *Vogue*. Her house was full of gathered treasures: a Nigerian medicine mask, a divining rod from a Botswanan witch doctor, prayer mats from Pakistan. She knew several languages, had outlived a beloved husband and could work round the clock; at seventy she had far more energy than anyone I knew.

'Don't be ridiculous, darling. You know I don't do holidays. Five?'

'Victoria!' The dean, his rotund face beaded with sweat, appeared from the crowd to take her elbow 'I need to ask you about the photographs for the parish magazine.'

She winked at me. 'Catch you later.'

The room was crammed now. Ophelia must have mixed London friends with neighbours, glamour ran through the group, a thread of glitter in a bolt of tweed. I spotted one or two of my patients. I used to wonder if social meetings would be awkward for them. I had listened to their fears, seen them crying, seen them naked, but I needn't have worried; unabashed, they sought me out at parties or waylaid me in the supermarket, wanting the answer to a new set of symptoms.

I turned to the drinks table at the same moment a child in pyjamas appeared at the door, his hand resting on the doorknob, head tilted to one side. A beautiful boy aged between eight and ten with fair curls, thick freckles and bare feet. He looked calmly round before stepping into the room and, reaching into a bowl on the table, took out a handful of little biscuits covered with caviar. He crammed them into his mouth and was lifting a glass of wine to his lips when Ophelia appeared from the hall. She took the glass from him with a smile, her hand lightly passing over his curls. The next second he'd vanished from sight. Ophelia's son; I'd imagined a much younger child, four years old at most. Ophelia looked too young to have a ten-year-old son. She must be one of those women who keep their looks intact, or perhaps she'd inherited lucky genes. Her eyes met mine briefly, her smile faded, she moved away. I had intruded into a private moment. I picked up two glasses from the table and turned to make my way towards Lizzie, which was when I saw my patient.

It was ridiculous to feel so jolted. It wasn't really surprising he was here; after all, he'd said he was restoring a house in Wiltshire and this must be the one. He was at the centre of a group. His audience were spellbound. I didn't recognize any of them but they were young, it was less likely I'd have met them at work; the young don't need doctors as often as the old.

He was wearing a black tie slung around his neck as if he'd forgotten what he'd been doing halfway through dressing. Today his face was unmarked by tears, but his mane of hair was longer, almost to his shoulders. In this polished setting he looked untamed, pacing up and down like a caged animal. I backed away. I didn't want him to catch me staring like a teenager at the class alpha male but the movement snagged his attention. He glanced up, smiled and walked towards me without a backward glance, as if he'd found an open door in the cage. I should have known then; I should

43

have taken that as a warning. Faces turned to follow him, noting me.

'I'd no idea you'd be here,' he said.

'How are you?' I hoped he wouldn't notice the wine trembling in the glasses, it was the unexpectedness of the encounter, I'd forgotten the French accent and the warmth of his voice.

'If I'd known you were coming, I'd have lain in wait.' He took one of the glasses from my hands.

'I'm here under false pretences,' I told him lightly. 'It's my husband they want, not me.'

'Why not you?' He raised a glass towards me as he spoke, an unspoken toast to that hour in the surgery.

'He's useful to them, a teacher at their son's school. The mother has pounced already.'

'That fits.' The dark eyes gleamed.

'You were the architect in charge of the restoration?'

'My brief was simple. I had to make sure nothing changed.'

'It must have involved more than that.' I nodded at the immaculate ceilings, the clean stone window sills, the deep window seats. 'I knew this house years ago. It looks better now, the rooms were very gloomy.'

'I regret the gloom; in my opinion houses aren't nearly gloomy enough nowadays.' He finished his wine and smiled at me. I'd forgotten how his smile transformed his face. 'My doctor would tell me not to drink with medication.'

'So would I, but then, I'm not your doctor.' It must have been the alcohol, but it was as though we had begun to dance together, a little waltz, keeping time.

'I think you'll find you are.' He put his drink down. 'I've stopped those tablets now. I wanted to tell you—'

'There you are, babe.' Ophelia appeared from the mass of people and took his arm. The jigsaw fell into place. It didn't have many pieces – it was surprising it had taken till now.

Her face was glowing with triumph; her party was going well. 'I see you've met the wife of Oscar's future history teacher.' A quick, bright smile in my direction. 'Come and meet the man himself, he's awesome.'

'Sorry, Ophelia, you'll have to excuse me.' He disengaged his arm from Ophelia's hand. 'The history teacher's wife turns out to be my doctor, she's called Rachel. I need her medical opinion.'

'Don't be too long, Luc.' A tiny wrinkle appeared on her smooth forehead. 'We need to circulate.'

She nodded in my direction; I wasn't a threat of course, just a nuisance. She turned away, bumping into the solid figure of the bishop, which drew another joyful exclamation. The pang of guilt I felt for accidentally criticizing Luc's wife to him vanished as he looked at me, a moment that lasted until Victoria put her hand on my arm.

'I'm off now, darling.' She kissed me and glanced at Luc, her eyes alive with interest.

I didn't want to introduce her as my next-door neighbour although that was true – it implied a friendship of convenience, one you hadn't chosen. Victoria had chosen me and it still felt miraculous.

'Vee, this is Luc Lefevre, our host. Luc, meet Victoria Jackson.'

I kept my voice casual, but she wouldn't be fooled; a photographer notices everything. She'd have seen the beat of the pulse in my neck, the way my fingers gripped the stem of the glass in my hand. Luc leant forward and kissed her. She'd register that he was attractive, that his gaze was unusually intense, but even Victoria wouldn't guess that two months ago he had sat before me, tears coursing down his face. What would he see when he looked at her? A glamorous seventy-year-old with pink-streaked hair, whose kohl-rimmed eyes missed nothing? That's probably untrue; I don't think he saw her at all.

'Bye, you two.' A smile that encompassed us both. 'Have fun.' And she was gone, leaving the scent of roses in the air.

Luc took my glass and put it down; he leant towards me. 'Follow me,' his voice in my ear raised goose bumps.

I glimpsed Nathan talking to Sarah, they seemed absorbed. Everyone was drinking and chatting, no one seemed to notice us slip quietly from the room. He went ahead down a flight of steps into a stone-floored passageway and opened a side door into the cool night, a lawn lit by flares thrust into the ground.

He glanced down. 'Shoes today, I'm relieved to see.'

Excitement crept through me, a tingling warmth spreading up from my toes. Through the windows I could see heads bent together or thrown back in laughter. I hoped Nathan would be so deep in conversation with Sarah that he wouldn't come to look for me, and that Blake had gone back to rescue Lizzie. No one knew we were here.

Don't be a fool, I told myself as I walked after Luc across the large, square lawn. You must be drunk. Don't begin to imagine he is interested in you, he has a glamorous wife half your age. You are a middle-aged woman with lines on your face and a grown-up child. A marriage of twenty-five years. Besides, he's a patient, you're a doctor, the boundaries are non-negotiable.

I stumbled against the stone lip at the end of the lawn; when he put out a hand to steady me, the warmth burnt. I tucked my hands deep in my pockets. I should go back to the party, seek out my husband, listen to the conversation with Sarah, join in, laughing at all the right moments, but I continued walking. I was watching the shadows that moved ahead of us on the grass. Luc's was tall, mine much smaller, wavering next to his.

He led the way through iron gates set in an old wall, then down the wide grass path flanked by beds, empty at this time of year. We didn't talk. He walked quickly, I had to hurry to keep up. A rushing sound came out of the darkness towards us, getting louder, coming closer. Ahead was a dark hedge and, through a pruned opening, a slippery deeper darkness. We were by the river, it was flowing high between its banks, the surface glassy in the moonlight. The noise was louder than you might expect, as if there was unseen turbulence beneath the calm surface, hidden currents, faster, greedier ones. The kind of place my mother would have pulled me back from as a child.

'The water meadows are just over there.' Luc gestured to the land the other side of the river, a string of lights in the distance. 'That lit-up place is a restaurant, Ophelia's favourite.'

I knew the Old Mill restaurant, I knew the water meadows and this river. He didn't need to explain anything, I'd been here before, years ago. I used to make little islands out of the weeds in the river with Cathy all summer holidays. Nowadays my evening run took me past the meadows and the restaurant whose lights were pricking the darkness. There were cattle grazing in the land between the mill and the river. I'd lived in this place all my life, but I wouldn't tell him that, it sounded too dull. In any case the landscape looked different in the dark, as if I'd found myself in unfamiliar territory, somewhere I'd never been before.

'This was why I agreed to this house in the end. Down here there's the illusion of peace, especially at night.' His eyes shone in the moonlight. 'You saved my life. You probably think that's nothing special. I expect it's the kind of thing you do every day, but I wanted to thank you somewhere quiet, not tossed into conversation in the middle of a party, as if it didn't matter.'

'Any doctor—'

'That's not true, not any doctor. Believe me, I know. Doctors don't really listen, but you did. You allowed me to talk. I felt reclaimed; it seemed to me that if the world contained such kindness, it couldn't be a bad place.'

Had it been kindness? Or had it been simply a case of having enough time for once? Of being drawn in, compelled by the story and the man telling it?

'I told Ophelia and Blake about you, but they didn't listen either. They never do. I was heading for a breakdown. I've had them before; did I tell you that? It could have all got much worse. I'm better now, you cured me. You're smiling, don't you believe me?'

'You do seem remarkably improved, though I can't take all the credit.'

'You look quite different when you smile.'

If patients give me compliments I deflect them, but this time it felt good, which was scary. It was as though one of the fences around me that normally kept me safe had broken, and I'd found myself nearer to the edge of a bank. I didn't reply, I wasn't sure what to say.

'I'm sorry.' It was too dark to see his expression, but he didn't sound sorry. 'Do I sound like some creepy patient?'

I shook my head and attempted a laugh, but his last words made me uneasy. They conjured Brian, that half smile, his whispery voice; even the sounds in this place were whispering: the rustling trees, the little noises the moorhens made in the rushes. There might be water rats coming ashore to forage for food, their long tails snaking over the grass. I shivered. Luc took off his jacket and put it around me; it was heavy on my shoulders, the silky lining warm from his body.

'We should go back,' I told him. 'It's your party, people will wonder where you are.'

He shook his head. 'It's Ophelia's party, definitely not mine.'

We began to walk back, side by side this time, towards

the flaring torches and the house, the sound of the river fading behind us.

'It's all her doing,' he continued. 'The people, the flowers, the décor. I asked her not to, I can't stand this sort of thing.' He was short-circuiting the rules again, as he had in the surgery, as if the usual ways into friendship took too long. 'I imagined it would be easier to ignore all this than it's proving to be.' He turned to me, his face pale in the moonlight. 'Once Ophelia and Blake discovered this place, they were determined to live here. I was too busy to think it through but it was a mistake. I don't want to live like this, that was never my aim.'

We were nearing the house which rose up in front of us in all its lamplit grandeur; towering above its ancient walls and gabled roof, the spire of the cathedral itself reached into the sky, a fairy-tale construction as thin and delicate as if made of icing sugar. Was Luc asking me to feel sorry for him amid such privileged splendour? He must have felt the question in my mind.

'It's stunning of course, but it's a house that was built for greedy men, the church at its most entitled. The men who actually built the house lived beyond the walls. I'd prefer that. An empty room, a sheet of paper, space outside the windows.'

'Your builders wouldn't have had much space outside their windows,' I couldn't resist pointing out. 'In fact, they wouldn't have had windows.'

'You're right of course. I meant I want less, not more.'

'So what would you draw on your sheet of paper?' His dream house probably, a modern construction he'd been waiting all his life to build.

'Trees and mountains and sky.'

'Not houses?'

'The house I want has been built already. It's in France,

remember? The south. You should come and see it. Would you, if I asked?'

It was the kind of invitation people toss out without meaning, he would be horrified if I took him at his word. I let myself imagine turning up at some pretty villa in the Côte d'Azur. He'd answer the door, politely disguising surprise and the fact he'd completely forgotten my name. The rest of the family and friends would be outside, sipping drinks in the sun, while their boy splashed in the pool with other children. Blake would appear with a glass of something cool and a show of friendliness, but Ophelia would look bored. I'd be invited in, but the atmosphere would be awkward. I wouldn't stay long.

Then we were back at the house; someone had locked the side door, so we went around to the front. People were leaving. I could hear Ophelia laughing and glimpsed her blonde head turn as we walked up the steps. She was talking to the bishop, I don't think she noticed me though she slipped an arm through Luc's, drawing him into a group of guests.

I found Nathan in the library; he was still talking to Sarah, their heads close together. Lizzie was nowhere in sight. I slipped off Luc's jacket and left it on a chair.

'Hi there.' My voice sounded louder than usual. 'Sorry.'

Nathan looked up, clearly startled. 'Why sorry?'

'I lost track of time. I've been admiring the gardens.'

Sarah looked at me, a distracted little glance with a trace of hostility. She and Nathan had been deep in their conversation and hadn't registered my absence. We needn't have come back after all.

'Gosh, yes; it must be time to go.' Nathan smiled at Sarah. 'See you at school tomorrow.'

Ophelia was at the front door, Luc had disappeared. Blake stood next to her, holding a glass in one hand and her arm

50

with the other, his fingers gripping tightly as if she was exhausted and he had to hold her up.

'You escaped,' he whispered as Nathan was thanking Ophelia. 'You and Luc. How clever of you.'

'A quick guided tour,' I smiled, wondering who else had noticed. 'I used to come here as a child. It's changed a lot; now I can't even find my own child.' I looked down the hall towards the kitchen, hoping to catch a glimpse of her.

'Oh, Lizzie's gone home, she was tired. What a sweet girl. She takes after her mother.'

I kept the smile on my face but a sharp little claw of worry scraped my mind. You shouldn't be walking the streets on your own at night, I wanted to tell her, even in a quiet town like Salisbury. We'd planned to walk you to your flat. We'd have chatted about the party, compared notes on Ophelia and Blake. I was looking forward to it, why didn't you wait? But I knew the answer already. It was simple. She was showing us and maybe Blake that she was independent; she might have come back to her hometown, but she certainly hadn't come home.

Then Blake laughed, breaking the silence. He leant forward and kissed me, and I felt better; froth, as my husband would say, but delicious and refreshing all the same. I warmed towards him, he'd remembered Lizzie's name.

'Time to go, darling.' Nathan took my hand. He nodded at Blake, who smiled as he emptied his glass.

Outside, the night seemed colder and darker than before. I glanced back at the lights shining from the windows – the house looked magical from here, an enchanted palace in an ancient fable. We walked quickly, our breath clouding the cold air.

Nathan pulled my arm through his. 'I enjoyed that, I hadn't thought I would.'

'But you talked to the same people you see all the time.'

'I expect that's why I enjoyed it,' he replied peaceably. 'My tribe. Did you find yours?'

Who did he imagine was my tribe? Other doctors? Middle-aged mothers, schoolteachers' wives? He was wrong anyway; I hadn't been in search of a tribe. I'd been looking for something quite different though I couldn't put it into words, something that had been part of the moonlit garden, the warmth of Luc's hand and the sound of the river rushing in the dark.

'I don't think we have much in common with our hosts,' Nathan said cheerfully as we walked along the road. 'Ophelia is very beautiful of course, one of those trophy wives that rich men acquire. I didn't like the fair-haired guy who was hanging round her, he was smiling too much.'

'You mean her brother?'

'I thought he was gloating, all that money on show.' He put his arm round me as we went through the Close gate into our quiet little street. We'd passed the shrubbery and I hadn't even noticed; perhaps it was as simple as having someone with me, preventing my imagination getting the better of me.

'We don't have to worry though.' He unlocked the door and stood back to let me in. 'It's not like we have to see them often.'

It was as though my mother was standing behind me, pulling me back from the edge of the river.

Chapter 6

In custody
June 2017

All the sounds in this place were threatening. The approach of footsteps in the morning, the turn of the key in a lock. The creak of the door opening and, worse, the thud of it closing. I made almost no noise, just the soft tap of my bare feet on the floor, the louder clicking when I put on shoes, the scrape of the chair when I sat down, the scratch of my pencil on paper. The hours on my own hung silently but then, I wanted to be by myself. I couldn't bear the thought of visitors. I didn't even want Nathan or Lizzie to see me, to be honest, I was ashamed.

When I was due to be interviewed, I was taken to another room down a narrow corridor. The Sri Lankan woman who led me was taller than I was, younger. She seemed kind and I wondered what it was that made me think so; it might have been her gentle manner of speaking or the careful way she touched me, her quiet smile perhaps. I was aware of all those things in here, they seemed more important than usual.

When the policeman arrived, he introduced himself straight

away. Detective Inspector Wainwright. Everything about him was square. His box-like face was wind-scalded, topped by a stiff hedge of pale hair, his hands were broad. He settled himself in a chair facing me, he looked anything but kind.

Luc's eyes were dark like peaty water in a Highland loch, Nathan had sea-water eyes – his thoughts were transparent all the way to the bottom, or so you might have thought. The inspector's were opaque like pond water, grey-green pond water solid with ice.

My lawyer, Judy Burns, arrived late and I caught the chemical scent of the deodorant she must have sprayed in her armpits before she put on the black suit hanging in her closet, dragging it out with the same set frown she was wearing now; being here sharpened my sense of smell, my sense of everything. Her eyes were like currants in a doughy face. Her suit was a size too small and one of her tights was laddered at the ankle; these things made me worried. I needed someone well-groomed, because in my mind, at least then, a perfect appearance went along with intelligence and success. At work I wear – wore – tidy clothes, though that changed.

Love changed me. After France I relaxed my grip on things I'd always held tight. I allowed myself more wine at night, I wore scent every day. I did less work in the evenings and read novels instead, the novels of my youth, *Anna Karenina*, *Women in Love*, *Middlemarch*. I devoured them greedily and left them open on the floor. I wore clothes to work I wouldn't have worn before, sleeveless dresses, shorter skirts, ankle boots, silky underwear. I didn't wear tights. Some of my patients sensed the difference. They commented that the colours were brighter, the fashion more edgy. Brian came more often still, like a dog who scents that a bitch is available. He leant closer, so close I could see the dirt encrusted in his ears and the dandruff at his hairline, little details that aren't meant to be criticisms, just the kind of things a doctor can't help noticing, they tell a story though, in his case, I should have read between the lines.

Judy smiled at me when she came in as if she was sorry for me. I guessed she was in her mid-twenties, Lizzie's age. Maybe she saw her mother when she looked at me, which would make it difficult for her if I was asked to talk about sex. Old people's sex lives, she might think, squirming a little. It was always hard to contemplate my parents in bed though as a child my mind strayed towards the thought, like touching a painful spot, away then back, as if compelled to pick at it. My father, the vicar, an attractive man in his youth, going by the pictures, my mother a physiotherapist, slim, pretty; all the same, a joke. Anything with a vicar in it could be a joke.

Did Lizzie think of sex between Nathan and me as a joke? My mind circled my daughter and the last time I saw her, probing the secret she'd been keeping, the new, astonishing one. It was obvious that her parents' sex lives would be the last thing on her mind. In any case there was hardly any sex now, or at least not good sex. The last time Nathan had made love to me had felt like rape and you can't make a joke out of that.

'So, take me back to the start,' Inspector Wainwright leant forward. 'When it all began.'

I told him about the evening Luc came to the surgery, but that didn't seem to satisfy him. I described the night of the party, but he looked away and scratched the back of his neck. I knew this because I was watching him carefully and I was good at reading people, it was what I did for a living. The inspector and I both, but my business was about healing people, his was about catching them out. I wanted to say whatever I needed to please him because that way I'd earn my freedom, if only on bail.

The real beginning was too far back to interest him. It

rang with the noise of a child's feet in wellingtons running over a bridge, above glittering ropes of water. The old mill, there was no restaurant in those days. I would have looked happy; in my hand was a bag of crusts and, around the corner, the millpond. Thrillingly I had power for once though I was only five. The ducks and geese clustered at my feet, my mother stood behind me, immobile, her black coat buttoned to her neck.

When I walked deeper into the pond, the water tugged my boots and she pulled me back. The way home completed a circle and led through the peaceful streets of Harnham, past playing fields and the industrial estate. At home, my mother took off her coat with a sigh, which I now know was one of relief. Years later, it was James, my cousin, who put me right about why she'd watched me so closely by the water. We smoked cigarettes behind the garden shed when my parents were out, and he told me the story of the bridge.

He said it used to be a thin timber thing, I was to imagine it swaying in the wind. One afternoon, many years ago, the weather was fierce. The chains that held the bridge in place had eroded the softened banks. A young child had hurried ahead of her mother who had gone the long way round from school so her daughter could feed the ducks. A fair-haired little girl, a beloved only child.

It had been stormy the night before, the river had mounted its banks, but the child had run ahead, and the mother met a friend and was chatting. She hadn't noticed the height of the brown water in the stream and, when she looked up to locate her daughter, the child seemed to be flying.

The mother must have been confused at first, not understanding the bridge had twisted itself free of its moorings, tossing the little girl into the air like a bird; she had leant from the bank, holding out her arms, but couldn't reach her. She jumped but couldn't find her.

And the child? I liked to think of her last moments as wonderful ones; when I listened to the story, I had wanted them for myself. I wanted to fly through the air and fall through the glittering surface and go deeper. I wanted to feel the dark pull of the current, be tumbled over and over in the grip of something larger than myself. I imagined how the cold water would fill my nose and throat. I wanted to know what happens beyond the bursting feeling when you hold your breath as long as you can. That was the beginning, but it's not the beginning that the detective wanted; he was looking for a story about fear, danger and sex. Most people are. We'll start with fear and danger; the sex comes later.

Chapter 7

May 2017

The wet tarmac glistened under my feet as I ran. I could just make out cows in the water meadows the other side of the stream that flowed to my left and, beyond, the cathedral spire splintering the sky. I stopped to retie the lace of my trainers and that's when I heard them again, the stealthy noise of footsteps behind me.

I had started my run later than usual, having had tea with Victoria before she left for New York to see her ninety-five-year-old mother. Gladys had emigrated to the States with her second husband thirty years ago. He had been a wealthy American businessman. When he died, she lived on in the flat they'd shared overlooking Central Park. I'd visited before, the views were magnificent. Now she was ill with a cough she couldn't shake. Victoria had tried her best to persuade me to go with her.

'God knows you need a break, you look exhausted,' she'd said, examining me with narrowed eyes, though she was probably more tired than I was. She'd spent the day photographing views of the Close for the parish magazine, climbing partway up the cathedral spire. We were having tea in her garden at the green tin table, as we did when she was at home and I was free. Cello music filtered down to us from her CD player through the open doors of her sitting room. We were wrapped in rugs and surrounded by tubs of crimson and orange wallflowers. It was early in May and still chilly. 'There will still be blossom in the park and we can visit the MoMA, we didn't have nearly long enough last time.'

'Gladys won't want visitors if she's feeling poorly. I'm booked to go to the Paris conference anyway, then there's Lizzie. She'll be missing Mike. I can't go far, she might need me.' It was unlikely but, if she called, I could easily get home from France.

'I saw her chatting to some bloke in a car yesterday, she looked very happy.' Victoria smiled at me. 'Relax for once.'

'A bloke in a car?' Discomfort tingled, the thin edge of panic. 'Did you see who it was?'

'Just his back view, he was wearing one of those beanies. They seemed intent on each other.'

Someone from the library? A date she'd arranged online? 'I hope she'll be careful, only she's just had a break-up—'

'If she was still in London you wouldn't have a clue who she was with and that's exactly how it should be. We should be glad she's making new friends. I'll phone her when I get back, there's a play at the Almeida I think she'd love.'

Victoria was Lizzie's godmother, she had no children of her own and they were close. Lizzie told her things she didn't share with me. I didn't mind, in fact I was grateful. It hadn't been easy for a young woman getting started in photography in the sixties; it was male-dominated back then. Victoria never talked about the aggressive sexism that came her way, the comments and the glances, but I'd seen them for myself, even now. She knew everything there was to know about fighting your corner with courage. Lizzie was lucky.

'Thanks Vee.'

As I hugged her goodbye, I could feel the sharp outline of her shoulder blades. She was more fragile than she looked. Her cure would be the opposite of mine; ideally she needed to stay home and rest, whereas I wanted escape.

The shock of the cool evening air emptied my mind; I lapped the towpath twice. The first time round there were still commuters walking home from the station, briefcases in hand. The second time round they'd all vanished. I was halfway from the town to the Old Mill when it began to rain. I stopped to tie my lace and that's when I heard the footsteps.

I straightened quickly and looked round with a prickling sense of disquiet. I'd put the memory of those footsteps out of my mind but now my skin stung with anxiety. It was more worrying this time, I was a long way from home, it was almost dark.

There were shadows on the path, thick ones between the trees that lined the fence, the water in the stream was black. I held my breath as I listened but there was no sound at all. Had I imagined the steps as I probably had before? I started running again and at once the sounds started up as though someone behind me was playing grandmother's footsteps. I turned instantly, catching a figure melting into the shadows behind a tree.

The shock was sickening.

A second later, I began to run as if for my life, my feet thudding on the tarmac, breath rasping in my throat, fear flooding my mind. At the end of the path, I raced over the bridge, past the side wall of the Old Mill and, turning right at the corner, ran straight into the solid body of a man. He was looking over the rail into the millpond a few yards from the front door of the restaurant, umbrella in hand. He staggered, then righted himself, putting an arm out to support me at the same time or I would have fallen.

'Rachel!'

It was Luc. His face lit with a smile, as if he had been waiting specially for me to round the corner at speed on that particular rainy evening in May. For a second I wondered if I had conjured him from my subconscious but the hand that grasped my arm was warm, the grip very firm.

'Sorry,' I gasped out.

'Are you running away or just running?' His glance took in my face, my mud-splattered leggings, my wet T-shirt. He looked interested, amused and concerned at the same time.

I was struggling for breath.

'Are you okay?' His smile disappeared, he sensed trouble.

'Someone's following me.' I could hardly speak.

'Are you sure?'

'I heard footsteps, then I saw someone, or the shadow of someone.' My words sounded mad even to myself, but he nodded seriously, he didn't think I was imagining anything.

'Wait here.' He gave me his umbrella and jogged around the corner of the Old Mill, disappearing quickly. The quiet closed in as the sound of his footsteps faded. The rain pattered on the dome of his umbrella. I could hear water flowing under the bridge, the reeds at the edge of the pond murmuring in the wind, like someone breathing in the dark. The water smelt dank as if something was rotting at the edges. The shadows under the trees by the bank were deep enough to hide a man, several men. The sudden squawking of a duck made me jump. I began to shiver.

Luc reappeared ten minutes later, out of breath. 'I ran all the way to the end of the towpath and back. Whoever was there has disappeared now.' He took my arm. 'You're cold. Let's go inside. We can ask if they've seen someone lurking around, then we'll phone the police.'

'No.' I took my arm away. I didn't want to go inside, I didn't want to call the police – Luc hadn't seen anyone. It was possible I'd been imagining things again, unease can get the upper hand in the dark. I'd seen it before; driving home after a late call I would sometimes brake to avoid a woman crossing the road from one side to the other for no apparent reason. I'd know it was because she thought there was someone behind her, even when there was no one there at all. Fear makes you behave like that.

'Did you see a face?' he asked.

'He was too far away. I could be completely wrong, it might have been shadows from the trees by the path.' I began to feel foolish, but all the same it was good to stand close, comforting and disconcerting at the same time. Luc was so near that the heat from his skin was warming mine.

'What are you doing here?' I asked, turning away to look out over the water; it was easier to talk that way.

'We're with friends in the restaurant but I wanted to get some air. I've been standing out here for a while. The sounds of a river are sharper at night, as if each one was outlined in light. Listen.'

I heard the quiet rustling of rain on the water, the faint noises of the cows moving in the fields, the birds settling among the reeds. Friendly sounds this time. I could have stood next to him, listening for hours.

'Come inside with me, join us for supper.'

I turned to look through the windows behind us. Candlelight shone on tables laid with glass and silver. A low glimmer of flames came from an open fire. It would be warm in there, the air would be scented with food.

'Is Blake with you?'

'Would you come in if he was?'

'He seemed so relaxed, he wouldn't notice if I wasn't dressed for the occasion.'

'No one will notice.'

'Of course they will.'

'You can sit next to me, I'll hide you.'

I tried to visualize how it would be if I walked in with Luc. Ophelia might be annoyed though she'd disguise it well, their friends would be agog. There would be raised eyebrows and suppressed amusement. He'd put me in a corner next to him, try to shield me from their curious glances, but I'd still be embarrassed, an interloper in their little group.

'I wouldn't get past the door.'

'Let me run you back then, keep you safe.'

At that moment the door of the restaurant opened. Ophelia stood there; backlit, her fair hair was lifting in the wind and floating around her head like a cloud. She was immaculate in a close-fitting black dress with high heels. She pulled out her phone and punched numbers in, I heard the answering vibration in Luc's pocket.

'Luc, where the hell are you?' Her voice was tense.

We were only a couple of metres away but her vision would be limited by the door frame on either side.

'James and Tilly are starving, we've ordered.'

I was unsure why we kept quiet, like naughty children hiding from the grown-ups. I had an absurd desire to giggle.

'For God's sake, hurry up.' She put the phone in her pocket, stepped back inside the restaurant and shut the door.

'I'm off,' I whispered, bending to retie the lace again. 'You need to join your party and I have to pack.'

'Why? Where are you going?'

'France.' I straightened and stepped back. I should hurry, Nathan might be waiting.

'Which part?' Luc seemed intrigued.

'Paris, medical conference.'

'I'll be in France from tomorrow.' His whisper was louder than mine. 'Blake's coming to visit.'

'That sounds fun.' And it did; I could see exactly why Luc would want his brother-in-law along. Blake would make the visit into a party, he'd bring wine and tell stories, insist on picnics. He'd crack amusing jokes and make everyone relax.

'Thanks for your help.' I touched his hand then jogged away fast. I'd lied. I didn't need to pack, the conference was in a couple of days' time, but nor did I want Ophelia to reappear and find us conferring in the dark. There was another reason which I trod underfoot as I ran; talking to Luc, standing near him, had felt seductively good, like some heady liquor you know you shouldn't be drinking even as it slides over your tongue, warmly intoxicating.

The way home was along lit pavements, but the fear had returned and I sprinted, glancing into every garden that I passed, half expecting to find someone crouching in the shadows. By the time I reached home Nathan was in the kitchen; he was bending over the table, a couple of salmon fillets spread in front of him, intent on preparation. I slipped my arms around his waist, leaning against his back as I caught my breath.

'Christ, Rachel.' He shifted sideways. 'You're soaking!'

'I was followed on the towpath.' I sat down at the table, my voice sounding flat, even to me. In our calm little kitchen, what had happened seemed unreal.

Nathan was taking tiny bones from the salmon, and didn't look up. 'See anybody this time?'

'I heard footsteps. I thought I saw someone disappearing behind a tree.' I felt my heart begin to thud as it had when I'd seen that shape merging into the shadows. 'I'll report it to the police tomorrow, that's twice it's happened now.'

'Better safe than sorry.' He started putting the bones into a neat pile one by one. 'But don't be disappointed if they fail to make much of it, it's difficult to investigate things when there's so little certainty.' He straightened. 'Both times have been in the evening when it's hard to see clearly.' He cut a lemon in half with a clean swipe of the knife. Nathan was an excellent cook, his approach was precise, patient, the opposite of mine. 'Didn't you say hallucinations are more common than people realize?' He squeezed lemon juice over the pink flesh.

I'd told him once that hallucinations can be triggered by hormonal change: pregnancy, childbirth and around the menopause. Once I'd been caught out by a fifty-five-year-old woman who insisted there was an intruder in her flat despite repeated searches by the police. Her symptoms disappeared on hormone replacement therapy. It was an intriguing story but now Nathan was applying it to me.

'It's fortunate that you're going to France soon,' he continued, sounding like a teacher, which of course he was. He ground black pepper over the fillets and scattered parsley evenly. 'A break, some sunshine, just what the doctor ordered.'

'Don't patronize me, Nathan, I know what I saw.'

Although I didn't, not exactly, and that was the trouble. Nathan was washing his hands; I wasn't sure if he'd heard. He'd resent that remark, he liked the last word. I went up for my shower.

My eyes blazed back at me from the bathroom mirror. Luc had believed me, he'd checked it out. I stripped off my wet clothes, leaving them in a muddy heap, and stepped into the shower. The hot water pounded my body and after a while I felt calmer. There were odd types around all the time, people who lingered in quiet places, who followed women for no other reason than curiosity or boredom, who would never cause harm. I probably wouldn't report it after all. What was the point? Even if the police decided to investigate, the man would be long gone.

The conference would be a chance to pull myself together, regroup, get a grip, all those words Nathan used to his pupils. I might appreciate him more after a little break, that meticulous attention to detail, his loyalty, the companionship, all the things I took for granted. I stood under the shower for a long time, longer than usual. I was rinsing off the mud, but it felt as though I was sluicing away something else that was clinging to me, an unfamiliar scent of some kind, forbidden, exotic, troubling.

Chapter 8

The glass doors of Salisbury library opened into the main concourse; inside, the building hummed with life. School children sat at tables, an old man with a straggling white beard read the paper in an armchair and three mothers with toddlers were sitting on bean bags in the children's section. One was reading in a hushed voice, a little boy with his hand on her knee stared up at her face as if it was the only one in the world.

Lizzie was at a counter on the first floor, talking to a small bunch of students, some were taking notes. A tall young man with glasses and dark hair at the back of the group was handing out pens and paper to those who didn't have them. They were listening to Lizzie with rapt attention. I couldn't hear the words but her voice had the cadence of a story and they were clearly entranced. Her hands described circles as she spoke. She appeared in her element; one of her jobs was explaining how to access library resources and she seemed to be turning that into a journey of discovery.

She looked different today: a new leather jacket and a

pretty skirt, her hair gleamed with highlights and her nails flashed red as she pointed to the screen. Lizzie never painted her nails. I leant against the wall, watching approvingly, conscious I was being hypocritical. I'd often glanced in the little mirror in my room at the surgery, noticing my untidy hair, my smudged or absent make-up. It was difficult to look good when you were busy; unimportant, I told myself, compared with the work itself and the need to hurry from patient to patient. All the same, I was glad my daughter had bothered. One day she'd catch sight of herself in the mirror and see her beauty had gone. She might find it impossible to believe that the tired face in front of her was her own; she'd be glad then that she made the most of her looks while she could.

After five minutes the students thanked her and left, the dark-haired man– a young teacher perhaps – lingering for an earnest-looking chat. Lizzie walked with him to the door, then turned with a smile that lasted until she saw me.

'What are you doing here, Mum?' she asked as I approached. 'Spying on me?'

It was a joke and not a joke; her lips had tightened.

'My half day. You were great with those kids—'

'I'm busy.' She looked around, then back at me. 'Working.'

'I wanted to ask you to lunch.' I began to wish I hadn't come; I was embarrassing her. If my own mother had watched me at work, I might have been mortified too. How stupid I'd been. 'I'm off tomorrow—'

'Fine.' She glanced at her desk.

'It's a conference in Paris,' I continued, though she hadn't asked. 'A long one. I'll be away for ten days so I thought we might have lunch today.'

'I've got a date already.'

Hence the highlights, the make-up. She sat down in front of the computer and examined the screen.

'Lizzie—' I was about to say, let's go for a holiday when I get back, somewhere hot. I'll sort it out, a girly weekend, it'll be fun. Just us. Then she looked up, eyebrows raised, hostility in her glance.

'What?'

'Oh . . . it's just that I think I was followed on a run yesterday. There are some weird types around, you need to take care.'

'Thanks. I can look after myself.'

She had stopped wanting me to kiss her years ago but some mothers wouldn't care, they would step right up and fling their arms around their daughter, no matter what she said. I stepped forward but she pulled herself nearer to the desk, the chair legs scraping on the floor. The old man glanced up from his paper. I walked to the door and turned back to wave but she was tapping on the keyboard and didn't look up.

On the way home, I passed an older woman and a much younger one eating chips from the same bag, a mother and daughter perhaps. They were chatting with their mouths full, pushing against each other, absorbed. I watched them, feeling jealous. I had been busy when Lizzie had needed me, I couldn't expect her to respond now. I hadn't earned the closeness. There was a time, when she was at university, that things improved – she adored her English degree and flourished at King's – but, since her return to Salisbury, everything I said was wrong. I could sense resentment below the surface like a rock underwater whose shape you can't make out, something you might bump into by mistake. I had to remember Lizzie had been returned to the place of her childhood just as she was finding her wings. Nathan could be right, she needed freedom and I might be hovering too close, getting in her way.

Nathan fell asleep on the sofa in front of the television

after supper. His half-moon glasses slid to the tip of his nose, so I took them off and put them on the table. His features had settled in sleep, there were new lines between his eyebrows; he looked faintly cross. We hadn't talked about my trip tomorrow. We would have done, years ago. We would have said we'd miss each other and planned a meal out on my return. We might have made love. Nowadays we rarely went out, and seldom made love. We didn't text when apart in case the other was busy. We had become like business partners, familiar and amicable, sharing the running of our careers, our daughter, the house, the garden, his mother, Lizzie's dog. Parallel lives, not clashing but never meeting. Nathan's head turned sideways, he began to snore.

There were things we could do, the kind of things I told my patients about: date nights, candlelit meals, holding each other in bed, even if we didn't have sex. I'd never used the vaginal oestrogen foam I'd got Debbie to prescribe for soreness. I went upstairs, took it from the bathroom cabinet and slipped it into my case. I'd have a few days in hand, we could sleep together when I got back. Perhaps it was as simple as that, one of those things you have to do to keep your life on track, like cooking supper or washing the clothes.

I began packing, something pretty for the evening, suits for the day, jeans for exploring Paris, a swimming costume – the conference centre housed a leisure complex. A blue cotton dress in case it was hot, Victoria said Paris could be hot in May. I was hot already; a wave of heat began to travel from my chest to my face and up into my hairline, this was happening often.

I opened the window and looked out in the dark. I might arrange for us to go to counselling or Relate, though Nathan would resist. I told my patients about these options and they listened because I was a professional, who wore tidy clothes and a calm smile, heard their stories and examined their bodies, who had a husband and a daughter, who could be seen on dog walks and jogging sometimes. A woman whose life seemed complete. The glowing spire of the cathedral reached up above the walls of the Close. The red light at the top was like an all-seeing eye, keeping watch over civilized life in a pretty market town where the days passed without drama and we all played by the rules.

I remembered this a week later when my civilized self watched my primitive self in a bedroom in the south of France, enthralled, naked, the hot sun slanting through the shutters onto my skin, onto my lover's skin.

We have arrived.

Chapter 9

May 2017

In films, the music changes when something important is about to happen; it gets faster or louder, there might be a drum roll. In real life the soundtrack is often muted, a door opening quietly, someone whispering in your ear, a text message arriving on your phone.

By mid-morning on the second day of the Paris conference the auditorium was stuffy, the air conditioning wasn't working. The subject was childhood precursors of adult bipolar disorder, interesting, even absorbing, but the thought of eight more days spent jammed with others in an overheated theatre was dispiriting. The conference was lengthy even by international standards. I was beginning to think I had made a mistake.

Dinner the night before had been lavish and tedious; trapped between a neurosurgeon from Texas and a French neurologist, my head had swum with tiredness. Afterwards I walked back through the streets, looking through lit windows at couples chatting together in cafes and glancing behind me every now and then. I was in another country and on a busy street, but I couldn't shake the feeling of being followed. I heard footsteps last thing at night, they had entered my dreams. I slept badly.

The voice of the lecturer was monotonous, seconds later I might have been asleep. I might not have felt my phone vibrate when the message arrived. The woman next to me made a little sound of disapproval as I slipped it from my pocket, feeling worried. It could be Nathan with a problem, something to do with Lizzie, perhaps she was sick. It must be serious, we only texted in emergencies. My mind flew to the mystery man in the car and worry spiralled. She could be in serious trouble of some kind, there might have been an injury, an assault, even a kidnap. The possibilities were endless.

'*C'est mon mari,*' I whispered to my neighbour. '*L'urgence.*'

She looked back at the lecturer, uninterested.

I lowered the phone to my lap and read the screen.

I need help with house project before Blake arrives. Sending ticket for train to Arles which leaves this afternoon. Details to follow. Luc

I had to read it twice, my heart slowing. It wasn't Lizzie in trouble, it wasn't Nathan either. I had jumped to the wrong conclusion. Luc was inviting me to his house, he'd kept my number, he'd remembered I was going to France. He needed my help, mysteriously ahead of his brother-in-law's arrival. There was an attachment, a blurred photograph of grey buildings surrounded by grass, a broken roof, a line of windows, shutters hanging crookedly. Mountains in the distance, a blue sky. Arles, the deep south, the place of sunflowers.

It was as though sunshine was seeping around the cracks of the lecture theatre doors. This was the kind of challenge I'd dreamt about; the sort of thing I'd thought wouldn't happen any more. The woman next to me tutted again, staring at my phone, but I stood up. I'd had enough of her, enough of the lecture and the conference. I'd escape for a day, maybe two, then come back. I stumbled over feet in the dark, apologizing in whispers.

Outside, I began to run, leaving the centre behind, weaving my way between shoppers and strolling tourists. People stared; it was raining, a light summer rain, but I didn't care. I felt as irresponsible as if I were my younger self again, intent on some crazy adventure.

Nathan had told me I needed a break, he knew I loved houses, especially old ones. He'd recommended sunshine, and I could feel it already, that southern heat on my skin. I ran in through the front door of the hotel and hurried past the receptionist. She looked up from the screen, plucked eyebrows raised – guests were normally out all day. I was stepping out of line. Another message pinged through as I was going up in the lift: there was a train from Gare de Lyon in an hour and a half. Luc had sent the ticket to my phone, taking a risk, as I was.

The maid was cleaning my room when I entered. She looked up in surprise from her hoovering. I told her I was leaving and not to bother tidying when she'd only have to clean again later. She shrugged and left, a tired-looking middle-aged woman with chapped hands. Not unattractive, just worn-out; we were probably the same age. She might feel trapped as well, but with far more reason.

I bundled my clothes into my case but some of the excitement had drained away. I folded some notes under the lamp as if to assuage guilt; I was hurrying to the south of France to meet a patient, a man I liked, who was nine years younger than me and married as I was. Rules were bending, snapping. I zipped up the case, glancing around the room. The small part of my life in this blank little space would be expunged; the sheets, the towels, the discarded toothpaste box in the wastepaper basket, everything would vanish as though it had never been. I'd forget it all, forget the tired woman who was going to clean after me. The next couple of days with Luc would vanish too, buried within the larger trip. I might tell Nathan one day in the future. I'd say that I managed to fit in an outing to help a friend with a house to restore; I might even tell him it was Luc. He would pretend to be jealous, we would laugh. By then I would have forgotten the way my heart was beating now, the excitement fluttering in my abdomen like a case full of butterflies.

My train was waiting on the platform. Everything was easy in the way that running down a slope is easy, your legs carry you effortlessly, you don't have time to think. I sat in the corner by the window; the train was peaceful as trains often are, despite other people sitting near.

We left the suburbs behind and the rain dragging sideways on the glass loosened the colours of the landscape like stains in the wash. Lime green, sage green, emerald. I glimpsed dovecotes and cows, white ones with large horns. Bungalows, grey roads, grey sky, women with umbrellas and children bundled against the weather. Neat apple orchards became fields of beet, woods scribbling at the edges, the dark green foliage delicate as if traced with the sharp point of a crayon. Five minutes later I was asleep.

When I woke my mouth was dry, the carriage had become more crowded. I was wedged between the window and a snoring man whose shoulder listed into mine. The light was sharper, warmer. There were olive trees in the gardens outside the windows, orange-tiled roofs. Two teenage girls perched on the seat opposite, their smooth faces bent to their phones. I turned back to the window, a wave of heat travelling from my chest to my face. The sweat was collecting along my neck. My face was reflected in the glass, the lines around my eyes and mouth clearly outlined. This was a mistake. Luc must be regretting his decision already, he'd probably expected me to say no. I'd let fantasy get the better of me, no one gets to retrace their steps at my age, much less take new ones.

When the train came to a halt at Arles, I stood and straightened my crumpled skirt, the lining sticking to my skin. In my haste I hadn't given myself time to change my clothes. I'd take the next train back and text Luc from the carriage to explain that I'd had to return, something had come up. I'd go home after that, settle back into my life. See more of Lizzie if she'd let me, arrange that holiday. I'd try to get closer to Nathan, I could learn more about gardening to keep him company or take up sketching again, all those sensible things women my age do.

The girls on the seat opposite jumped down from the train door to the platform; landing gracefully, they ran up the platform together. I watched as they dodged round other passengers, giggling; perhaps they had boyfriends waiting by the barrier. Lovely girls, loose-limbed, happy, very young. I needn't go as far as the barrier; there was a train waiting on the other side of the platform. I'd buy my ticket on board and change trains further up the line. I pulled my case across the platform, my hands slipping on the handle, the heat already making me sweat. My heels caught on the step as I mounted. I stumbled and a hand closed on my elbow, preventing a fall.

I looked up into Luc's face.

Chapter 10

May 2017

Nowadays I can only visualize his face as it was in the paper when they came for him weeks later. There was a bruise on his forehead in those grainy images, his skin was splashed with blood. What he looked like that afternoon in Arles station, the exact expression as he gazed down at me, has disappeared from my memory, which is odd because I can still hear his voice. The words themselves were difficult to make out above the noise of the guards, the slamming of doors and the blowing of whistles, but I can feel the warmth of his hand even now. I'd guessed he would meet the train, but I hadn't thought he would be on the platform itself. He didn't ask why I had been about to board a train going back to Paris. Just then the train began to move and it was too late for second thoughts, too late for escape.

We stood very still, staring at each other. A woman knocked him with her handbag as she hurried past but he didn't seem to notice. He wore a paint-splattered shirt with rolled-up sleeves. His skin was deep brown as though he had spent all the days since I'd seen him in the sun, the hair on his arms was golden.

Then he smiled and so did I. He took my case, and with his other hand held mine as if it was a completely natural thing to do. The knit of our fingers seemed to me to be at the centre of the station and the crowds, part of the swirl of language, the desire to laugh. The desire. Hot and new, painful as if I had lost a layer of skin. Even the light seemed to sting. The woman ticket collector, indifferent and thickly made-up, examined the ticket on my phone and nodded us through, then smiled unexpectedly, her face transformed in the instant. A good omen surely.

Then we were outside in brilliant sunshine. I remember three women with bulging plastic bags across a little complex of roads and paving. They must have been shopping and had come back on the train, and were now climbing into a dusty blue bus, a dark-haired little boy clambering up in their wake. An old man stood by the taxi rank, a bunch of bright yellow roses in his hand. Later in the summer, the station would look different, with queues of holiday-makers jostling for taxis, but just now I had the impression of ordinary life. I could pretend I belonged here too, that we were a couple. I was being picked up after a day of shopping. I would settle myself in the car, we would talk about our day and what was for supper. There'd be no tension or worry, no sick anticipation in the pit of my stomach. He might rest his hand on my thigh as we drove, I would cover it with mine.

Then we were by a pick-up truck. Luc unlocked the door, jolting me from my daydream. A battered green truck would not have been Ophelia's choice, but I could see it fitted Luc perfectly.

'This came with the house when my grandpapa died three years ago.' He opened the door. 'He left everything to me. Blake thinks it's time something was done.'

A sharp note glinted beneath his words; maybe Blake was possessive of Ophelia or Luc was. I didn't know much about family rivalries, Nathan had no siblings and nor did I. It would have been a luxury to have had a sister. I could almost understand Blake; if I'd had a sister I loved, I might have been jealous of her husband too.

A small dog was curled on the red leather of the passenger seat, a black and white terrier of some kind, who woke when I opened the door.

'Meet Coco.' Luc's face softened as he lifted her down.

She nosed his feet, squatted to pee by the wheel of the truck then climbed back up the steps, clambered onto my lap and sat upright, staring out. One small ear was up, the other down. I kept very still, a hand resting on her warm little back.

'She likes you.'

Luc started the truck. Behind the front seats there was a clutter of paint pots and rope, batteries, a ladder, buckets, hammers in a box, a crate of wine. An easel on its side. The smell of turpentine and faintly, not unpleasantly, the salty tang of freshly caught fish.

'Coco belongs to my neighbours; she turns up when I arrive. I'd love a dog of my own, but Ophelia says we're too busy. She's probably right.'

Ophelia was in the car with us then, her blonde hair drawn off her face, remote but watchful. There was a little barrier between us now, so far but no further.

'Nathan says the same, we look after my daughter's spaniel sometimes.' There. I'd mentioned Nathan too; the barrier grew higher. I bent my face to Coco's head. She smelt of fresh air and grass. My eyes filled with ridiculous tears. 'I wish we had our own too.'

'Wishes are powerful things.' Luc turned to smile at me, a generous smile, the kind you can't help returning. I felt better, it was possible that one day when Nathan and I were older and both retired, my wish might come true. Nathan, if pressed, would choose a Labrador, obedient and reliable, but I'd prefer a rescue animal, less predictable, in need of love. There would be time to look after a dog, we would both be at home, cooking meals and listening to music. I'd draw the trees in the Close, the Cloisters in summer or Odstock woods in the spring when the bluebells were under the trees. Safe, pretty things. I wouldn't attempt the dark water of a river rising at its bank, nor the crowded station at Arles, nor the man who sat next to me, his large hands curved on the wheel. Nathan and I would take our dog around the Old Mill on sunny days. If the warm shock of Luc's hand in the station came to me, I would never share that memory for fear of disturbing the peace. We would live safely according to a routine, reputations intact.

'You're very quiet.' Luc was watching a motorbike that had cut in front of him and didn't look at me. We were passing through a stone-walled village with a pretty church and narrow roads, he had to concentrate. 'You must be wondering exactly what you are doing here.' His voice was matter-of-fact as if stating something obvious, even boring.

I didn't want to give him the chance to say he was sorry, that he'd made a mistake, he'd invited me on an impulse he had thought better of since. I turned to him with a laugh, as if this was merely an outing to pass the time, a trivial escapade to humour a friend I didn't know very well.

'I have to give a talk about what I learnt on my trip to my medical colleagues when I get back; what on earth am I going to say?'

'Talk about the light.' He gestured through the windows at the shining olive groves, the distant gleam of a river. 'People have always come here for that; tell them it has healing properties.'

84

We turned a corner and the gear stick pushed into my leg as he wrenched at it.

'Sorry.' He picked up speed and left the streets and the church behind. He began to tell me about the house his grandfather had left him, untouched for years. Blake was arriving in five days' time with extravagant plans to update it before letting it out. Luc couldn't bear the idea of change but he was too close to tell, an objective viewpoint would help. He smiled and drew out to pass a caravan piled high with bikes. The movement aligned with the deft swerve in his conversation, an impersonal note, complications avoided, except that there were no complications. This was about Luc assessing his house before his brother-in-law arrived, he wasn't interested in me, not in that way. I'd dreamt it all up.

I looked out of the window; we were passing fields of sunflowers with tight green centres, a faint dusting of lemon, the yellow petals not yet unfolded. I saw my room at the surgery as it had been the evening I met him, I saw myself listening, consoling. He had valued that, he'd said so. How stupid to have imagined anything else.

My face burnt and I kept my head turned towards the window. 'I'll do my best but I can't stay long.' Smile, I told myself, it will make your voice sound light-hearted. 'Actually your call came at the right time, I wanted a little escape. I'd attended the lecture I needed to.'

'What was it about?'

'Oh, precursors of mental health problems . . .' I stopped talking abruptly. I was straying into forbidden territory, bringing back that evening in the surgery.

He put his hand on mine, briefly, burningly. 'You want to leave the doctor self behind and I'm making that difficult.'

On the contrary, it felt easy to leave my other self behind, frighteningly easy. I sat back and stroked Coco's rough little head. I'd help Luc with whatever decision he had to make and leave long before Blake was due to arrive. I could skip the rest of the conference and go straight home. I'd text Nathan that I was returning early. He'd meet me at the station, he'd be pleased. Life would resume as normal and the sting of this memory would fade.

We passed a road sign to Saint-Rémy de Provence, then Luc turned right onto a smaller road by an intricately carved stone arch on the left, a museum entrance on the right. Half a mile later he slowed to turn right again past a shuttered mansion behind a pair of elaborately wrought iron gates. I saw a pointed tower and shuttered windows. Dark green cypress trees were visible over a high wall.

'Who lives there?'

The road was rough, the bottles of wine in the crate were rattling noisily, and Luc didn't hear my question. The trees grew closer together as he drove, the road narrowed between high banks. He swung the car left through a gap in the trees and for a while we bumped along a narrow track in green-gold shadow, trees stretching back either side into darkness. The heat was stifling. I lowered the window and the scent of hot pine entered the car. There was a final, jarring lurch, and we were there. His house, lying in a curve of land. A group of buildings in the shapes a child might draw, two rectangles, one on its side, one upright with a square between them. Ivy spread over the grey stone in a dense green triangle, pink roses tangling among the glossy leaves. There was grass to the walls, mountains in the distance. The car ticked to silence. The only sounds were the clear high call of a bird and dense twittering from the trees.

'It was a medieval convent.' Luc pointed to a row of windows high on the wall. One was wide open and it was easy to imagine a young nun leaning her elbows on the sill, looking towards the mountains with the sun on her face.

I followed Luc to the door which had been left ajar, Coco trotting at my heels. Birds were flying in the vaulted space inside. The air was full of the clapping of wings, the floor lit up by sun in slabs of gold. There was a stone shelf and sink under a window, a fireplace like a cave, a table, chairs and a fridge towards the back along with a cooker and an old-fashioned metal safe propped against the wall. A battered chair was positioned by the fireplace, its leather split, the stuffing protruding. A folded paper lay on the seat; this must be where Luc sat at night reading, with the dog on his lap. The high windows were wide open, letting in the smell of grass and lavender.

'It's incredible, Luc.'

His face relaxed, he took my hand again; it felt easy this time, friendly.

'Come with me, I want to show you the view from upstairs.'

Each bedroom was simply furnished with an iron bed frame and an old armoire, timeless things that had been left behind, as though the nuns had simply walked out of the rooms, down the stairs and out of the door, vanishing into history.

'This is yours.' He walked ahead of me into a sunny room, a bed in the corner with a patchwork quilt, wildflowers in a glass jar on the sill and, through the open window, the mountains beyond fields of olives and vines. There was an old dovecote to the side of the lawn near the house, water glimmered between the trees. Luc joined me by the window.

'I slept on that lawn when I was a boy. Grandpapa cooked everything outside. He was an artist, as his grandpapa had been; he was the one who encouraged me to paint. My parents left me here in the summers, the best months of my life.' Luc's shoulder was touching mine, the warmth of his skin through his shirt seemed part of the birdsong and cicadas and the smell of warm grass. 'I know he wouldn't want changes; it's meant to be as it always was.' He was silent for a while, his eyes following a white dove fluttering to the dovecote. 'Blake and Ophelia want to bring it up to date.'

'Do you have to do what they say?'

'We need money. Ophelia likes to live in style, so does Blake. There are school fees to pay, we've run through my inheritance already. They think we could make a fortune on holiday lets, I suppose they could be right.'

I could imagine how easily the house could be spoilt: the walls straightened, double-glazed windows put in against the winter, a Jacuzzi on the lawn, the dovecote removed to make way for a pool, the hum of filters and pumps drowning out birdsong.

'Be very careful,' I told him. 'It's perfect as it is.'

He looked down at me, nodding slowly. 'That's all I needed to hear. Thank you.' Then he smiled. 'Let's have a swim. There's a towel in the cupboard. Come down when you're ready.'

I watched him from the window as I changed, he was moving logs from a stack by the trees to a pit at the back of the house, Coco running alongside, back and forth, tail wagging. Luc had stripped to his shorts, he was tanned and muscled with wide shoulders, young-looking. I was conscious of my white skin, my breasts which were slacker than they used to be, the way my thighs must look compared to a younger woman's, compared to Ophelia's. I wrapped myself in the large towel, the red varnish on my toenails giving me courage.

As I hurried barefoot down the corridor, I passed the open door of a larger room on the left that I hadn't noticed before. There were paintings on the floor and on a table, taped to the wall and on the shutters, hundreds of paintings.

The colours were vivid, brilliant yellows and greens. Some were landscapes, glittering olive trees in the foreground, the mountains behind, white against the sky. Most were unfinished, olive trees in rows, paintings of leaves on torn sheets of paper, some mere splashes, others finely detailed; more drawings of bark and shells. There were several of Coco asleep by the door in the sun. One sheet was covered in blocks of colours in different shades of green, another with the image of a man picking cherries from a small tree, repeated several times as if the painter had kept trying for an effect he couldn't quite reach.

'I meant to shut the door.' Luc had come to find me, I hadn't heard him enter the room. 'I don't usually let anyone see my work.'

'I'm sorry.' My cheeks felt hot. 'The colours drew me in, I didn't mean to pry.'

'Have a look if you want. You can tell me what you think.'

I went close to a sheet of paper on the table near the window, a painting of lemons in a brown bowl on a blue tablecloth. The colours were so sharp I could almost taste them.

'You have a gift, Luc, you should be painting, not designing houses.'

'Have a word with my wife.' He smiled a little bitterly.

Ophelia was with us again as clearly as if she was standing beside him, a hand on his shoulder, her blonde hair shining in the sun. *My wife*. The doubts and desire, the way he smiled at me, the warmth of his hand, none of that mattered. How I looked compared to her was irrelevant, Luc was taken. Regret twisted in my stomach, which was crazy – he didn't want me anyway. Even if he did, I wasn't free either.

'Where is Ophelia now?'

'She doesn't come here as often as I do; she keeps an eye

89

on an art gallery she helps to run, and then there's Oscar. They'll be here in August, I expect. School holidays.' Then he grinned. 'Come on, that swim.'

Coco had been sitting in the shade but ran to me as if I was an old friend already. I picked her up and her solid little body was warm against mine, obscurely comforting.

We walked across the lawn and through the pine trees, our feet crunching on dried needles. The pond was just beyond, round and large like a pond in an English village. It was fed by irrigation channels running between banks of wildflowers, I half expected ducks to swim out of the reeds. The still surface reflected the grass, the trees and the sky. I dropped the towel and slid down the bank, a frog jumping away under my elbow, a flash of iridescent skin and webbed feet. The water was cool, we floated face up in the sun as Coco settled on the bank and went to sleep. The sun was warm on my face, the beat of the cicadas and the sound of birds were soothing. There was nothing else in my mind, not the darkened room of the conference I'd escaped, not Ophelia, Nathan or even Lizzie, just moments of pure sensation ticking past in the sunlight.

Afterwards Luc showed me a bucket shower at the back of the house under a lean-to that smelt of hot pine. A swallow flew out as I entered, a barbed arrow in navy and red. In the shard of mirror propped against the ledge, my eyes were puffy with water. I'd caught the sun and my body was tingling all over as if stung back to life. Back in my bedroom I pulled out the blue dress; brushing my hair I could hear quiet, creaking noises around me. Even here, even now, I felt a frisson of fear. Luc was whistling in the garden as he laid out a rug, setting glasses on the low stone wall, lighting the logs in the fire pit, a bucket of fish by his side. I hurried down. He poured wine and we tipped glasses.

'I could hear the house settling down just now, almost as if it was talking to itself.' I wouldn't mention the fear – he'd have forgotten the footsteps by now and the shadows on the path.

'That'll be the ghosts.' He winked at me as he sipped his wine; he hadn't forgotten, he was making it into a joke, and I relaxed. 'They'll be the first to go if Blake has his way.'

'He's American; they pay for them, don't they?' I replied, though Luc could be right, it sounded as though Blake would rip out what was old and secret, even if by mistake.

The scar beside Luc's mouth dragged his lips a little as he smiled. The bones of his jaw seemed to widen; people with wide faces appear more open, a trick of anatomy maybe. The wine was making me light-headed. I sat on the rug, while he laid out the fish on a rack above the fire and tipped a stream of golden oil over the skin as it cooked, spluttering above the white-hot coals.

While we ate, he told me about other places he loved, where the past breathed through ancient stones: Haddon Hall in Derbyshire, the Parthenon in the early morning, the mosaic dog on the floor of the house of Caecilius in Pompeii. Fragile, potent places where the past was present in a dipped step or the dark patch on a kitchen sideboard where bread had been made for centuries.

'Houses that you love, love you back. I've always felt that here, even as a boy.' Luc glanced at me. 'Does that sound stupid?'

I knew exactly what he meant. In the evenings at home after work, my gaze rests on the way the light pools on the dresser and the row of my mother's old cookery books, the shape of the wall as it curves to the ceiling; familiar things like arms around me, the house where I'd grown up and where I felt safe, the keep of my castle.

'I paint better here than anywhere else in the world.' Luc poured another glass of wine for me. 'That building where

91

you work must constrain you, all those low ceilings and long corridors. I'd feel claustrophobic.'

My other life was with us then, a breath away in the shadows. My thinking had to be constrained at work, that was the point. I had to ignore the outside world and concentrate on my patients, patients like Luc, who had come to me for help. Roger's concentration was legendary. What would he say if he could see me now?

I glanced around at the dark trees. Nathan would be pouring a solitary drink before walking out into our garden, checking on his flowers. He would heat something from the freezer, eat in the silent kitchen and then watch television on his own. He hadn't phoned, by agreement, but he would be thinking about me, he might be wondering what I was doing at this very moment. He would be missing me just as Ophelia might be missing Luc.

'We can't talk about where I work.'

'Because I was your patient? I'm with Dr Morris now.'

'You're still a patient in the practice.'

Bats were flying low in the sky, tipping and tilting as they sped above us. The flames in the barbecue had died down, it was chilly. The temperature drops near the Mediterranean after a hot day. I shouldn't have come. I'd followed a crazy impulse; the kind you get away with when you're young. I'd allowed myself to forget my family and Luc's, my work and my age.

'It's been a long day.' I smiled though my lips were trembling. 'I'll have to make an early start tomorrow, perhaps you can drive me to the station.' My voice sounded ridiculously formal but I'd already made myself ridiculous, I should have stuck to the rules. 'I'll say goodnight. Don't get up, I'll see you in the morning.'

'Wait.' He moved so that his eyes were level with mine, his knee tipped my wine and it spilt on the grass. The heat from his body was intense, it made me want to shut my eyes. This close I could smell him, a deep smoky scent.

'I lied to you. I didn't need your help with the house though Blake is coming, that part's quite true.'

My heart began to thud, everything was shifting around me. I put my hand on the rough surface of the wall next to me, it was warm from the heat of the day. I remember registering that and the sound of the cicadas, the sweet, peppery scent of the lavender, stronger in the dark; all those irrelevant things that the senses absorb no matter what's happening.

'It was a trick, a ruse, to bring you here.'

This was what Luc did, he cut through to the truth. But I'm older than you, I wanted to say. I'm not like those kids on the train, I'm not supple like them. My skin is more fragile, everything is. I can't do this, I'm scared.

'I fell in love the moment you took your shoes off in the surgery.' He took my hands. 'I love the way you listen as if you don't want to miss one word.' He was very near now, filling my vision. 'I love your eyes and the shape of your mouth.'

Love. The word seemed extravagant. I hadn't called it that, not even to myself. I'd felt a connection when we met, excitement at the party, a reckless attraction when he'd taken my hand in the station. Love grew slowly over the years, surely, it was low-key, steady, reliable. It wasn't this painful uncertainty, this desire, the way my heart was thumping right now.

I don't remember what happened next, the order of things. Did I move first? Was it my hand on his arm or his on my face? What words were spoken or murmured? Perhaps there were no words, just the heat of his skin, the shine of his eyes, the feel of his body and his hands. His mouth was hot. It was dangerous and safe, wrong and right, it had been waiting for me since I walked into my surgery three months ago and found him crying in my room. I can't blame him for what happened, it was my fault. I was older than him, I should have known better. Nathan didn't appear in my mind, nor did Lizzie. Ophelia vanished. Everything fell away. I went further back, the way you do in dreams. I pulled free of my mother's hand and stepped over the bank of the river.

Chapter 11

In custody
June 2017

'How would you describe your relationship with the accused?'

Detective Inspector Wainwright was searching in a pile of documents on the desk between us. His fingers, flicking impatiently between the papers, were freckled and covered with sandy hair. The nails were split, his lips looked chapped. He must have been in the sun at the weekend. I could see him standing four-square on the deck of a sailing boat, a fishing rod in his hands, shouting commands to his wife. I wondered if she would resist him, huddling with their children in the back of the boat, or if she would do whatever he told her to, because she had learnt it was easier that way.

'That depends what you mean,' I replied.

He glanced up. 'He was your partner for a while, wasn't he?'

He was reeling me in bit by bit. There was no impatience in his tone, it was as if he had all the time in the world, though Judy had told me he hadn't. He had applied for the full ninety-six hours before he had to charge me with a crime but now there were just two days left. After that I'd be incarcerated until the trial or let go on bail.

I shook my head. That word partner conjures work, my GP partners, Roger and Debbie. We supported each other, puzzled over patients, joked over coffee, backed each other's decisions. We knew each other's families. I didn't love them in the way he was implying but I trusted them. It was the other way around with Luc. I wasn't sure if I trusted him, though that hadn't mattered at the time; trust had taken second place to desire.

Behind the bland expression on Inspector Wainwright's face, there would be other thoughts skidding through his brain just as there were in mine. He might be thinking of the next weekend's sailing or about taxing the car, how best to advance his career, but, given those gimlet eyes, he was doubtless planning exactly how to trap me.

'How would you describe your relationship then?'

Deep, warm, open; words that would be too simple for him. Luc and I were open to each other, our minds and our bodies, there was a warmth between us that heated my skin when we touched. I'd forgotten about sex; the depth of the pleasure, the extremes of it, the way you felt as though opened up, emptied out, part of each other. Conversation, companionship, respect, all those things I had already, or thought I did; what happened with Luc was different, it was those things too but more than them. If the inspector wanted a word that summed it up, I could give him miraculous, but I doubted he'd know what to do with that.

'We were friends,' I said and that felt true. Friends rescue you and I'd been rescued, the feeling of incredulity when I looked in the mirror, the knowledge that I had been chosen, however briefly; I, a forty-nine-year-old woman, over his glamorous, much younger wife.

'Friends.' The inspector sounded contemptuous. 'You were much closer than that, weren't you?'

He wanted my confession, but he was on the wrong track. Close was another word that didn't quite capture it. After that first night we were inseparable. I don't think we walked anywhere without touching; we were making up for lost time, past and future time.

There are moments in life that you savour like wine. I can still taste them. The way my head fitted between Luc's chin and his shoulder, the warmth of his palm as he cupped my breast. The smoky smell of him, the knit of our hands. The heat of his mouth. The weight of his body on mine, the aching afterwards. The secrets we shared. I told him every-thing about my life and he told me things he'd never mentioned to anyone before, how he went mad with grief when his grandfather died, holed up at the house or walking on the beaches of the Camargue.

That was where he met Ophelia, sitting by the waves as though waiting for him, her little boy turning cartwheels in the sand. She was travelling and asked for a room. She turned up the next day with her child whose father was a secret, though some calamity seemed to smoke out from the past. Oscar attached himself to Luc. It seemed to work, Luc was less lonely and Ophelia, apparently happier. They became a couple though he could never work out quite when it began, he was still adrift with grief. When Ophelia proposed, everything happened with bewildering speed – at least, it bewildered him. He hadn't real-ized he'd accepted but then her friends arrived, there were parties, celebrations, gifts. Blake joined them. Luc's father approved of the glowing Americans, their enthusiasm for the house, the grounds, the furniture, Luc's work, even the old family painting that had hung on the wall for years. A date was set for the wedding; it became too late to turn back.

I have that family painting and several of Luc's. No one can take them away because no one knows where they are, hidden in plain sight. My secret.

'I want you to have them,' he'd said.

We were in a hurry. I'd stayed five days, much longer than planned, and suddenly Blake was coming within hours. I had to leave. We were late for my train, but Luc insisted on giving me his paintings. I'd need to remind myself of our days here, he said, in case I forgot. He chose my favourites: a painting of the house, the dovecote, several others of the view from the window, the olive trees and the mountains, the lemons in the bowl. The wildflowers by the pond. Two of Coco. He put numbers into a dial on the door of the safe, opened it and took out a leather satchel, slipped in the paintings and handed it over. It was heavy so I looked inside, glimpsing a flat metal box fastened with clasps.

'Did you know this was here?'

'Of course. It contains a painting of the view by my great-great-grandpa.' The green in Luc's eyes seemed to deepen. 'He was a psychiatrist, one of the early ones. The story goes, as he grew older, he'd recoup from the stress of his work by painting. He would paint for hours, a glass of wine at his elbow, a cat by his feet and a few Van Gogh prints spread out beside him for inspiration. He worshipped Van Gogh; the colours are the ones he used, you'll see.' His voice dropped, almost as if he sensed someone would hear him. 'I don't trust Blake. He knows I love that picture, it hung in the kitchen for years, but that wouldn't stop him. I've seen him throw the entire contents of a house into a skip before now. Keep it safe for me.'

We had to run to the car. I could look at the painting at home, he said, taking my time.

'I'll speak plainly.' DI Wainwright's voice became loud in

the little room and Judy stirred beside me; she might have thought he was bullying me. 'It was an affair.'

It was the wrong word again. He had no proof and, besides, Luc had been clear it wasn't an affair.

We had been standing together on the station platform in Arles, next to a cart. *Glaces à Vendre* printed on a tin sign. The ice creams shone in the shade of the stripy parasol: lemon and pistachio, mango and the deep red of raspberry, like frozen blood, those bags that are stored for patients who are bleeding to death. He looped the satchel over my shoulder as we stood there – it dragged a little on my sunburnt skin – then he put his arms around me.

'We can't call this an affair, that sounds so trite, so temporary,' he said. 'This is just the beginning.'

'No, my love, it's the end. It has to be.' My eyes stung with tears.

We'd talked through the night; his marriage and mine, our children. My career, his. The impossibility of a future without destroying the past. I thought we'd agreed. We'd washed the sheets and cleaned the barbecue, my damp swimming costume had been collected from the line and packed away in my case. I was wearing my suit skirt again despite the heat, and carrying the jacket. I'd go straight to the conference for the three remaining days it had yet to run. Luc would shop for food and meet Blake back at the station. Blake's train was due a couple of hours after mine had left. We'd worked it out carefully, Blake would have no idea that I'd been here, no one would ever know. It was over. We would draw a clear line; we wouldn't meet or talk or even text. It would be easier that way.

'You think you would be destroying a marriage that's perfect but it's not.' Luc spoke rapidly, there was so little time. 'I told you; Ophelia and I never—'

'Don't.' I turned my head away, I could hear the train, we had seconds left. I didn't want to waste them; if we talked about all the things that weren't perfect in our marriages, they would grow into something unbearable, and we had to go on bearing them for the rest of our lives. I couldn't take him from his wife or his stepson. I had borrowed him for a while, that was all, and now I had to give him back.

'We've had five incredible days.' I touched his cheek. 'I'll never forget them.'

He closed his eyes and, like a fool, I thought that meant he agreed that it was over.

'Right.' Detective Inspector Wainwright glanced at the clock. He pushed his chair back from the table and stood up. 'You admit, finally, it was an affair?'

I shook my head. I agreed with Luc; the word was unbearably trite.

The inspector sighed and left the room, it seemed like an admission of defeat. I didn't know then that he was only just getting started.

Chapter 12

June 2017

'You look well.' Nathan kissed me, taking my case.

I felt well. It had been three days since I'd left Luc and returned to the conference, but I was still soaked in the memories of our time together, filled to the brim with them. I hadn't yet begun to miss him.

'How's Lizzie?'

'Fine.'

May had turned into June while I was away. It was early evening and the sun was low in the sky. It was also raining and the platform at Salisbury station was crammed with tourists in bright anoraks, pointing out the spire of the cathedral above the rooftops. There might have been a rainbow, but I didn't look. I was trying to keep up with Nathan who was walking quickly, his gait seemed jauntier than usual. We hurried through the underpass, which smelt as it always did, of metal, stone and urine.

'I wasn't expecting you to collect me,' I said as we approached his car, neatly parked in the short-stay car park.

'Sarah's holding the fort but I'll have to go back to school.' He put my case in the boot, the leather satchel hidden deep inside. He would have noticed it otherwise, Nathan noticed everything. It might have been difficult to explain away a battered old satchel; not the sort of thing you're given when you attend a medical conference sponsored by a drug company, unlike the pens, the little torches and the patella hammers that are freely handed around.

'You're very quiet.' Nathan glanced at me as we drove out of the car park.

'I'm tired after the journey.'

'Good trip?'

'Very.'

'You've a tan.' Another sideways glance; if I felt I was being assessed, it was because I was conscious of guilt and conscious of happiness, trying to hide both.

'We had lunch outside every day, it was sunny.' It was surprising how easy it was to avoid lying by keeping to the facts.

'You must have learnt a lot in ten days.'

He was looking at the road and didn't seem to need an answer, which was lucky because I would have struggled. The things I'd learnt had nothing to do with medicine. I couldn't talk about the abacus of Luc's fingers, the shape of his nails, the muscles that swelled under his thumb. The way his biceps curved into deltoid, the dip in his nose from boxing at school. The width of his hands, the manner of his walk and the quality of his silences, the way he lifted Coco onto his lap and stroked her. Loss hovered, like a headache you sense will become a migraine.

I turned to Nathan. 'Tell me more about Lizzie.'

On the train home, I'd googled spas in Greece. We'd go for a long weekend, just Lizzie and me. We'd swim and sunbathe, eat delicious food. There would be time to talk.

'I haven't seen her, but she texted. Busy of course, happy, I think.'

'I'm hoping to persuade her to have a little holiday with me. I've seen this hotel in Corfu by a beach—'

'She's already booked a trip with a friend in a month's time.' He started the windscreen wipers, the rain was falling harder now.

'Ah.' The sunlit images of Lizzie and me on a beach began to fade. 'Which friend?'

'I didn't cross-examine her, isn't that your department?'

I let that go. It didn't matter; it would be one of her old friends or maybe a new one. I should be glad for her, it would be more fun than with her mother. Nathan was focusing on the traffic, he looked calm, but his eyes were bright, his lips pursed as though stopping himself from smiling. There must be a surprise in store, something he'd been saving up to tell me.

'How's things at work?'

'That housemaster's job comes vacant at the end of the year. Simon's dropped hints that I'm to be appointed.'

So that was it. 'How wonderful.'

He nodded, glancing at me, eyebrows raised as if expecting something more.

'Are you sure that's what you want, Nathan?'

'You know it is.' He looked back at the road, his voice quiet as if with disappointment.

'Of course, sorry. Congratulations, darling.'

The job was exactly what he'd always wanted. He'd been working towards that position for a very long time; no doubt he envisaged our lives stretching ahead in exactly the same way for years to come: the same routines, the same meals and walks and bedtimes. I looked down to hide my panic catching the dull gleam of gold, a small cylinder rolling around the foot well of the passenger seat. I shifted my feet and picked it up, a cigarette lighter.

'Don't tell me Lizzie has started to smoke.'

'I gave a lift to some boys yesterday on the way to a match.' Nathan braked, narrowly missing the car ahead which had stopped at a zebra crossing. 'One of them must have dropped it.'

It was a pretty thing, with its fluted casing and solid feel, a little band of red near the top. 'Doesn't look like a boy's lighter to me.'

'Nicked from someone's mother, I expect.'

Nathan was a bad liar, even his ears were pink. Perhaps he was protecting Lizzie, but who was I to talk about deceit? The lighter might belong to someone else and my mind flew to Sarah, uncovering images I hadn't realized were there already: Nathan's head near hers at Ophelia's party, her glance at me, her voice on the phone asking for him. She was the first person who helped him out with a staffing problem, the one he always turned to. Sarah was holding the fort right now.

The streets of Salisbury narrowed as Nathan navigated the one-way system that led to the Close, a spider's web of lies seeming to tighten around us the further we went. I was lying to Nathan but was he lying to me too? I glanced at his face, surprised at my surprise. It seemed so obvious now. They wouldn't have slept together, I knew that. My husband was ambitious; an affair with the headmaster's wife would be career-ending. They'd have kissed, it wouldn't have gone much further than that. They were both much too careful. I felt jarred but not angry, I was far guiltier than he was.

Our row of houses looked smaller than I remembered as Nathan drew up outside, more ordinary. Helen Densham was opening her door as we parked, she waved and smiled, a bag of shopping in her hand. I waved back. Colin would be waiting in their kitchen, he'd put the paper down, switch the kettle on and they would unpack the shopping together.

She'd say how crowded it was at the shops, he'd tell her about a phone call he'd received from their son. Our neighbours; a normal, happy couple, no secrets between them.

In the courtyard, a few flower heads had appeared on the magnolia tree, splashes of pink against the brick. Nathan carried my case inside; if he noticed it was heavier than when he'd put it on the train ten days ago, he said nothing.

The kitchen was the same, the same tea towels by the stove, the same cups upside down on the draining board. This was the home I loved, I reminded myself, my place of safety, but now it was like meeting an old friend after a long time, you had less in common than you'd thought, some connection had been lost. Pepper's basket was empty; Lizzie must have taken him back.

Nathan went into his study and I unpacked, looping the satchel on the hook behind our bedroom door and replacing my dressing gown over it. I hardly wore it these days. Nathan thought it sloppy to walk about in dressing gowns and in any case there was rarely time. After my morning shower I would towel-dry then quickly dress in work clothes, at night I changed into pyjamas and slid straight into bed. To the best of my knowledge, Nathan hadn't touched that dressing gown once in twenty-five years, he probably no longer saw it at all. It was quilted, a little bulky, made of silk and cotton and stiff with brocade, given me by my mother when we got engaged just before she died. Perhaps she envisaged Nathan putting it tenderly around my shoulders or even taking it off; she would have had no idea how impossible it would be to imagine that now. The satchel would be safe beneath those heavy folds until I found somewhere better.

My blue dress was grass-stained. I put it in the kitchen sink to soak, then dried my hands and took out my phone. The screen was empty, no messages. Luc was sticking to the rules, my rules. I trod down disappointment and slipped it back in my pocket when I heard footsteps in the hall.

'I need to pop back to school.' Nathan appeared in the kitchen doorway, briefcase in hand. 'Prep time.'

He looked tired. He had organized his day so he could be free to fetch his unfaithful wife from the station and now he had to go back to work although it was late and getting dark.

'I'll come with you.'

He began to say something then he nodded; it was possible he wanted to see Sarah. I slung on a mac, took his arm and we walked into the Close together. Anybody watching us would think I had slotted back into my place, that nothing different had happened to us and perhaps it hadn't. I was still Nathan's wife. I would go on being his wife, go on being a mother and a doctor. I might have changed, he might have changed too, but the framework around us hadn't.

We walked down the path by the shrubbery, through the gate to the Green, then turned right past the west front of the cathedral and across the grass to the far steps in the corner over the low wall; the shortest route to the Cathedral School entrance. The rain was still falling, that light rain which leaches the smell of summer from the ground. The tourists had long gone and the Close was empty. The beautiful houses I'd known as friends all my life seemed to stand sentinel in the gathering dusk, watchful today rather than friendly.

We said goodbye at the school gate. I kissed him just as he was turning away, my mouth against the side of his, slithering off. He nodded awkwardly and we parted.

On the way back I walked near the cathedral, so close that my shoulder brushed against the stone. The floodlights had been switched on. Looking up at the spire and the red light at the top, it loomed over me, seeming to tilt towards my face. The spire had terrified me as a child, I'd always thought it was about to fall and crush me. I put my hand on the wall. I used to imagine secrets buried in the stone and that I could feel their rough edges under my fingertips, secrets whispered into the wall for safekeeping. I'd never thought back then I'd have secrets of my own that I needed to hide, nor how guilty that might make me feel.

I was handed a leaflet by the guide at the door and took it automatically. I hadn't been inside for months. I passed the fourteenth-century clock with its turning wheels, the thud of the cogs beating out the seconds like a vast iron heart. The floodlight was filtering through the deep blue glass in the Lady Chapel at the far end of the nave behind the altar, it was where we had been married. It had been a small service; my parents had died that year.

I sat on one of the old rush chairs, losing track of time as I remembered back to that day. Nathan had folded my hand in his by the altar, steadying me. He'd always been steady. Blue light shone on the stone floor at my feet, blue for fidelity. Family life was supposed to be sacred. I'd never thought I'd be unfaithful or step across that deep divide between doctor and patient, but both had been easy when it came to it, the easiest thing in the world. At the last moment, I'd leapt across without a second thought. Nathan wouldn't have, I knew that. What kind of wife did that make me, what kind of doctor?

The heat began to rise from my neck to my face. A woman I knew came towards me with a vase in her hands; Margaret somebody, she arranged flowers in the cathedral. She had the inquisitive face of a squirrel, Lizzie used to imitate her darting head movements. She peered at me as she drew closer, my cheeks were probably bright red by now and blotchy with heat. I got up and left the chapel, my feet ringing on the stone as I hurried out of the great west door into the rain. Water was pouring from the mouths of the gargoyles that framed the archway above, the grotesque stone faces leering down as if mocking me.

The wind blew rain in my face; walking back towards the shrubbery I felt cooler, calmer. The broken vows were in a separate compartment of my life. I could keep those five days hidden, like a miser keeps his jewels, locked up and secret. I'd look at them from time to time, hold them up to the light, turn them to catch the sun, then put them back. I glanced across at the North Canonry and, as I watched, a light went on, pricking the evening, cheerful, domestic, innocent. I couldn't destroy Luc's family; I shouldn't destroy my own. Nathan must have sensed something different about me for a while. I'd unsettled him so he'd turned towards someone else. Our family was at risk.

It was quite dark now; I'd spent longer in the cathedral than I thought. Nathan might be at home already. How stupid to let myself be alone on the stretch of path again.

The footsteps were buried inside other sounds at first, the noise of rain pattering on leaves and the branches moving up and down in the wind, a lorry in the distance on the Blandford road. I thought I was hearing things again, those things that Nathan had told me weren't really here.

I began to hurry. The footsteps were louder now, closer. They sounded real. My skin crawled as if a swarm of ants were making their way from my collar up into my hair. I wanted to put my hand to the back of my neck but I was afraid of other fingers reaching to touch mine.

I skirted a puddle; a few seconds later there was a little splash as a heavy foot landed in the water. I began to run although I could hardly breathe for the fear that was gripping me, like a vice round my chest. I swung through the Close gate so quickly I half slipped on the wet cobbles under the arch and stumbled to my knees.

Chapter 13

June 2017

I scrambled to my feet and a second later I was at our door, my wet fingers fumbling with the key. When the door opened, I ran inside and slammed the door behind me.

The house was silent. I wanted to talk to Luc with a longing that hurt my chest but how could I phone him when I'd made him promise not to phone me? He'd be with Blake in any case, and Blake might overhear. I tried Nathan but he didn't pick up. I phoned Lizzie, I wasn't going to tell her about the footsteps, but I'd warn her not to go out on her own after dark, I'd ask her to humour me. She didn't pick up either. I made a cup of tea, spilling the milk on the sideboard, crashing the bottle back in the fridge, the sugar scattering on the table as I spooned it in. I didn't usually take sugar, but I needed it now.

I called the police and stood behind the half-opened door of the sitting room, staring out of the window at the back of the house, in case whoever had followed me had found his way into the garden. When the phone was answered, I was asked what the problem was and had to wait again. The man who came on had a kindly voice, a little condescending; it was easier to pick up these things by phone. He asked if I was safe. I told him I was, though I didn't feel safe. Did I know my stalker? That's what the man on the end of the phone was calling him. My stalker. It sounded worse than a follower; the words implied intent.

When I admitted I had no idea who he was, I was asked if there'd been phone calls or notes through the door. Had there been a history of threats or violence? Did anyone bear a grudge? I said no to all the questions, conscious the voice on the phone was changing with my replies, that I was slipping down a list, urgent to less urgent. The triaging process had begun, those who can wait and those who can't. We do the same in medicine all the time. The woman who came on the phone after that had a soft Irish voice; she asked me if I was frightened and, once she knew my profession, if any of my patients had been angry or vengeful or whether they had shown signs of obsession. Could they have been after drugs?

She told me to document sightings, to be in touch if I was threatened; when I told her I felt threatened already the voice became factual, checking that there had been no shouting, confrontation, physical damage or weapons. I hadn't been threatened according to her, just frightened. A specially trained police officer would contact me; what had happened to me, while disconcerting, wasn't an emergency. There were women in danger of their lives out there, she said, who had been targeted, stalked by known abusers with a history of violent crime, obsessives, rapists. It was possible she meant to be comforting. She gave me a number to call for counselling.

Nathan came back after an hour; his phone had run out of charge. By then I'd drunk two glasses of red wine and the edge of terror had dulled. We sat at the kitchen table, the bottle between us. We had sat like this a thousand times over the years, talking through issues as they came up: Lizzie's run of childhood illnesses, normal and terrifying at the same time, whether she was happy at school, her friends, her exams, her university choices. We'd discussed Nathan's work and mine, any work problems we faced. Sitting here felt as though we had matters in hand.

'Let's go through things logically.' Nathan poured me a third glass of wine; it was thick enough to leave a viscous trail of crimson in the glass as I drank. 'The police suggested it could be a patient after drugs, which makes sense. Has this happened to Roger or Debbie?'

'Roger was trailed to a house in Harnham by some kids once, they managed to get his bag.'

'So the police could have been right, whoever followed you might have been after drugs?'

'I wasn't carrying my bag.'

'Maybe someone was following you because he thought you keep drugs at home. Do you have addicts on your list?'

'There is a clinic for addicts, but I'm not involved.'

'Does anyone bear a grudge?'

'Nothing stands out.' I'd never thought of my patients as dangerous; I'd hoped we were on the same side.

'She mentioned obsessives, does anyone fit that label?'

Brian bobbed up to the surface of my mind, like a body that's been pushed deep underwater and suddenly released. That creepy little smile, the way he sat so close, his lizard-like tongue, the whispery voice.

'There's a patient called Brian who books in to see me all the time, usually with different symptoms. Sometimes I think he makes them up as an excuse to come in.'

'Did you tell the police about him?'

I shook my head. 'On second thoughts, I don't know why I mentioned him. Brian wouldn't stalk anyone.'

111

Nathan sipped his wine, looking sceptical. 'What makes you think he wouldn't?'

'He's short-sighted and overweight for a start. He's fitter than he pretends to be, but I can't see him running.'

'Tell the police.'

'They wouldn't be interested in someone like Brian.'

'He could be dangerous. Tell them and then refuse to see him any more. Don't go for walks on your own in the evenings.'

He was being kind, I told myself, kinder than I deserved. I got up and put my arms round him. 'I'm sorry.'

'For what, exactly?' He tipped his head back and looked up at me, a curious, glinting look as if expecting me to tell him something interesting.

I almost confessed, I wanted to. I was tired and drunk, but not quite drunk enough. 'For spilling out my worries and not asking about yours. Did you finish what you needed to at school?'

He nodded and, from nowhere, a picture of Sarah came into my mind, Nathan and Sarah standing in an empty classroom, a little apart. Nathan might have talked about me, he might have said he'd missed me after all, told her things could go no further because he loved his wife and his daughter. He wouldn't have mentioned his career, though that would have been at the forefront of his mind, the looming promotion.

I phoned Lizzie again, the need to warn her was filling my mind. I watched Nathan beating eggs, adding salt, pepper, a few chopped thyme leaves. His face was calm, but he looked at me from time to time, little glances which made me think he was hiding something but it was hard to tell. I might have been oversensitive; after all, I was hiding something too.

There was a recorded answer on Lizzie's phone, she sounded unusually blithe. I left an invitation to lunch the next day. I could tell her to take care face to face, it would be less dramatic that way. She might share her news about the mysterious man in the car, her happiness would be something I could hold close to my heart, compensation for my unhappiness.

Nathan set the table, halved the omelette and slid a perfect yellow envelope onto a plate which he set in front of me. I didn't feel hungry though I had hardly eaten in the last three days. I could still taste the food we'd had in Provence: the white flakes of barbecued fish, the peaches that were so ripe the juice ran down to our elbows, apricot jam on warm croissants in the morning sun, the mellow depth of red wine.

Nathan ate my omelette in the end, he put my lack of appetite down to worry. I drank tea instead. I thought he might want to make love as we used to after trips away, his or mine, but he had a splitting headache, the excuse that I was going to give; too much wine, he muttered as he turned away. I was glad, if surprised. I'd betrayed my husband but sex with him now would have been a betrayal of Luc and that felt worse.

I lay still as the memories returned; the flowers clambering up the walls of Luc's house seemed so real the smell was in the bed with me. The missing began in earnest. In the silence there was nothing to stop the details trickling back: Luc's hands as he cut the wood, the smile he gave in the morning when he opened his eyes and remembered I was there, the warmth of his skin, the feel of him inside me. The cathedral clock sounded each quarter hour and the minutes between passed slowly. The heat built until the sheets underneath me were sodden. When I heard the muffled noise of a window banging in the wind, I took my phone and crept downstairs.

In the sitting room the window had become unlatched and a breeze was blowing in, the room felt beautifully cool. Outside, beyond the glass doors, the moon shone into the garden and the moving branches of the trees cast shadows over the ground. Hundreds of miles away, Luc was thinking about me. I whispered goodnight and imagined him saying it back. That's how I would get through the days until the loss settled, by imagination, by fantasy. I held my phone as if it were his hand and lay down on the sofa, sliding a cushion under my head.

I felt myself sinking into sleep, descending as through water into some deep place, but a snapping noise jerked me awake. I pushed myself up, confused by the furniture of the room, not sure whether I was at Luc's house in France or the hotel in Paris and remembering a beat later that I was at home but downstairs. The noise must have been a cat or fox but as I watched the garden, waiting for an animal to emerge from the undergrowth, the shadows under the apple tree began to waver and then to grow.

The gooseflesh rose on my arms as the shape unfolded from a crouching position, straightened and became a man.

My stalker was the other side of the glass door.

I stood up, sick with fear, calling for Nathan and backing from the window until I bumped into the wall. My legs gave way and I slid to the floor. I could hear Nathan stumble down the stairs, he ran into the room, stubbing his toe on a chair in the dark.

'Fuck. What's the matter, Rach?'

I pointed into the garden; my hand was shaking. 'There's a man out there, under the tree.'

'What? Where?' He unlocked the door and stepped out, barefooted. 'I can't see a bloody thing.'

'Wait.' I grabbed the poker from the fireplace and stood next to him on the step. 'Listen.'

The garden was silent apart from the rustling scurry of a small creature in the bushes. The silver birch trees glinted in the moonlight. Nothing moved. Nathan took the poker and walked around every bush and every tree, disappearing briefly at the back of the shed. He came back, shut the doors behind us then locked them again.

'There's nothing there. What were you even doing down here?'

'I couldn't sleep so I came downstairs. I must have dozed on the sofa. I was woken by a noise.' My mouth was dry. 'He was standing there, almost as if he wanted me to see him.'

'He?'

'The man who's been following me. My stalker.'

'Where did he go?'

'I don't know, I didn't see.'

'There's no one there now.' Nathan shook his head. 'It's unlikely that anyone was there to be honest. We're enclosed by gardens either side and the wall at the back is ten-foot high; he would have to be an athlete to scale that.'

'I saw a man out there, I swear it.'

'Perhaps you should phone the police, see what they say.' He replaced the poker and made me a cup of tea while I talked to the police. The man who took the call noted my previous contact, but it had the opposite effect to the one I'd been expecting; it was as though I was prone to fantasy and this was another instance. He asked if I could still see the moving shadows but in careful tones as if I was a child who'd had a nightmare. Once he knew Nathan had been outside and found nothing, he told me to be sure I'd locked the doors and phone back in the morning. He probably didn't believe me. My conviction began to waver. It was true I'd woken in a different place, true I'd been momentarily confused, but the man in the garden had seemed utterly real.

'I'm tired, Rachel. Let's sleep now.'

I followed Nathan up the stairs. He was asleep in five minutes while I lay awake, unsure which was the more frightening possibility: that a stalker had been staring at me from our garden in the early hours of the morning, or that the policeman's inference was correct, and I had simply imagined it all.

Chapter 14

June 2017

'I'll have to go; it sounds worse than usual.'

I was waiting for someone from Wiltshire police to pick up but Nathan sounded so miserable that I put the phone down and turned on the kettle instead. It was breakfast time and he was sitting at the table but he hadn't touched his toast.

The early morning garden had been peaceful. There were no signs of intrusion when I walked around as the sun was rising, no footprints, no broken twigs or damaged flower-pots. It was hard to convince myself that there'd been a man crouching under the trees a few hours ago. Nathan was right, it would have been impossible for anyone to vault a ten-foot wall. His mother was the priority; if she was in trouble, of course he should go.

'Why did she fall?'

'God knows, she's confused. She was crying when Annie found her, she must have been on the floor for hours.'

Annie was his mother's cleaner. She'd looked after Ada since Peter died two years ago as her dementia slowly advanced. I gave Nathan his coffee and adjusted his tie, it was half undone. A new one, silky grey with little stars, an improvement on the usual stripes. His mother must have sent it and he was wearing it in her honour, not that she'd remember.

'She left the hob on all night, the kitchen was roasting.'

'We know she has atrial fibrillation.' I put my hand over his. 'Perhaps it was her heart, we should organize a few tests. Her GP—'

'Thanks, Rach. I don't need a medical lecture. I'll sort it.' He withdrew his hand and stood up. A new Nathan, irritable, maybe guilty. Ada lived on her own in Reading, he hadn't visited for a while.

'What can I do?'

'You? Nothing.' Again, that new sharp tone. 'Luckily it's Friday. I'll delegate. Sarah will probably pitch in.'

Sarah again. He walked out of the room, punching in a number. I'd washed the cups, set them to dry and found my coat by the time he came back into the kitchen. His frown had gone.

'Sarah's taking over. I'll throw a few things together and be off.'

She would have been happy to help. She might have given him the tie herself, a coded plea for something she couldn't have.

'Nathan—'

'It might take me a few days to sort things out. Sarah said to take as much time as I needed so I could look at some nursing homes.'

'Shouldn't we do this together? It's the weekend tomorrow. I might be able to get away early today if you can wait a few hours.'

'I'll cope on my own, I'd rather.' He must have caught the amazement in my face because his tone softened and he touched my shoulder. 'Your list will be full with Debbie on maternity leave and I need to go right now.' He started towards the stairs then turned back. 'Didn't I hear you on the phone last night asking Lizzie for lunch?'

Lunch with Lizzie had totally slipped my mind, I'd forgotten Debbie was on maternity leave too. Worry stung; there wasn't time for forgetfulness, not now, not yet.

'Don't tell her about Granny till we know what's what.' He shook his head. 'No point in upsetting her.' His glance swept me. 'You look different today, can't work out what it is.'

I'd put on a green summer dress, a sleeveless one made of linen, discarding the suit I usually wore along with the tights – they felt like a uniform now, one that belonged to someone else. I'd left my hair loose for a change, I liked the feel of it on my shoulders.

'Sexier,' Nathan said, a little smile playing over his face as he studied me. He probably thought I was dressing for him.

I kissed him. 'Good luck with Ada, give her my love.'

In the end I left before he did. On the way to work I pulled over to check my phone. No messages. The disappointment was sharp, like the stab of the needles I'd used for liver biopsies as a house officer; patients had cried out in pain and disbelief as I wanted to now but what the hell had I been expecting? I'd set the rules. We weren't to communicate. I had to carry on as though nothing had happened although everything had; Luc had turned my world upside down and I had to wait until it righted itself. I put my head back and closed my eyes against tears until a car hooted behind me. The woman gesticulated as she went by, her lips working angrily.

The morning was busy, Debbie's patients swelling the list. Asthma, sick notes, hypertension, a woman with a breast lump who needed rapid referral, migraine. I worked fast,

119

glad of the problems that filled my mind, until Brian came in. He was the last patient on the list, he was always the last patient. Maybe he thought he'd get extra time that way. It was shortness of breath this time. He hunched over, putting a hand to his chest, his nails were longer today, even dirtier.

'There's something stopping me breathing.' He licked his lips, that reptilian little tic. 'I can't take a proper breath in, my chest doesn't let me.'

I examined him; most patients this close gaze over my shoulder, avoiding eye contact, but Brian stared straight at me and smiled his creepy half smile. I looked away. I didn't want him to see the fear in my eyes. I focused on his chest instead, the metal disc of the stethoscope sank into the doughy flesh but his lungs were clear.

I put the stethoscope on the desk, a loop of tubing hanging over the edge; when Brian sat down he took the tubing in his pale fingers and folded it tightly, patting it firmly into place, all the while smiling that knowing little smile.

I scrolled rapidly through his notes, Brian had been Roger's patient originally; I'd seen him first about four months ago because Roger was away at the time. Since then, Brian had been in every week and the visits were increasing.

My skin prickled. Could Nathan have been right about Brian?

'It's easy to feel worried about breathing,' I told him. 'At worst this will be a viral infection. Luckily it's not causing any signs in your chest that need treatment at the moment.'

As he was leaving, he turned round at the door and took out his phone. 'You look very nice today.' His face was flushed. 'Could I take your picture?'

'Of course you can't, Brian. There are privacy rules about things like that.'

I had no idea if there were but, if not, there should be.

He pocketed his phone with a little shrug and the door closed softly behind him.

I watched him cross the car park from my window, parting the slats of the blind and peering out. My own chest felt tight. Had I been wrong to think he was harmless? It might have been Brian in the garden last night; it was hard to see how he would have managed it but people with obsessions can do things which seem impossible.

Carol bustled in without knocking, she had come to collect my notes, her pungent scent of lily of the valley filled the room. She glanced at me and I dropped the slat.

'There was just one visit today and Roger's picked that up as your surgery was running late.' She looked round the room, as if expecting to see someone still with me.

'The last patient took longer than usual.' I turned off my computer, wondering why I felt I had to explain myself to her.

She crossed her arms. 'It might not be sensible to give a man who is so clearly obsessed quite so much time.'

I felt breathless with surprise. 'Brian has complex problems; his mental health—'

'Liam Chambers had mental health issues, but you stuck to time with him; you haven't since, I notice. It's Roger I feel sorry for.'

Her bob trembled as she swept from the room with the notes. The door banged behind her. The brutal truth caught me by surprise: I was overcompensating. I dropped the stethoscope into my bag and stood up. I wanted to go home.

I walked past Carol without saying goodbye, ridiculously I felt like crying. She was staring at notes and didn't look up – it was difficult to see her expression but her cheeks were flushed. She might be feeling triumphant but her comments had hit home even harder than she'd meant; if I'd spent extra time with Liam, he might still be alive. The guilt tasted bitter in my mouth.

The sun was hot now and the streets were crammed with tourists taking up the pavements, trodden sandwiches lying on the cobbles of the pedestrianized high street. In France, just a few days ago, Luc and I would have retreated from the garden by now, stepping from the sun into cool shadows, climbing the stairs to the bedroom, my hand on his shoulder, already breathless. Another world, a different self. I would have given anything to have him with me now. The wave of longing was so strong I put my hand to the glass of a shop window and that's when I caught the reflection of someone dodging between the tourists, a dark shape moving towards me.

I turned to search the sea of faces, but the figure had disappeared. I began to hurry, bumping into a man's shoulder in my haste. He turned, bellowing in surprise, the face of a bull under a curly thatch. I held up a hand in apology as I twisted past him and through the high street gates which funnelled the crowds towards the cathedral. I glanced behind again, this time glimpsing the same figure moving towards me among the tourists, a hat pulled low, a scarf hiding his face.

I tore towards the constable's hut, cutting across the path of the mass of people, and tried the door, but it was locked. I looked back but the man had disappeared as if he had never been. My heart was beating so hard it made a noise in my ears, so I didn't hear my name until it sounded loud in my ears. I turned, an arm raised to fend off the attack.

Chapter 15

June 2017

'Woah.' A familiar voice, American, amused.

For a moment I didn't recognize him and then I did. Ophelia's brother, Blake. He was smiling, as relaxed as he'd been at the party where we'd first met.

'Blake!' I almost threw my arms around him. It was good to see him; it seemed at that moment as if Luc must be here too, just out of sight, waiting to come forward with his arms outstretched. I had to stop myself looking round.

'I was mailing a letter when you flew by, didn't you hear me call?'

I shook my head. 'I'm so glad to see you.' Surprised too, I'd thought he would still be in France, though of course I couldn't tell him that.

'Where were you off to in such a hurry?' The American accent gave his voice a carefree edge; it reminded me of the laconic hero in a cowboy film, the one who saves the day with a lasso and a lopsided grin.

'Home.' My voice trembled on that word. He stepped forward and took my hands. His were small, smooth and cool, unlike his brother-in-law's; Luc's were large, rough-skinned and very warm.

'What's up?' He seemed genuinely interested; I'd forgotten how friendly he was.

I wanted to tell him what had just happened, but felt afraid he might discuss me with Ophelia. I imagined her cool amusement. I shook my head and tried to smile.

'You're white as a sheet, have you seen a ghost?' He searched my face with his bright blue eyes, so blue they reminded me of Californian swimming pools. I could see him lounging by an oval of glittering water in the sunshine, drinking wine and surrounded by women. 'Why don't you come for a drink?'

'Now?'

'Of course now.' One of his dimples was deeper than the other, it added to the charm. 'I was off to the bookies, but I'd rather have a drink with a gorgeous doctor.'

Going for a drink at lunchtime would be normal for Blake, for many people. I had been outside normal for a while. At home the rooms would be silent; Nathan was with his mother, Victoria in New York and Pepper back with Lizzie. I wondered what Roger would say if I went to the pub. He'd be making his house visit now, his gangly frame folded into a chair, painstakingly taking a history, but, looking at Blake's smiling face, I decided I needn't feel guilty. His company was exactly what I needed.

'Why not?'

'Let's go to the Haunch of Venison, they make ace sandwiches.'

The Haunch of Venison was the oldest pub in Salisbury, a city of old pubs. I hadn't been inside for years. I remembered a dark interior, wooden panelling and vast fireplaces. We walked back through the Close gates together and into the town; with Blake chatting easily by my side I felt safe.

124

He asked me about the practice as we went, about the people I worked with. Carol's remarks were still echoing in my mind. I began to tell him about her, cautiously at first, but as he listened and nodded it poured out in a stream: the way she hero-worshipped Roger but criticized me, the little jabs about timekeeping, the hurtful remarks today. I couldn't help it; like my loose hair, the dress I was wearing and even the sun on my limbs, it felt transgressive and irresistibly good.

'She sounds like a bitch.' Blake's eyes were warm with sympathy. 'What do your patients say?'

'Oh, they all feel sorry for me.'

He laughed. I felt triumphant but guilty; Carol was devoted to the practice, she was respected by the patients and Roger adored her. I should talk to her more often instead of complaining about her behaviour, find common ground, but all the same, by the time we reached the Haunch of Venison, I felt much better for opening up.

The pub wasn't crowded – most people were jammed into the courtyard garden at the back under sun umbrellas. I sat in a large leather chair, watching Blake order drinks at the bar. He was flirting with the young girl serving him, her pleasant, freckled face creased in a broad grin. I remembered how Lizzie had looked when she met him; Blake was the kind of man who made women smile.

He brought the drinks to the table, white wine for me, two large glasses of beer for him.

The pub was dark and cool. An old couple sipping beer were doing a crossword puzzle at a table in the corner. Three women watched a game of football on television, a little terrier sleeping by their feet. The way her nose tucked neatly into her paws was so like Coco, I felt tears sting. I looked away quickly.

'It's nice here.' I smiled at Blake across the table. 'I'd forgotten about pubs; we don't go to pubs often enough.'

'So what does a doctor like you do for kicks around here?' He drank swiftly, then put his glass down and settled back, his eyes on mine, bright with curiosity.

'Dog walks, cooking, reading. I sketch sometimes. Nathan likes gardening.' Ordinary, everyday things, they sounded boring even to me. I wondered whether this cool American pitied me my middle-aged life. I had an urge, instantly repressed, to tell him that the dull little world I was describing had cracked wide open a week ago, revealing a different one, replete with warmth, sunshine, tenderness, sex.

'And what do property restorers do when they find themselves in Salisbury?' I asked as the sandwiches were brought to the table, with another glass of beer for Nathan.

'I was hoping for some tips.'

'There's a good theatre, concerts in the cathedral, a literary festival.' The wine was restorative. I was feeling better, almost back to normal. 'And all the old houses you could want.'

'I've found one of those already.' He started the second pint.

'Oh? Where?' I put my glass down on the table in case he noticed my hand had begun to tremble.

'*La belle Provence*,' he replied, leaning back again, as relaxed as if sitting against the stone walls of Luc's house with the mountains shining in the distance beyond the olive trees. 'Luc inherited a crumbling pile, it's a mess but, with the right input, it could make us some serious cash.'

'Us?'

'Luc, Ophelia and yours truly.' He leant forward. 'It needs gutting, new walls and windows, new flooring, the works. There are some old sheds that should be demolished.'

I took a bite of my sandwich but put it down again. The bread was dry after all, unappetizing.

'The kind of people we're aiming at are used to luxury.' He continued, his voice warming up, 'I'm thinking lots more bathrooms, a modern kitchen. A gym, a swimming pool of course . . .'

The pub door opened and banged shut. I glanced up, then stared. Brian was standing just inside. His head was bent and that half smile was on his face although he wasn't looking at me. Blake was still talking but now his voice seemed to be coming from a long way away. I felt sick. I should have listened to Nathan. Brian had been different in surgery today, that should have alerted me. He must have doubled back and loitered outside the waiting room then pursued me as I emerged from the practice. He would have watched when I met Blake and then followed us here. I shrank back as he made his way to a table by the window and slid into the chair behind, putting his newspaper down on the surface as if to claim the territory.

'What do you think?' Blake was watching me, his chin lifted expectantly.

I turned my chair towards him, away from Brian.

'About what?'

'You haven't heard a word, have you?' He shook his head, smiling. He drained the second glass of beer and started the third, one of those people who seem able to drink quantities and yet remain unaffected. 'We might sell it after a few years, there's already interest from the States.'

A chair scraped noisily on the floor, then Brian walked past us to the bar. I turned my head away as he passed us on the way back, beer in one hand, three packets of crisps in another.

'What's wrong?' Blake's tone had become kinder, less gossipy.

I hesitated but Brian had followed me, he had already broken one of the rules that exist between a doctor and her patient, which meant I could break one too.

'Don't look now.' I whispered, 'That bloke who's just sat

127

down, the one on his own in the corner reading the paper? He's a patient. Nathan thinks he's obsessed with me. I've been aware of someone following me, I think it might be him.'

The dimples reappeared. 'Can't say I blame him.'

'Be serious, Blake.' My skin was prickling again. 'Brian's creepy. He comes in to see me several times a week. He was my last patient this morning, afterwards I was pursued down the street and now he turns up here. I don't believe in coincidences.'

'Those kind of people need to be confronted and stopped. If someone was stalking my sister, I'd beat his ass. I'll speak to him.' He sounded quite different, a little cold and utterly determined. Determination is contagious, my fear vanished. He was right, this had to stop.

'I'll do it.' I got up and walked over to Brian's table. He was reading the paper and glanced up as I approached, then stared. A blotchy stain spread slowly over his face.

'Hello there, Brian. I need to speak to you for a moment.' I pulled out a stool and sat opposite him.

'I know what you're going to say.' Brian put his glass down clumsily, spilling beer over his paper. He lowered his voice. 'I shouldn't be in a pub drinking beer and eating crisps.'

'Did you follow me here?'

'What d'you mean?' He sounded confused. 'I've been coming here every day since Mum died. It's my local. Ask them, they know me.' The red stain deepened. 'The same people come every day. I thought, one day someone would say hello and then we could begin to talk. I might make a friend.'

'Have you been following me at other times too?'

He started to pick at the skin around his thumbnail. The nail fold was red and inflamed; it must have been a habit, something he did under stress.

'I didn't mean anything by it.'

'When?' I stared at him, the admission was so simple. I could have asked him a while ago and put a stop to it much earlier.

'Once I followed you through the Close in my car though I felt dreadful after, I might have run you over by mistake. One Sunday, I walked down that gravel path behind you, the one with trees by the cathedral – you had a dog with you – and once by the path to the Old Mill.'

'There've been other times too, haven't there?'

He shook his head and held up three fingers. 'I promised myself I'd stop after three.'

'Why are you doing this?'

'I wanted to see where you live. You're my friend, I haven't got many, just people in the practice.' His voice dropped to a whisper. 'My mum used to say you should always know where your friends live.'

I began to feel very cold. We should have sat outside in the warm June sunshine after all. 'I'm your doctor, that's different.'

He kept picking at the sore place around his nail, it had begun to bleed.

'Why did you follow me to the Old Mill?'

'I was in the Elizabethan gardens, feeding the ducks, when you ran by. It was getting dark. I was worried something might happen to you, something nasty. I tried to run after you but you were too fast for me. I'm not used to running. I hid when you turned round, I was frightened you'd be cross with me.'

'You scared me. I told the police.'

'I don't mean anything by it, I haven't done it since then, honestly.' His forehead was beaded with sweat.

'That's not true though. You followed me in the Close again.' I tried to speak calmly, a doctor to a patient. 'I saw you in my garden last night. And you tracked me just now.

129

If it happens once again, I'll tell the police and, this time, they could arrest you.' I didn't know if that was true, but nor would he.

He shook his head but his eyes glistened. 'I sit in my car at the surgery sometimes, waiting till you go home, but that's only to make sure you're okay. I would never hurt you. I haven't got anyone else to care about except you and Carol and the nurses. It's not like I want anything.'

A hand dropped lightly on my shoulder, Blake glanced down at Brian. 'Hi mate. I'm Blake.' He held out his hand, the blue eyes twinkled. 'Great choice of pub.'

Brian flushed, ignoring the gesture. 'My local,' he mumbled.

'Mine too.' Blake took my arm. 'And now I'm going to walk my favourite doctor home.'

Brian looked down, he began picking at the skin around his nails again.

Blake turned to me outside. 'What did he say?'

'He admitted following me. He says he's concerned for my safety, that's all. He seems harmless enough, I can't help feeling sorry for him. He doesn't seem to want anything.'

'Everyone wants something.' Blake's voice had hardened. 'It's always power. As the doctor, you hold more than he does, he'd resent that. Scaring you would make him feel dominant, it's why men hurt women. It's not very complicated.'

We walked side by side in silence until we reached the Close. As we passed the cathedral I was aware of its power bearing down on me; the air felt differently charged as it does in the presence of a cliff or a great tree. People flocked to the cathedral, walking close to the walls as if for comfort but it wasn't a comforting place to me. When I was little I'd been frightened of the towering height, the grinning gargoyles, and the gaping entrance, the dark hush inside. Today it seemed austere, menacing. Was it possible Brian wished to hurt me?

'So what are you up to this afternoon?' I wanted to change the subject, fear was exhausting.

'Me?' The blue eyes sparkled. 'Playing cricket with my nephew.'

Ophelia's son, Luc's stepson, the little family I had blundered into. I looked up at the spire shining like a sword in the hot afternoon light, I didn't want Blake to catch the guilt in my eyes.

'I saw him at the housewarming.' I mustered a smile. 'He's what, ten years old? Ophelia looks far too young to be his mother.'

'I'll tell her you said that, she'll be so happy. She's older than she looks, though I'm not allowed to say more.'

She was still years younger than me. Luc must have compared us if only subconsciously. If it was a contest based on looks, I'd lose every round. It didn't matter now of course, I'd given him back, not that he was ever mine to give.

'She's very lovely.' Would Blake wonder why my voice was so flat?

'Hence Oscar's looks.' Blake's face seemed to melt. 'I'm indecently proud of that kid, he's one of the reasons I stick around.'

Oscar had seemed happy; he was lucky to have Blake as an uncle. Perhaps, if I'd had a brother, Lizzie would be happier too, a larger family around her, compensating for my mistakes. We were passing the row of dark trees, the tall pines and short scrubby bushes crowding together. The ancient murder had taken place in the dark, but it was a disconcerting place even in sunshine. The shadows between the trees were thick, an ideal place for someone to hide. I moved closer to Blake and he put his arm around me, as if sensing my fear. Ophelia was fortunate to have a brother like him, more fortunate than she knew. He felt like a friend already, someone who'd

131

arrived at the right time, with all the careless generosity of a man who'd grown up surrounded by wealth.

At the door of the house, I turned to face him. I didn't want him to go. His cheerfulness, his very casualness were soothing, as if everything was bound to turn out all right and nothing mattered very much.

'Coffee?'

He glanced at his watch. 'Sorry. After cricket I'm going straight back to France, taking Ophelia with me this time; we want to finalize plans. We're dropping Oscar with friends on the way.'

Luc must have thought he'd seen off the danger when Blake left. Perhaps they were planning to take him by surprise, but they couldn't make him do what he didn't want to, surely.

Blake kissed me twice, first on one cheek, then the other. He smelt of lemons and cinnamon.

'Thanks for lunch.' I put my hand on his sleeve. 'And for being so kind.'

'My pleasure. And don't worry, I think Brian will behave himself in future.'

He meant well but the low hum of concern started up again. I watched him saunter through the gate, raising his hand in a salute without turning round. Casual, charming Blake, as tall and golden as a film star, off to play cricket with his nephew on a summer afternoon. It made him nicer still, luckier somehow, the kind of man who strolls through life enjoying the good things on offer.

He and Ophelia would fly to France this evening. I could imagine them walking around the house. Ophelia might open cupboards, Blake would put his hand against the wall for damp. They would go upstairs. They might glance at the vase on the sill in the room where we'd slept, though the flowers would be dead by now. They would stand at the window, gazing at the view just as we had done. Luc would cook, maybe a barbecue. Blake would call down to him with an outrageous idea for improvement and Luc would smile and shake his head, he'd stoke the fire and pour the wine. He might lay the rug on the lawn where he put it for us. I was swept with a longing so fierce that tears rose. I had to get inside and pull myself together.

As I put the key in the lock, I felt warm breath on my neck at exactly the same moment I saw a dark reflection in the paint of the door.

Chapter 16

June 2017

I whirled round. It was Lizzie, her face was very close to mine.

'Jesus, Lizzie, you gave me a fright.'

She was so near I could see the lines where her fingers had smoothed the foundation over her cheeks, the glitter embedded in her dark eyeshadow. She looked familiar and not familiar.

When Lizzie was a child, she'd followed me to work several times. Carol had brought her into my room, seven years old and tearful. She wanted to be with me and didn't understand why she couldn't stay. It was so long ago I'd forgotten; was it conceivable it had started again?

'Have you been following me, darling?'

'Of course not.' She stepped back, her face stiff with distaste. 'Do you know how ridiculous you looked? That man is half your age.'

'Blake? But you know him, you met him at Ophelia's party.' I was confused. 'We'd just had lunch in the pub.'

'You arranged lunch with me. I've been waiting for you.'

Her face was flushed beneath the make-up, her voice trembling with anger.

'Oh no.' I stared at her in disbelief. 'I completely forgot.'

'You phoned me last night.'

'The thing is, I was being followed.'

'By Blake?'

'Of course not. I bumped into him as I was running away. I was so terrified I couldn't think straight. He thought a drink and a sandwich would help, that's all.'

'You had your hand on his sleeve.'

'I was thanking him.'

'Don't suggest lunch again, unless you're sure you can spare the time.'

'Sweetheart, come in and have coffee. I'll explain exactly what happened. It's really important, I wanted to warn you—'

She turned away, opened her car door, slid in and slammed it, driving away fast. She hadn't believed a word. Her coil pot was still on the kitchen table; Nathan had filled it with white roses this time. I sat down slowly. I should face it: the bookish little girl who had made things for me and followed me to work had vanished. There was no trace of her now, grown-up Lizzie was irrevocably different. She always seemed angry but I couldn't blame her this time. She'd come as I'd asked, I'd forgotten and, worse, I'd looked ridiculous. I wouldn't get another chance.

I was glad of evening surgery, glad there was a long list and results to file. As usual, I was the last doctor to leave. Keith, Carol's husband, ex-army, blazered and upright, was reading a tattered edition of Country Life. I lingered by the counter as she crossed off her jobs.

'Carol, I wondered if we could talk about Brian—'

'Finished, are you?' She took the notes from my arms and disappeared between the shelves, heels ringing.

She'd be in a better mood after the weekend. On Monday

I'd tell her Brian been following me and ask her to transfer him back to Roger's list, though I doubted she'd believe there was cause for concern. I greeted Keith, who stood up with a tired sigh. He had her coat over his arm and was holding a large brown envelope, stamped with her name in blue print. I felt a pang of sympathy for Carol; she might be breaking the rules herself, sneaking notes home to sort out in her spare time. She worked harder than most of us. Keith must have lost track of the times he'd waited with her belongings to drive her home at the end of the day. He frowned as if he thought it was my fault she was late so often. He would be right, it probably was.

At home I poured a large glass of red wine and phoned Nathan. I wanted to tell him about being followed and about Lizzie. He didn't pick up so I phoned his mother.

'How wonderful to hear you.' Ada's voice quavered. 'When are you coming to see me?'

'Soon, Ada.' Timid, pretty Ada with a halo of white hair, her milky eyes and soft pink cardigan. 'Are you better?'

'Better?'

'From your fall.'

'Did I fall?'

'That's why Nathan's come to see you, darling. Can I speak to him?'

'Is he here?' She sounded fearful and guilty at the same time, as if she had mislaid him by mistake.

'He must be. He left this morning to come and visit you.'

'Oh my goodness, maybe he's lost his way.' She sounded near to tears.

'He'll be in the kitchen, sweetheart, can you ask him to phone me?'

'Of course I will, dear.'

I refilled my glass. The dementia was worse than I'd thought; Nathan's plan to see nursing homes made sense.

The house was quiet. Victoria was still away, no cello music filtered through the walls to keep me company. I paced the rooms, looking at the garden through the glass doors as the light ebbed. I didn't turn on the lights – what if Brian was out there looking in, despite his promises? Blake might be right, there could be a hidden side to him, a damaged man concealed inside the timid one. I sat in the dark waiting for Nathan to phone, I didn't read a book or watch television. I tapped out a lengthy message to Luc on my phone instead. I told him I missed him, needed him, longed for him body and soul, that he was in my mind all the time. I admitted he was right and that I'd made a mistake, it was obvious we should be together.

And then I deleted every single word. I thought about him instead; the moment we'd met and the moments since, those perfect days in the sun and the warmth of the nights. I lived them again and again until I thought I'd go mad. In the end I was too tired to watch the garden. I went to bed and read *Anna Karenina* until I fell asleep. I surfaced once near morning to the fading noise of a police siren then slept again.

The heat woke me. The sun lay in thick stripes on the bed, it was late but it was Saturday, it didn't matter. I looked at my phone; nothing from Luc or even Nathan, no messages, no missed calls. I showered and dressed, then walked into the garden with my book and a coffee, wincing at the light. It was one of those hot, still June mornings. The leaves hung limply from the trees, the roses were already drooping. A headache had begun and I felt faintly shivery like the very beginning of flu. It didn't bother me much, I was used to contracting viruses from work. I had the weekend to get better, I'd read and rest. When my phone went I snatched it up, but it wasn't Luc; of course it wasn't him.

'Rachel?' Nathan sounded different, odd. Upset.

'Are you okay? Only Ada said she hadn't seen you.'

'She forgets me as soon as I leave the room.' He paused, then continued in a little rush, 'Have you heard the news?'

'What news?' My mouth dried, it was his wary tone. 'Is Lizzie okay?'

'She's fine. Sit down, baby. It's all over the internet. I'm surprised you don't know.'

'Know what?' Nathan never called me baby; was he trying to break something to me very gently? A car accident in France, a green truck overturned outside Saint-Rémy-de-Provence. Would that be on the internet? Even if it was, Nathan wouldn't have understood the significance. I sat down on the bottom step of the stairs, holding the banisters tightly.

'Something's happened in the Close to a friend of yours. I'm sorry, it's bad.'

Why are people taught to break bad news slowly? You need it fast once you know it's coming.

'For Christ's sake, Nathan, tell me.' The blood was pounding in my ears so loudly, I couldn't hear and missed the name after all.

Chapter 17

'. . . killed last night.'

'Who?'

'Carol.'

'Carol?'

My Carol? How could she be dead? I'd seen her yesterday, she'd been vibrantly alive with her immaculate hair, her high heels, her red Biro. The idea was obscene. My mind scrambled, thoughts trying to get a foothold. Keith must be devastated. Roger wouldn't believe it.

'Her body was found this morning by a dog walker.'

Why are bodies always found by dog walkers? Are we the only people in the world who go for walks? But I knew the answer; a dog is persistent, he searches in the undergrowth, smelling out an unusual scent, tugging at a shape under the leaves, licking at a pale hand.

'Does anyone know what happened to her?'

'The internet is buzzing with rumours. It seems he put a bag over her head, there were stab wounds in her back. He

. . . he cut off four fingers. They say the signs are that she struggled up then collapsed.'

Once I'd been knocked over by a huge wave and thrown onto the beach, winded. It felt like that now. I groped for bearings. 'We have to warn Lizzie; if there's a killer on the loose—'

'We spoke just now, she's fine. She's in her flat with a friend.'

I closed my eyes in relief but the image of Carol wounded and bleeding was painted in bright colours beneath my lids.

Nathan was still talking. '. . . think he knew her, hence the bag over her head. It means he didn't want her to recognize and report him, and therefore that he might not have meant to kill her. If he had, he wouldn't have bothered to prevent her seeing him.'

Carol's life had been rigorously conventional; her savage death was difficult to comprehend.

'Apparently the police have been crawling all over the Close for hours. I'm surprised you haven't heard anything.'

I remembered the dying wail of a siren in the early morning, help that had come too late. Carol's fear and anguish was hard to imagine. He must have removed her fingers after he stabbed her, or she would have fought him; perhaps the first shock would have obliterated the second.

'Where was she?' But I guessed what was coming before he told me.

'The shrubbery.'

I was back by the trees then, and those menacing shadows. I knew exactly what it was like to hear footsteps on the gravel as Carol must have, the sickening fear.

'You must tell the police you were followed in that very place, by that patient of yours.' Nathan had kept pace with my thoughts.

'The police were useless, you were there when I made that call.'

'It's different now, they'll take you seriously.'

If I reminded the police, they would question my patients and they would find their way to Brian; under pressure he might admit to following me. He'd be arrested, accused, destroyed, and it couldn't be him. Brian might be creepy but he would be incapable of doing this, I was sure of that.

'I'll come back, you won't want to be on your own,' Nathan said after a short pause.

'Have you found a nursing home yet?'

'God, no. There's four days' worth of booked visits yet to do.'

'You must stay in that case. Ada needs your help more than I do. I'll be fine.'

'Well, if you're sure.' A quiet sigh of relief; those visits would have taken time to arrange. 'Promise me you won't walk anywhere on your own.'

'I promise. Lizzie—'

'I told you, she knows. She's okay, leave her be. Ada's calling for me, I have to go. Tell the police about your patient.' He hung up.

I stayed where I was on the bottom step of the stairs. Nathan had been curt at the end of the call, in a rush, but I understood. He was worried about Ada and worried about me. I should get up but I felt too dizzy.

Perhaps Carol hadn't run fast enough or maybe she'd been braver than I was. She would have tried to turn around which was when he'd have slipped the bag over her head and pushed her into the undergrowth, her face hitting the mud, stones tearing the skin. The twigs would have snagged her tights. She might for a second, a millisecond, have registered that, minded about the mud stains on her clothes and her torn tights, until she felt the knife in her back. Each

143

breath after that would have been agonizing. She wouldn't have been able to scream, not even when he removed her fingers, but her mind would have been screaming in the last seconds of her life.

The phone buzzed in my hand.

'How are you?' Roger spoke in a different voice from his usual one, deeper, louder, disguising tears. In his book, men were tough, women were to be protected. He had protected me from Carol, Carol from me.

'Is Nathan with you?'

'On his way home.' A necessary lie, Roger would worry otherwise, he'd offer to come round.

'I've been with Keith since the news came through. He's drinking cup after cup of tea. I don't think he believes it yet.'

I could see Carol's husband clearly, bolt upright and bewildered on a chintzy sofa in a sitting room that still smelt of lily of the valley. I hoped Roger would put whisky in the tea.

'Betty will stand in next week,' Roger said unsteadily.

Betty, Roger's wife, the calm centre of his life. At parties she was a homely figure in the background, a little dumpy, easy to overlook, but her food was delicious and imaginative, she chatted to the shy intern on the edge of the group and she always remembered my birthday. Tonight, I was enormously glad he had Betty in his life.

Despite what Nathan said, I texted Lizzie. I couldn't help it.

Hope you're okay darling. Don't go out on your own.

My longing for Luc was visceral, constant. I had a thumping headache now and my limbs had begun to ache, so I did what my tidy mother had done when she was upset, I began to throw things away. Nothing made sense so I tried to create order, if only of possessions. I started in the loft and worked downwards, tossing out clothes and cleaning the empty cupboards afterwards. I chucked away garments from childhood, student clothes kept for Lizzie, my old pregnancy dresses. They were outdated now, it was stupid to think she'd want them. I opened an old cardboard box, finding Lizzie's christening gown, made of fine wool, now shredded by moths. It was hard to let that go; she'd been so tiny. I'd held her against me in that huge cathedral, one of those moments in life that feel complete, a fusion of happiness and love. Nathan had taken a photo but I'd given it to Lizzie a long time ago, I hadn't seen it for years. She would have lost it by now, being close to me was the last thing on her mind; if anything, she wanted to get further away.

I put the wrecked gown with other clothes into bags, then threw the bags down the stairs. I hoovered the loft and started on my room, discarding shrunken cardigans and ancient plimsolls. I wiped paintwork and door handles but when I came to the back of our bedroom door I stopped. The satchel was still behind my dressing gown, a hiding place so perfect I'd forgotten about it myself. I removed the dressing gown and lifted the satchel off the hook – my paintings from Luc, at the moment I needed them most.

I sat on the bed and slid out the sheets one by one: the house in the sun with its line of windows, sketches of Coco, olive trees, swallows in the sky, lemons in a bowl. The view to the mountains. It was as though he was beside me at the bedroom window again, his shoulder against mine. It was only when I was replacing them in the satchel that my finger-tips brushed against the case. I'd forgotten that too. The family painting by his great-great-grandfather. I took out the case and snapped open the clasps. The contents were encased in layers of black paper and plastic; unwrapped, it was the view from the window, in the style of Van Gogh and nothing like Luc's. Olive trees twisted into the distance, but these weren't green and grey like his, instead wide blue circles whirled on ochre branches, ivory mountains crumpled against a yellow sky. The grass was blue, violet, red and green; bare canvas was visible between the strokes, as if the painter had been in a hurry to capture the scene before the light changed. The painting was breathtakingly powerful, almost hallucinogenic.

When the doorbell rang I didn't answer it, I was far away in the Provençal heat, listening to the wind rustling in the olive trees, watching the light flicker like flames on the leaves. After a while I layered the black paper then the plastic around the painting, replaced it in the box and put the box in the satchel. I slipped the satchel back on the hook and arranged the dressing gown over it carefully. It vanished again.

Lizzie's old room was next but it felt empty already. She had cleared her dressing table and her wardrobe, taking the clothes she wanted with her. Her childhood things had been left behind, the teddy bear with the torn ear, a sketch I'd drawn of the cathedral years ago, the shell necklace from Granny Ada. I picked up the teddy and held him as I texted Lizzie again.

Take care my Lizzie. Please don't go out on your own.

A text pinged back. *Take a break Mum, stop texting me!*

I put my phone down. What had I expected? Nathan had told me to leave her alone, I should have listened. Lizzie was fine, that was the main thing. I cleaned every room and was trembling with exhaustion by the time I'd scrubbed out the last cupboard in the kitchen. The bell rang again as I was emptying the bucket of soapy water. Victoria stood on the doorstep, taking in my dusty dungarees and tearstained face. She was wearing her wide yellow culottes and rough-edged navy jacket; the very sight of her was soothing.

'I'm just back, you're having supper with me,' she announced calmly. 'Abby told me what happened.'

'I've got some bug starting, Vee, what if you catch it?'

'My immune system is rock solid, sweetie, that's no excuse.'

Her bags were still in the hall, the little sponge bag she packed for travel propped on top, full of Victoria emergencies: her scarlet lipstick and scent along with toothbrush and soap and face cream.

'How's your mum?'

'Good news.' Victoria's smile was bright, too bright. 'It turns out to be a tiny treatable cancer, in her left lung.'

Lung cancer is always bad news. 'What can I do?'

'Nothing. The doctor says we mustn't worry.' Victoria laughed, her usual full-throated laugh. 'She'll outlive us all.'

'If you'd rather she was near you, we'll look after her in the surgery, find an oncologist—'

'Thanks, my love, but she's better where she is. She's started treatment and all her friends are over there. I'll go back when she needs me.' She put a glass of wine into my hands and led the way into the sitting room. 'Now, tell me how you are after that terrible happening.'

I told her what I knew about Carol's death, stumbling a little over the words, while Victoria lit candles and put a lace cloth on the table.

'She wouldn't have known much about it,' she said as we sat down. She had prepared a fragrant curry of monkfish and prawns, flecked with coriander, but I couldn't eat much. My face had begun to burn, the fever was building.

'Terror speeds things up, it would have been over quickly.' Victoria filled my glass with wine.

Would it? I wasn't sure I agreed. Terror slows things down for me, images become sharper, the silhouette of a crooked branch, the metallic gleam of a puddle, a shadow's dark edge. Sounds get louder, the crunch of footsteps on gravel, the pistol crack of a snapping twig. What about the blade of a knife? It would have burnt as it slid between her ribs, there would have been the taste of iron in her mouth as the blood bubbled up in her throat. I pushed my plate aside, reaching for my glass instead.

After supper, sitting on the floor on deep cushions, Victoria lit a roll-up made of Turkish tobacco and the pungent scent filled the room. 'Now, you don't have to tell me a thing sweetie, but if it helps to share, go right ahead.'

The room glowed around us, the screams of the swifts came in through the open garden door. I told her everything, from Luc's first visit to the surgery to the days in France and the days since. Ada's fall and Nathan's absence, how Brian had followed me and Blake had come to my rescue. Lizzie's anger.

She listened, then relit her roll-up. 'You've had an unforgettable love affair, that's rare. Hardly anyone gets that.' There was a little silence. She'd been married to her husband for thirty years before he died, they travelled everywhere together, they'd adored each other. It had taken great strength to carry on, though few would have realized that. 'In fact, if I didn't love you as I do, I'd be madly jealous.' Then she laughed again, her throaty little laugh. 'The man who's been following you turns out to be a harmless patient. My godchild is cross because like every daughter she wants to be free of her mother but hasn't yet worked out how.' She began coughing and stubbed out the roll-up in an enamelled ashtray brought back from Russia.

'You need to stop smoking, Vee.' What was happening to her mother hovered between us.

'Bloody doctors.' The ghost of a wink. 'I'm off to Edinburgh tomorrow to shoot some interiors for *Vogue*, back in a few days. I'll check on you then.'

The house was dark when I returned, the images of Carol started to circle again, and in spite of the warm night I began to shiver. The virus was gaining ground, my hands were icy. I was running my wrists under warm water when a text pinged through on my phone.

Just heard horrible news. Sending thoughts from France. Stay strong, Blake xxx

I was glad Blake was away, or he might have come round; kind though he was, I didn't want fuss. I needed my thoughts to settle in peace but, twenty minutes later, the bell rang, ripping the silence. I was beginning to feel very ill and I let it ring. After the third time it occurred to me that it could be Lizzie, breaking her promise to stay safe, needing comfort after all or come to comfort me. These thoughts blocked out a quieter, saner voice that was whispering at me not to answer the door at midnight when there could be a murderer about.

As if it were a sunny day, as if I were welcoming my daughter, I opened the front door wide into darkness. There was no one there. I stepped back into the courtyard and began to shut the door as my stupidity became clear to me. At that moment Luc stepped inside.

Chapter 18

June 2017

He was the same and not the same. He looked exhausted, thinner, taller even. There was a little muscle below his left eye that was ticking. He wasn't smiling. I wasn't either, I was trying not to cry.

'Come inside.'

We crossed the courtyard, I ushered him into the house and locked the door; it never occurred to me that I was ushering in danger, locking it in with me, though now, too late, I see that's exactly what I was doing. I took him into the kitchen, poured glasses of wine. I hardly knew what I was doing, the wine splashed onto the table. He looked around the kitchen, as if wondering where my husband was this late on a Saturday evening.

'Nathan's with his mother in Reading.'

We were standing either side of the table like strangers, though if we were strangers, we would probably have smiled at each other. I knew him deeply, intimately, in the way animals know each other, by instinct and by heart, but, in terms of everything else, hardly at all. All the facts that come with friendship, the hinterland behind the people you trust, there hadn't been time for any of that.

'I'm sorry.' His voice was so familiar, so warm, it made me want to cry.

'Why sorry?' My voice sounded unsteady.

'For not being in touch and now, for turning up unexpectedly.' He walked round the table, coming closer. 'I can't get it out of my head that it could have been you that was found by that dog walker.'

I could feel the heat from him, inhale that smoky smell. His presence was overwhelming. I closed my eyes, but all those processes were clicking into place again: my heart rate was accelerating and my mouth drying, my hands were slippery with sweat, it was difficult to breathe.

He put his arms around me, at the same time that my teeth began chattering. He half carried me to the sofa. He was hot whereas I was very cold. I could feel his heart galloping against my chest, or it might have been mine against his. He began to kiss me. I lost all sense of time as we sank into love, hours could have passed.

'Why did you come back?' I put my palm against his face, the skin was damp with sweat. 'You were in France; you shouldn't be here.'

'Why do you think? Blake told me you'd been followed.'

'Why would he tell you that?' I sat up. 'Does he know about us?'

'Of course not. He remembered I'd been your patient, he mentioned he'd bumped into you and that you were scared because a patient was following you.' He got up abruptly, walked to the window and back again. He was talking much faster than usual. 'I had a bad feeling about it immediately. I was afraid you wouldn't take my call so I caught a late flight back yesterday, I had to warn you to take care. When I heard the news this morning, it felt as if my worst fears were coming true. I came round earlier but you didn't answer the bell.' He came closer. 'Don't you see? The killer could have been the man who followed you, that patient of yours. It happened in the same place, didn't it? By those trees? What's his name?'

The words were spilling from him so quickly it was difficult to keep pace.

'He's called Brian, but he's harmless. Carol was his friend, one of the few he had.' I felt worse now, my teeth were chattering again, there was a rug on the back of the sofa, and I wrapped it around me. 'Stop pacing, Luc, you're frightening me.'

'How do you know it wasn't him?'

'He's just not the type.'

'He managed to terrify you.'

'I terrified myself.' I reached for Luc and pulled him down to sit next to me. I spoke slowly to calm him, 'Brian's a very lonely man. He's followed me a few times but that's it, he wouldn't be capable of anything else. I don't think he realizes how frightening it is to be followed. I was convinced I was in danger, so I started running—'

'She didn't though.'

'Who didn't?'

'Your receptionist; she didn't run so he caught her.' He was sweating, looking wildly around the room, caught in some make-believe world, imagining a murder committed by someone I knew to be innocent.

I took his hand. 'You're not listening to me. Brian wouldn't have killed Carol. He wouldn't harm me either, though he managed to scare me. I've been so scared I actually thought there was a man in the garden the other day. Fear does that, it makes you see things that aren't there.' Another patient came to mind as I spoke, I'm not sure why I hadn't remembered this before. 'It can even happen if your

153

eyesight is faulty. I had a patient who saw a figure out of the corner of his eye whenever he moved his head, in the end it was discovered to be an artefact; his retina was detaching.' I turned my head swiftly to demonstrate and nearly cried out. There was a shadow in the garden, in exactly the same place as I'd seen it before, a shadow crouching under the apple tree.

Fear was turning me insane or perhaps my own retina was detaching. I should get my eyes checked. I got up carefully and slowly as if the ground itself was unsteady and closed the curtains. I hadn't wanted curtains, I preferred the clean lines of the old windows so light could stream in unimpeded on sunny days, but this wasn't a sunny day. It was night-time and my eyes were playing tricks. I'd make an appointment with the optician. I was glad now that Nathan had chosen thick, dark curtains. I snapped on the light and the shadows in the room sprang away. My body was shuddering, my face felt burning hot.

'I don't want you to catch this thing, you should go.'

'I don't have to. There's no one at home.'

My thoughts twisted like snakes. Go, I told him silently. We've survived the past without knowing each other, we can survive the future apart, but I wanted to say the opposite. I wanted to beg him to stay. In the end I didn't say anything. He moved closer and held me as I began to cry, fever and fear and desire melting together.

Chapter 19

We woke late on Sunday morning, the light stung my eyes. My temperature had climbed overnight and a pulse was hammering in my ears, the sheets hurt my skin. I began to cough. I fell down when I got up then crawled to the phone. I left a message on Nathan's phone to tell him I was tired out and not to contact me unless there was an emergency, I needed sleep.

Luc got up but I stayed where I was. I hadn't been in bed during the daytime since childhood; it felt indulgent, everyday life receded. The window was open and the warm air came in. The phone rang once but I ignored it, sinking back on the pillow into sleep. I came back to the surface at times to the fear that Luc had gone. The world stopped like a clock that's run down, until a noise set it ticking again: the whistle of the kettle, the rattling of cutlery as he searched for a teaspoon, or the sound of pacing between rooms. He brought me water, tea, lemonade, lemons in a brown bowl, he muttered. Sometimes he lay down next to me and held my hand. I wasn't sure whether the heat was from me or from him; I could feel his pulse going faster than mine or perhaps it was mine that I felt. Two people, one heartbeat. When night came again I tried to keep him lying down.

'Don't get up,' I told him. 'You must be exhausted.'

'The exact opposite. I feel like a plane revving up.' His eyes gleamed in the dark. 'Speeding down the runway, about to take off.'

I knew that feeling; sometimes after nights up in casualty during training, I'd felt exhilarated, powerful, my mind racing until tiredness caught me out and my thoughts became muddled.

'Sleep, Luc.'

But he got up again, he wanted to see his great-great-grandfather's painting. I told him where it was, and he unwrapped it and laid it on the bed. We stared at it together.

'I'm glad it's safe,' he whispered. 'It's the essence of Vincent, you do see that, don't you?' He gripped my hand; his was burning. 'The thickness in those brushstrokes, the way he's layered the paint. That energy, the extraordinary light. Look at the colours he used, look at the sky. I've seen that yellow in the sky above Saint-Rémy but he was the first to capture it.' He wrapped the painting up again and put it back, arranging the folds of the dressing gown to hide it once more.

'It's as though he's watching me from the corner of the room.' He looked round then shook his head. 'No, it's as though I've swallowed him.'

'Who?'

'Vincent, of course. I need to paint. Can I use a spare room?'

'We don't have any paints.' I couldn't take him seriously, I was too tired. 'You sound crazy, my love. Sleep.' I slipped back into peaceful darkness again and, if he answered, I didn't hear.

I lost track of time. I surfaced hours later into a different light, a whole night must have passed, but if anything I felt worse. It was Monday morning. I texted Roger with a shaking hand to say I was poorly, but would come in later. He texted back with strict instructions that I should stay in bed. Two clinics had been cancelled anyway, they would manage.

I heard Luc moving furniture in the room above, Lizzie's old room. He was running up and downstairs, muttering to himself. Through the open bedroom door, I saw a splash of yellow on his hand on the turn of the banisters. I didn't have the heart to question him. He was full of energy, completely alive. I was exhausted anyway, too ill.

The curtains in my room were patterned with red and blue flowers which swelled then shrank as my temperature climbed. Luc came in and I tried to show him. He had knives in his hand; he told me he had things to cut up, shapes to make. He laid a damp flannel on my forehead and opened the window wide. When I woke again it was later, the room was cooler, the light was going. Shadows had gathered. The curtains moved in the wind, billowing and flattening. Then I saw the curtains didn't flatten completely, there was something in the way behind them.

Something that was the shape and size of a man.

I reared up in bed, my mind drenched in fear. The shadowy figure from the garden had come inside. Terror beat in my skull like a drum.

My stalker was with me in the room.

'Who's that?' My voice was hoarse with terror. 'Brian, is that you?'

The figure was completely silent, but I could make out the shape of the head and torso, the line of the arms.

I'd been wrong to be so complacent, wrong to think I was safe when all the time I was in danger. I half fell out of bed and crawled over the floor, then started to scramble

157

up the stairs on all fours, calling for Luc. He opened the door, came down the stairs two at a time, lifted me up and carried me back to the bed.

'Behind the curtains.' I pointed to the windows, feeling hollow with fear.

Luc ripped the curtains aside so violently one of them tore off at the hooks.

There was nothing there. No one.

He looked out of the window. 'How could anyone get up this high?'

'I saw someone, I know I did. Brian knows where I live, you could be right after all.'

Luc stroked my hair. 'It's the fever, no one could have got up here or disappear so quickly.'

'I'm calling the police,' I whispered.

He didn't answer, we both knew I couldn't call the police. Our secret would be out, our families destroyed, my career over. Luc went downstairs to check for signs of a break-in. I sat very still, hands clenched, teeth chattering. I could hear him locking windows and checking doors. He returned, shaking his head.

'Nothing. It was your imagination, my love.'

'Don't go,' I whispered. 'Stay with me.'

I laced my fingers with his, trying to hold on though mine were trembling. He stroked my forehead and I slept though I hadn't thought I would. I dreamt of Carol frowning at me, she had a red pen in her hand and was making lines across a piece of paper, back and forth, deep lines that gouged bloody tracks. Her make-up was smudged; she had rings around her eyes. Dark shapes moved behind her and she began screaming loudly. I woke with a jolt that shook the bed frame, the sheets were wet. The window was locked now, the curtains drawn back, hanging limply by a few hooks. Luc was upstairs, I could hear him moving around.

I lay drenched in sweat with my face toward the door. I could just make out the outline of the satchel under my dressing gown; even the shape was comforting.

He lay down next to me sometime around midnight.

'I'm so glad you're here,' I whispered, but I don't think he heard me. He was muttering again, as if talking to someone, his hands deep in my hair. The next morning, he had gone.

Chapter 20

In custody
June 2017

The bad things about a police cell are not what you might think: it's not the bed, or the food or even the locked door; it's the thoughts in your head. People say they want to be alone for the peace, but they can't have thought that through. Ideas become noisier in the silence, imagination more toxic. When it was time to meet Detective Inspector Wainwright for the third time, it meant company, I was almost pleased. He didn't say anything though, a traditional ploy but still disconcerting. I think he meant to keep his face expressionless, but I noticed a new eagerness in the way he leant forwards and in the swift glance at my face as he removed a photograph from a plastic wallet in his hand.

The quality wasn't perfect; it was nothing like Victoria's. Her photos were deftly composed, they led your eyes to the central point, a narrative began; but all the same, as I looked at the image on the table in front of me, I could detect the start of a story. The photograph was of a crowded room lined by books. It took a few seconds to recognize the library in the North Canonry. Luc was at the centre of the frame and my profile was visible to the left; he wasn't gazing at the camera, though those around him were. He was staring at me and I was looking back. It was like a dance or the beginning of one and I remembered that's how it had felt. I knew now that at that moment I was falling in love.

It was very simple, the truth often is, though it can take a while to reach it. I hoped Inspector Wainwright wouldn't understand what seemed so obvious to me, that the photographer had unwittingly captured the beginning of a love story though no one was aware of what was happening at the time, least of all the protagonists in the story.

Chapter 21

June 2017

Tuesday morning announced itself on the radio to a silent room. I called Luc's name but I knew he had gone, the house felt so empty. Betty answered the phone when I called the surgery, they had cancelled my morning antenatal clinic already. Roger had left strict instructions that I wasn't to return until I was well.

The doors and windows were locked, the house was airless but I felt safe though exhausted, depleted, too tired to think of anything. I slept all that day. Nathan left a text message, he was busy with visits to nursing homes. On Wednesday morning I pushed myself out of bed and into the bathroom. My face looked thinner in the mirror, my hair in greasy tangles. I turned on the taps and sat on the edge of the bath, gripping the enamel curve. The cold travelled up through my palms into my wrists and higher. I sat very still as the bath ran while the minutes ticked by. I imagined Carol telling me to pull myself together, she would remind me Roger needed help, there were queues of patients waiting. You'll manage, she'd say, continuing to run her pen through the list without looking up; you always manage, Rachel.

I had my bath, washed my hair, put on a dark blue linen dress and make-up, applied scent as if following Carol's orders to carry on. My face was pale with mauve lines under my eyes, but I could still be, or pretend to be, a doctor in control of her life. I stripped the bed of the sweat-soaked sheets and replaced them with fresh ones, smoothing the surface with my hand until they lay perfectly flat. Nathan must never know. I would hold Luc's visit close to my heart, a secret to comfort me; he couldn't come back. We had taken a risk but nothing had changed, we belonged to the lives we had chosen before we met, our obligations were still the same. We had got away with it all by some lucky chance but we couldn't expect to be together again, ever.

The kitchen was as immaculate as it had been when I'd cleaned it four days ago. A couple of glasses stood in the sink but nothing more, either Luc had cleared it all away or he'd eaten nothing. There was two days' worth of post on the floor, bills, a white envelope bearing the Cathedral School logo addressed to Nathan, a sheet of service times for the cathedral and an A4 brown envelope for me bearing the faint print of a man's shoe. Luc must have stepped on it when he left yesterday, unseeing, preoccupied, exhausted. I laid the bills to one side and slipped the envelope into my bag to open at work; my appraisal documents probably, it was that time of year.

It was a hot day, groundsmen were cutting the grass as I drove through the Close, the mowers travelling back and forth, leaving stripes of light and darker emerald, the scent got into the car, the raw essence of English summer. The North Canonry looked quiet as I passed. I searched the top windows, finding one which was open. It might be Luc's, he'd been ill with exhaustion, almost out of control.

I imagined him asleep up there, stretched out on the bed, still unconscious to the world. His face would be turned sideways, one arm tucked under his head, birdsong coming through the windows, a glass of water on the bedside table. He would wake restored. He'd remember the days we'd just spent together as one does a dream, intense but irretrievable. He'd know we couldn't go back. We must never see each other again, it was too dangerous, for us, for everyone.

Betty was in reception, sorting post into piles. Her grey hair had been cut close to her head in a neat cap; in her beige jersey and tweed skirt, she radiated motherly calm. Her daughter was on the phone, Rose, a sweet-faced medical student, a younger edition of her mother. They looked up as I passed and Betty came out to give me a hug. I asked her to phone Brian and invite him in for an appointment. I had decided to question him privately about the break-in, then tell him I was removing him from the practice. The atmosphere was surprisingly normal as though it was simply another day and Carol just out of sight, filing a stack of notes behind the shelves.

My room was tidy, tidier than usual. Someone, Betty probably, had stacked the pads of paper and messages neatly and put the scripts ready for printing. The post had been sorted. I remembered the envelope and slid it from my bag, slitting it open with the paperknife I kept on the desk in a pot along with paper clips and rubber bands. The phone rang at that exact moment so the envelope went back in my bag, saved for later when I had more time.

The list was long, some patients came to offer condolences, but Brian wasn't among them. He'd be skulking at home, ashamed. He'd know he had gone too far. Nathan had been right, and I'd been wrong, even Luc had warned me. Betty messaged that she hadn't been able to reach him; I tried the number myself several times with no success. In the end I left a message informing him I was removing him from the practice and that, unless he got in touch soon, I'd be obliged to tell the police he'd been following me and that it was likely he'd gained access to my house.

'How are you coping?' Betty touched my shoulder when she brought in a cup of coffee. 'Don't work too hard, you've been so poorly.'

I had an overwhelming desire to confess everything. I could ask her to sit down and she would comply, a little puzzled, but smiling, wanting to be helpful, her plump hands folded in her lap. The flesh of her fourth finger was swollen around her wedding ring so the band of gold was sunk into her skin, she would be unable to remove it even if she wanted to. If I leant forward and blurted out that I'd slept with a patient, a younger man, married like me and who'd come for help, her face would change. I might try to explain that I'd been swept away by a wave of feeling unlike any I'd ever known, but she wouldn't understand. Her smile would fade, she'd walk out. Later, discreetly, I'd be asked to leave the practice. Later still, there'd be a letter from the General Medical Council. My career would be over.

When I sought him later, Roger was in his room, the space was in greater disarray than usual. He was trying to tidy his desk and stood up when I came in, one arm accidentally dislodging a pile of papers which slid to the floor. I bent to help him but, straightening, the room swam. I groped for a chair. He ran me a glass of water and put it in my hand.

'You came back to work too soon.' He looked older close up, his face more deeply lined. His eyes behind the glasses were full of tears.

'It's okay, Roger, I'm fine.'

'I can't get Carol out of my mind.' He took off his glasses and wiped his eyes with his wrists. 'She didn't deserve to die like that, no one does of course, but somehow Carol . . .'

He fumbled for the crumpled hanky he kept in his jacket pocket and blew his nose loudly. 'The police think her death was a mistake.'

'That's what Nathan said but she was stabbed, her lungs were probably punctured.'

'He left her alive; if he'd meant to kill her immediately, they say he would have done.'

'Do they have any ideas who it might have been?'

'Only that he was off his head.' He straightened his shoulders and put his glasses back on. 'I've cancelled the Wednesday lunch meeting. I'm going back to see Keith.'

There were no visits. I made an appointment with the optician then walked to the library through the streets in humid sunshine, the pavements gritty underfoot. I was desperate to see Lizzie and breathe her in. I'd try not to nag and I wouldn't stay long. I glanced behind constantly, the low buzz of fear in my head blocking the noise of traffic. I was fearful of the murderer and fearful of Brian. I searched the faces I passed for a dark fringe and pebble glasses. He'd know from my calls that I suspected him of breaking in, he would be scared of the consequences. Who knew what terror might make him do? Each twisting alleyway seemed dark with menace.

My back was wet with sweat by the time I arrived at the library. I walked slowly up the stairs, the remnants of my illness dragging at my legs. Lizzie was at her desk on the first floor. She was talking to the man I'd seen before, the tall dark-haired guy I'd taken for a young teacher, who had lingered to chat to her the last time I was here, the one who'd made her smile. They were bending over the desk together; she was leafing rapidly through a book searching for something. A swathe of hair fell across her cheek. He seemed a little younger than her and was gazing at her in awe as if hanging on her every word. She looked glorious, a little fatter maybe but it suited her, she'd always been too thin. Everything she was wearing was new, at least to me, a loose checked dress, cowboy boots, new hoop earrings. She swung her hair back and smiled at him, a wide, unfamiliar smile. She put her hand on his arm and began to talk, he bent to listen. Their absorption was complete. It had been a long time since I'd seen her like this, so full of happiness.

I turned to go. I mustn't interrupt, they were in their own world. I retraced my steps to the surgery, looking around as I went, watching the men in the street, those behind me and across the road, but I felt happier. My daughter was in love and, despite my fear and sorrow, things felt different, more hopeful. A text came through from Nathan as I arrived back, he was returning this evening but unsure of the time.

Several patients were waiting already. Betty handed me the notes for the afternoon but, turning round, I almost dropped them. Ophelia was sitting in one of the chairs with her son. She wore a light blue shirt dress, a thick rope of silver around her neck. She was smiling faintly as she leafed through a magazine, her fair hair gathered back in a smooth ponytail, one tanned leg crossed over the other. I tried to imagine how her face would change if I told her that her husband had made love to me in their house in France, that we had spent five days entwined and shared every secret we knew. That he'd been to see me since and had left just yesterday. I doubted she'd believe me; if anything her smile might deepen, she would consider it a joke, albeit a tasteless one.

Oscar was wearing red shorts and a navy jersey. He leant into her shoulder as he played on his phone, his curly hair seemed full of light. He whispered something to his mother, she nodded calmly. Guilt rose; they were members of a family unit they believed to be intact. I wanted to retreat but there was nowhere to go and my surgery began in a few minutes. I walked over instead, my heart beating fast.

168

'Hello there.' My voice sounded higher than usual. 'Are you coming to see me?'

Ophelia looked up, her amused expression didn't alter as she shook her head, releasing a faint scent of freesias. She and Oscar were both smoothly tanned as if coated in honey. Compared to the white-faced woman slumped in the next row of seats whose eyes were closed and whose kids were arguing over an iPad, Ophelia and Oscar looked in radiant health; privilege like an invisible wall, separating them from everyone else in the room.

Oscar slid off his seat and stood as if to attention. 'We're going to see Dr Morris, for my headaches. I may need glasses.' His eyes sparkled like his uncle's, even their smiles were the same.

'Sit down, Oscar.' Ophelia put her hand on her son's back, her long fingers were scarlet-tipped and ringed with diamonds and I wondered if she bought them for herself or if Luc had given them to her in the past. 'Dr Goodchild is busy.' Ophelia smiled down at Oscar, ignoring me.

'You'll like Dr Morris, he's very nice.' I told Oscar, 'I'm sure he won't be long.'

He nodded vigorously and sat down with his mother, leaning into her again, absorbed by his phone.

'Good luck with the glasses. I hope they sort the headaches.'

Oscar grinned at me, revealing braces. Ophelia didn't look up.

I walked to my room and sat at my desk while my heart slowed. She couldn't know, we had been so careful to leave no trace. That stylish scented woman would have no idea her husband had been my lover. Luc and I were the only ones who had suffered, I needn't feel so guilty. After a few minutes I rang Brian's phone number again, but he didn't answer. My first patient came in, the woman I'd seen with her quarrelling children. She started crying and the afternoon began.

The waiting room was empty by the time I emerged after surgery. Roger was with Betty in reception. He looked tired and was frowning at a bundle of notes in his hand, his wife bustling quietly around him. They would go home to a meal that she had cooked earlier, their daughter might be there. Roger would sit down, a drink would be produced, he'd be left in peace to listen to blues music, his favourite. He would close his eyes and the day might begin to fade.

My home was the opposite of Roger's. Without Luc it felt deserted, dark and silent, far lonelier than before. I felt the ghost of his presence in the empty house; if I were to turn round, I might even see him, leaning against the kitchen wall, his dark eyes on mine. I snapped the kettle on and let my bag fall to my feet. I was very tired. A faint smell of paint lingered in the hall. I poured a glass of wine and walked slowly upstairs and opened the door into Lizzie's old room.

Chapter 22

June 2017

I thought at first the sun was shining; there was yellow everywhere. Yellow on the cut-up newspapers that were stuck to the floor, yellow on the torn paper that half obscured the windows. A book lay open on a chair, a history textbook, one of Nathan's. The pages had been thickly painted with yellow. Torn-out pages of text had been blackened, cut into jagged shapes and threaded with cotton suspended from the light shade in the middle of the room. Tins of paint stood about the floor. Luc must have found the paint in the understairs cupboard where we stored old pots, brushes balanced on the lids. I'd chosen yellow for Lizzie's room when she was a baby, but Nathan hadn't liked it and we didn't use it in the end.

The colour, the whole crazy installation, spoke of frenzy and freedom, although when I turned, the wall behind me was covered with black sheets cut into triangles. I was somewhere different in this room, a beach in the sun with black rocks at the edge, Van Gogh's cornfield with crows, a desert landscape sharp with jagged shadows. Had this been Luc's

171

intention? Colour and shapes to take me somewhere else completely? Or had sleeplessness tipped him over the edge?

My head fizzed with anxiety. This had the hallmarks of madness but perhaps that was the point. Van Gogh, his ancestor's idol, had often been psychotic when he painted. Luc might think he had to step out of reason as well, to create his best work. I didn't have time to think it through. I had to remove it all, scrape the yellow paper off the walls and the paint from the windows, scrub the floor.

Why hadn't he told me what he'd done? It had almost destroyed Lizzie's room, it could destroy my marriage and his. My anger grew as I hurried up and down with buckets of water, growing breathless. I scraped and scrubbed, it took two hours to remove every trace. My hands were raw. I stuffed the torn, damp paper into black plastic bags, snapped the cotton threads from the lights and wiped the chair. By the time I finished, the windows were smeared but washed clear of paint, the floorboards wet but clean. The walls looked patchy but they would dry.

It was dark outside, I had to hurry. The house phone rang but I didn't answer, there wasn't time. Nathan could be back any moment. I hauled the bags downstairs and into the bins in the courtyard. I was in the bathroom scouring my nails when I heard the outer door of the courtyard open and footsteps cross to the front door. My heart began to thud, my skin to creep with dread. I crept downstairs, picked up the poker from the sitting room and tiptoed to the front door, feeling sick.

A second later the door was unlocked and Nathan walked in.

We stared at each other in surprise, as you might if you bumped into a stranger, then I dropped the poker and stepped forward to hug him. He felt different, slimmer, he even smelt different.

'It must have been awful for you.' He drew back and inspected my face. 'Are you all right?'

I've never been quite sure why the unharmed are asked if they are all right after someone else's calamity. I hadn't been dragged into the undergrowth, stabbed and mutilated then left to die. Without waiting for an answer, Nathan took my hand and led me into the kitchen.

'I've been so worried about you.' He let go of me and opened the fridge, withdrawing a half-finished bottle of white wine. He poured us each a glass and sat down. 'I phoned several times, but you didn't pick up.'

'I've been unwell.'

'Have you told the police you were followed in the same place that Carol was murdered? It's obviously crucial now.'

I sat opposite him and the wine slid down my gullet, cold, a little sour. I hadn't yet phoned the police but, all the same, I nodded. I was too weary to be nagged and it wasn't really a lie, or at least it wouldn't be tomorrow once I had contacted the police station.

'Did you choose a nursing home?'

He drained his glass and set it down with care. 'Ada isn't going to a nursing home.'

'But I thought that was why you stayed on.' I stared at him, surprised.

'It turns out she doesn't want to leave the house she's lived in all her life. That's understandable, isn't it?'

'Her dementia is advancing, Nathan. She didn't even know you were there when I phoned.'

'I'm organizing help, leave it to me.' It was his turn to stare at me, a narrow-eyed assessment. 'You look different somehow, thinner.'

'I've been unwell,' I told him again. 'I'm much better now.'

'If I'd known, I would have come back.'

'I didn't want you to come back, Ada needed you more than me.'

He poured out a second glass of wine, finishing the bottle, and got up to fetch another from the fridge. His movements were elastic; he looked different too. If I hadn't known he'd spent several days with his dementing mother, I'd have said he looked healthier somehow. He seemed younger. For a second, less than that, I wondered if Sarah had been with him. He glanced at me again, sensing my scrutiny.

'What?'

'You look so much better than you did.'

'It must have been the break.'

'Looking after Ada was a break?'

'From work – which reminds me, I have to call into school.' He shrugged on his jacket. 'Matron's sick and Sarah's been covering since I left. I promised I'd take over as soon as I got back. Don't wait supper.'

Sarah hadn't accompanied him, of course she hadn't. I'd deceived Nathan, it didn't mean he was capable of deceiving me. I stood up, touched his arm.

'Be careful, there's a killer about.'

'Are you worried about me?' He smiled, and for a second it was the old Nathan, Nathan from a long time ago. I hadn't realized how little he smiled these days. He turned to wave through the window as he crossed the courtyard. The family photo on the windowsill in the kitchen had been there so long I'd ceased to look at it. After I'd rinsed the wine glasses, I held the photo in its frame to the light. Lizzie was between us, she had her arms around Pepper who'd been a puppy then, about ten years ago. She was laughing. Nathan was grinning at the camera; I was smiling at Lizzie. We looked unassailable. I sat down with the photo in my hands, trying to recall what had been in my mind at the time, but it had vanished completely.

Luc had come too late. My life was here with my family, my past and future lives. Nathan might be flirting with Sarah and Lizzie absorbed with her boyfriend, but the framework held, just. If the affair continued, it would disintegrate, our family life would be destroyed. Lizzie would lose faith in me, in marriage itself. Ophelia would suffer and so would Oscar. Two families wrecked. I put the photo down. The life I had triumphed over the life I wanted. I stood up and felt giddy, put my hand to the wall. I should take care not to get up too quickly, take care not to walk in the dark on my own, take care not to follow my heart. Lizzie and Nathan's happiness were more important than my own. Lizzie had a lifetime ahead of her, marriage and children. What example would I be setting if the affair continued? I sat in the chair in the sitting room by the window until the shadows gathered. When Nathan came back, he switched on the lights and I flinched.

'Sorry it took so long.' He must have run home; he was out of breath. 'The boys were a handful.'

'It's okay, I've been busy, the time went quickly.'

It's strange to think now that we were both lying.

Chapter 23

June 2017

Nathan came to bed later than me. I could hear him in the kitchen opening and shutting cupboards as if putting things away or searching for something he'd lost. Eventually he came upstairs, smelling strongly of wine. His presence in bed didn't bother me at first. I was so used to him, his accustomed shape and the sounds of his breathing were as familiar as the furniture in the room.

I turned away but for once he turned after me and, curling into me from behind, pulled me to him. I was surprised, did he need comfort, or had he sensed a difference, a latent heat, my woken-up body? He slid his hand under my pyjama top and squeezed my breast hard. I murmured a protest and began to struggle but he took no notice, perhaps he thought I was joining in, playing a game. He rolled me over and roughly pulling down my pyjamas parted my legs with his knee, kissing my neck. I turned my head away, but he didn't notice, his head moving from one breast to another, his spit was wet, cold. I tried to push him away, but he held me tighter. It was happening so quickly. I was more astounded

177

than outraged. Was he drunk? He pushed himself deep into me, his pelvis grinding into mine; rougher than he used to be, groaning. I clenched my jaw. This wasn't an assault, I told myself, this was what some women put up with in marriage, hundreds of women endured this after they'd cooked supper and washed it up, sorted the laundry and locked the doors. Unwanted sex with their husband, the last in a list of tasks for the day, there are even jokes about it, though it didn't feel remotely funny. Nathan didn't seem like my husband, more like a stranger who had broken into the house. I wanted to push him off me but that would prolong what was happening. When it was over, he rolled off me.

'Okay?' He sounded sleepy now, lazily satisfied.

I turned away without answering. Was it possible he thought this had been pleasurable? Or had I forgotten what sex with Nathan was like? Compared with making love with Luc, sex with my husband had felt like rape. He was snoring in five minutes; it was all I could do not to get up and leave him, leave the house.

He went to work early the next morning, he took the school assembly on Thursdays and he always departed in good time. He placed a cup of tea by the bedside before he left. He looked content as though nothing out of the ordinary had happened. I didn't speak to him but he didn't seem to notice. I got out of bed once he'd gone, stumbling a little; it hurt to walk. I spent a long time in the shower, there were bruises on my arm, one on my left breast. Blood was trickling down my leg. As the warm water thundered down on my head, it occurred to me that I could take photos of the bruises and the blood, go to the police and file a complaint of sexual assault against my husband. I could say it was rape, it had felt like that. He would deny it of course. He might employ lawyers who could turn up evidence of my affair with Luc; even without that, the newspapers would have a field day. I imagined the tabloid headlines – 'Middle-aged family doctor accuses teacher husband of rape' – and the effect it would have on Lizzie. The cost would be very high.

A good divorce lawyer might suggest we talk instead. We would be advised to discuss it dispassionately, perhaps with a therapist. I'd point out that Nathan had been different recently, distant, irritable. He might say I had been as well, and that this was my fault; I'd put off sex for so long it had become an act of desperation, a way of shocking me back to him. I might not immediately counter with the truth, though to me it was obvious, that what happened last night had wrenched us apart. That hairline fracture had become a break, the plate was in separate pieces now – even if glued back together, it could never be the same.

I found a pad in a drawer in Lizzie's room and put on a cotton dress the colour of sand with a slim leather belt. A summer cardigan to hide the bruises on my arm.

We'd put this behind us or pretend to. I applied make-up with unsteady hands: eyeliner, mascara, lipstick. A spray of scent. Because of our daughter, I would continue to be Nathan's wife, at least in name. I would sleep in the spare room but we would be civil. I brushed my hair with fierce strokes. Focus on the day ahead, think of Carol and what she suffered. I would manage. *You always manage, Rachel.*

I took a cup of coffee into the garden. It was hot already but the sky wasn't blue like yesterday; clouds had appeared overnight, split into thin crimson streaks on a grey background. It might rain at last. I went back inside, locked the garden door and rinsed my cup. Nathan had left the kitchen tidy as usual though there was a chair out of place, up against the tall cupboard, as if he'd wanted to reach to the very top. I pushed it back under the table and took my bag to the car. As I unlocked the car door, I felt a tap on my shoulder. Victoria.

'Hello you.' She kissed my cheek. 'You're looking peaky, sweetheart. Lovely of course, but a bit washed out somehow.' She put a bunch of orange roses in my arms.

I bent my head to the flowers, still dew-studded. I felt tears rise, it took all my restraint not to blurt out what had happened during the night.

'I've been ill but I'm better now. These are gorgeous.'

'I have to tell you something, unless you've heard?'

My heart leapt painfully. 'Lizzie?'

'Not Lizzie,' she said quickly. 'She's fine. I invited her to supper this evening, and both of you of course. The Denshams are coming too.'

She led me inside her courtyard. There were two blue chairs set on the cobbles, put there for people who needed to catch their breath when they arrived, a very Victoria thing to do. I put my hand on the back of one as I waited.

'Just tell me, Vee.'

'Abby phoned; it was on the news.' She put a hand on my arm. 'A patient at your surgery has been killed; they think

it happened a couple of days ago but his body was only discovered late last night. Dr Morris had to attend.'

'Which patient?'

'A Brian Alder.'

'That's not possible,' I said stupidly. 'I phoned him several times yesterday.' He hadn't answered but I'd taken that to mean he was avoiding the phone. It couldn't be Brian, he wasn't the sort who got murdered, no one would wish him dead. It would be someone else with a similar name, we had hundreds of patients, thousands.

'I'm sorry, darling. It's been confirmed.'

The geraniums in her courtyard blurred, becoming a pool of crimson. I was conscious of Victoria's hand on my shoulder, pushing me down to sit in the chair.

'. . . found at his home. I tried to phone you. Actually I've been trying to phone you for a few days. I was worried, are you okay?'

'I heard it ring yesterday but I didn't get to the phone. Before that, I was ill but Luc was with me, Nathan only got back last night.' I looked up at her. 'What happened?'

Victoria sat in the accompanying chair. 'There were no signs of forced entry, they think he must have recognized his attacker.'

He would have opened the door wide, glad to have a caller for once; he might have offered him a cup of tea. I prayed it had been quick, a gun or a knife.

'How did he die?'

'The police say it was the work of someone who wasn't sane.'

'Why?'

'His face was unrecognizable.' She paused. 'A hand was missing.'

Her voice continued but it seemed to be coming from a long way away. 'The police think it was late on Tuesday. When he failed to turn up with the paper yesterday morning, the neighbour's daughter looked through a gap in the curtains. There was blood on the walls. The poor girl was scared she'd be blamed, she only told her mother late last night.'

While I was ringing his phone yesterday, waiting in vain for him to pick up, Brian's body had been lying on the floor since the evening before, ripped tendons glistening at the severed wrist.

The blood would have pooled around his body. He hated having his blood taken by the nurse, he said it made him feel faint.

'The police have no leads but they're linking his death with Carol's, a trophy was taken each time.' Victoria's voice deepened with concern. 'You look awful, darling, I'm sorry. I wanted to let you know before you heard it on the radio, but it was too sudden.'

'I must tell Lizzie.' I fumbled for my phone. 'She has to stay home.'

'I told her, when I rang about supper. She said she could look after herself, though I had the feeling she was a bit distracted. She promised to come tonight.'

I stood up and the courtyard seemed to tip. I grasped the back of the chair.

'You look as if you might faint any moment, do you have to go to work?'

'Of course. I'll be fine.' The courtyard settled gradually.

She walked out to the car with me. 'Go carefully. Don't forget, supper here. We all need each other now.'

I drove very slowly through the Close, I couldn't see or think clearly. I almost missed the ambulance and the three police cars lined up outside the North Canonry, I almost drove straight by.

Chapter 24

June 2017

I stopped the car and got out, the police cars and the ambulance filling me with terror. What was I about to encounter? Luc lying on the floor with horrific injuries? A hand hacked off? Both hands? The trophies had got larger each time. It was hard to walk forward, hard to breathe.

It would be something else, it had to be. Blake had crashed the car, maybe injured someone – that wasn't far-fetched, he drank like a fish. It could be Oscar having had a tumble from his bike and Ophelia overreacting. I'd offer help which would be politely refused, and then retreat. I pushed the gates wider and walked through to the drive.

The shock was immediate, a punch to the guts.

Three policemen were trying to contain a man struggling in their grasp. The sounds he was making were low, animal. It took a beat of time to recognize Luc, unshaven and dirty with bare feet, trousers stained at the crotch and a snarl on his face. There was a bruise on his forehead and blood on his cheek. He had changed beyond all telling in just two days. As I watched, one of his arms came free; he punched the taller policeman with force, the man lurched backwards, a hand to his nose, blood spurting through his fingers. The other put his arm around Luc's neck, while the third pinned his hands behind him and snapped on handcuffs, pushing Luc to his knees. I don't remember moving but I must have, because a second later I was next to the largest policeman, a thickset man whose shirt was dark with sweat.

'This man is my patient. He's ill. Let him go.'

He wasn't my patient any more, but how could that matter?

'Step out the way please, madam.'

'He's clearly psychotic. You're making him worse.'

How had I failed to see this coming? Looking back, it was blindingly obvious: the lack of sleep, the desperate restlessness, the sweating, the tachycardia. That mad room of yellow paper. Any doctor would have seen his patient was becoming manic, any doctor who wasn't in love with him.

'You can't do this, you need a Section 135.'

'Sorted.'

The policeman was pressing hard down on Luc's shoulders.

'And two health professionals, you'll have to wait for them.'

It was all I could do not to wrench the man's hands from Luc and push him out of the way.

'We did.' The man's voice was curt, he didn't look up.

I glanced at the porch where Ophelia was standing with Blake by her side, both looking grim. Whoever had allowed this to happen must have already left or be inside somewhere.

I knelt beside Luc, his wild glance pierced like a sword.

'I'll find you,' I whispered, I had only seconds before the police would push me aside. 'I'll find you wherever you are.'

'Move away.' The policeman spoke to me as he might to a criminal. Luc was pulled to his feet and led stumbling into the police car, his head pushed down as he was manhandled into the back seat. Two policemen got in, one each side, and the car drew away, followed by the second police car and then the ambulance.

Ophelia hadn't moved. Her face was expressionless as if deeply shocked or not shocked at all. Her hair was pulled back into a ponytail, she was wearing a dressing gown, silky and patterned with embossed peacocks. Her face, devoid of make-up, was still perfect. Blake stood beside her, his arm closely around her, holding her so firmly she was tipping into him, her feet raised almost off the ground. It occurred to me this was the first time I'd seen him without a smile.

'Are you all right?' I walked towards them.

'I'm just happy Oscar's not here to see this.' Ophelia's voice was emotionless.

'The GP's gone,' Blake told me. 'It was Ophelia's physician, a great guy. Henry's inside though, come and meet him.'

Henry? I followed Blake who led the way into the house, still holding Ophelia. I hoped my face showed concern rather than dismay, though when I saw Abby in the hall in tears, my resolve weakened. I went towards her but she glanced at Ophelia and began to pick up upended chairs, flung shoes and torn paper scattered like confetti all over the floor.

Blake turned to me. 'Luc returned from France some time before us, he said he had things to do. We came back yesterday morning but he was nowhere in sight. Oscar had a doctor's appointment. Luc must have showed up in the early hours of this morning while we were still asleep. We woke to this mess.'

Ophelia walked ahead of us into the sitting room where a figure rose out of a deep leather chair to greet us, a tall red-headed man in his sixties, crinkly hair flattened, he was kitted out in a waistcoat and bow tie, clothes that could have come from a dressing-up box for a nineteenth-century physician. I recognized him. He'd arrived after us on the night of Ophelia's party, the second time I'd met Luc.

'Henry.' Ophelia went close to him and nodded towards me 'This Dr Rachel Goodchild, she saw Luc in her surgery some months ago.'

He shook my hand firmly. His palm was dry and cool, mine was damp.

'I'm Luc's psychiatrist,' he said pleasantly, eyeing me through his bifocals. 'I've looked after him for a number of years now.'

Luc's psychiatrist?

'Henry arrived an hour ago.' Ophelia chose a high-backed chair and sat upright, a queen among her courtiers. 'We suspected Luc must be ill again when we saw the state of the house; as soon as we noticed there was blood on his shirt, we knew for sure. We rang Henry and he set off as soon as he could.'

'Blood on his shirt?' What had I missed? I sat down on the edge of the sofa, hoping the trembling in my voice wasn't obvious.

'Blake helped him change, that wasn't easy.'

Had he injured himself then? No one had attended to his wounds, instead he'd been bundled into the car like a criminal.

Blake poured whisky, the dark gold reaching high in cut-glass tumblers. Henry accepted with a smile but when Blake offered me one, Ophelia frowned.

'Don't be ridiculous, Blake,' she said evenly. 'Rachel must be on her way to work.'

'He didn't tell me he had a psychiatrist when I saw him in my surgery.' I was bewildered, heartbroken, guilty, trying not to let it show. He had mentioned past breakdowns at Ophelia's party but lightly, in passing, as though they had been trivial. Nothing like this.

'Luc's not in the habit of revealing his entire story to strangers,' Blake said. 'Even charming medically qualified ones.' He raised his glass to me, though he didn't smile.

186

Henry leant forwards, directing his gaze towards me. 'Luc's been bipolar for years but he's reticent about the diagnosis.' He was very calm, as if discussing the weather. 'He's ashamed, like many manic depressives he tends to keep his condition secret.'

A secret from me?

'His last episode was at the time of his grandfather's death, about three years ago.' Ophelia spoke coolly, her eyes on my face. 'He's been high recently, but I had no idea this meltdown was brewing. He's been hiding out in the cathedral since he returned from France five days ago, doing God knows what.'

She was wrong. If he'd been in hiding, it was for two days at most, he had been with me for the three days before that, albeit restless, erratic, possessed. Mania in evolution, I saw that now. My illness had clouded my judgement, that and love. I hadn't questioned or analysed, I'd failed to apply everything I knew.

Ophelia looked at Henry. 'The police found his sleeping bag behind a stack of planks in a corner of the Cloisters. He'd been camping out while we were away, though how he escaped notice for so long is beyond me.'

'He was clearly terrified.' I stared round at the little group, they seemed so composed: Henry sipping his whisky, Blake leaning over the back of Ophelia's chair gazing down at her as if her welfare was his responsibility. She was studying me calmly. No one seemed to be upset that Luc had just been dragged from his house like a dog. 'We have to help him.'

'We?' Ophelia's voice was very cool. 'It's thoughtful of you to include yourself, Rachel, but this isn't your concern.'

I stood up too quickly and the room spun. 'As a doctor—'

'You're not his doctor though, are you?'

I didn't really know her at all. I just thought I did, because

187

she was married to the man I loved and her face had haunted my dreams. To her, I was a neighbour who happened to be a doctor, someone who had seen her husband in the surgery once, months ago. She was under no obligation to consider my feelings.

'Please let me know if there is anything I can do.'

'You've done enough,' Ophelia replied. 'More than could be expected.'

I glanced at her but she was looking at Henry again.

Blake took me to the front door then left me as he ran down the steps to talk to a policeman who was waiting by the gates with a bag in his hands; there was a quiet exchange of words before he hurried back.

'What was that about?' I asked.

Blake's gaze followed the man as he put the bag in the boot of the police car.

'Abby showed the police to Luc's room. They wanted to pick up a change of clothes for him but they're concerned because they found his bloodstained shirt on the floor. The crime squad will come back to pick it up and do a search with their forensic kit. They'll want to know what he's been doing.' Blake looked sombre.

'Their forensic kit? What do you mean?' Blood was a medical concern surely, not a police matter. 'Aren't you worried about him, Blake?'

He smiled and put his arm round me. 'Are you like this about all your ex-patients?'

'No, but—'

'Don't you worry. He's strong, he'll recover, he has before.'

If I'd known about his illness, I would have calmed him down and helped him sleep. I could have asked him to make an appointment with Roger for medication and a psychiatric referral. But I hadn't known, I hadn't even guessed. I could share none of these thoughts with Blake but his grip was comforting, I didn't want to move.

'I'll let you know what happens.' He tightened his hug. 'He's been doing too much; we need to find him a simpler life.' He let me go and turned to go to the house then turned back again. 'Forgive my sister, she can seem a little chilly when she's worried.'

At the practice I parked the car but I didn't move. Victoria's roses on the seat next to me were wilting already, losing their bloom. My breath was coming fast in ragged bursts of panting. My fingertips began to tingle. A panic attack, I knew the signs, I've treated plenty. Just a few months ago I was hurrying into the practice, nodding to Carol, steeling myself for her sarcasms, inwardly groaning when I saw Brian's name on my list. A few months ago, I hadn't even heard of Luc.

Chapter 25

In custody
June 2017

DI Wainwright settled in his chair. I was aware, as one is with a lover, of every little gesture: the way he sat with his legs wide apart, and the squaring movements of his shoulders once he'd settled into his chair. Nathan always folded himself tightly inside a chair whereas Luc was relaxed, or had been, arms hooked over the back, his hands open, as if he trusted the space around him. Wainwright was upright, elbows on the table, hands clenched. He didn't trust the space at all, he wanted to dominate it.

'What relationship did you have with Brian Alder?'

'A professional one, he was my patient.'

'He followed you on a couple of occasions at least.'

Who told him that? Nathan? Blake? Luc? No one else knew. When I'd told the police I'd been followed along the shrubbery, I'd had no idea it was Brian.

'Don't answer that,' Judy said.

'You didn't tell the police that Brian had been

following you, even after Carol White's body was discovered in the same place. Why not?'

'Don't answer that either.' Judy leant close, so close I could smell the chemical scent of her lipstick. 'You have no need to answer any questions that you don't want to.'

She was right and, for a few minutes, I felt safe. I even felt safe when Inspector Wainwright leant down to the bag at his feet and took out a brown envelope. He drew out a pack of photographs then spread them over the table in the shape of a fan, as if revealing a winning hand of cards.

They were all of Luc and me, naked, together. My head swam as I looked at them. I wanted to put my hands over them, hide them, they surely belonged only to us.

'You've seen these before, of course.' He was watching me closely.

I shook my head.

'They were in an envelope that was found in a doctor's bag at your home, addressed to you and postmarked last Monday. It had been opened, you must have seen them.'

I looked at the envelope again and this time I saw the faded print of a shoe, fainter than before but unmistakable.

'You are right,' I spoke slowly, it felt dangerous to agree with the inspector, as though I was admitting guilt by mistake. 'That envelope was delivered to my home, I'm not sure when. I didn't see it until Wednesday when I picked it up and took it to work. I even opened it when I got there but I didn't look inside, I ran out of time so I put it in my bag and then forgot all about it.'

It had been a long Wednesday. After the clinic I'd arrived home to a room full of yellow paint to clear up, and later my husband had sex with me that had felt like rape. The envelope had slipped my mind, but those weren't the kind of excuses that would count in my defence.

'Please examine the photographs now.' The inspector sounded contemptuous, it was clear he didn't believe me. 'Can you confirm it is you and the accused engaged in sexual intercourse?'

The focus was perfect. Luc and I were lying on the sofa in the sitting room in the act of love, but it wasn't wicked as my mother might have said, or obscene as the detective might have thought. My body was half hidden by Luc's, my neck arched back, his bent down. Circles within circles: the curve of his back and the circle of my legs around him, my arms around his neck. Even now, even here, I felt that deep sexual punch. There were other pictures, Luc stroking my hair, his lips close to my ear. If the photographer had wanted sensationalism, he hadn't got it; this was tenderness. My eyes filled with tears.

'Yes, it's me and Luc.'

Inspector Wainwright shuffled the pictures together and replaced them in the envelope. He had tucked his chin down, but he couldn't hide the glimmer of satisfaction; now he could call his wife and children from the back of the boat where they'd been cowering all this time. He'd want them to admire the catch he'd finally reeled in, as it lay on the deck before him, helpless and gasping for breath.

Chapter 26

June 2017

The double doors to Victoria's garden were wide open, the honey scent of roses coming into the sitting room along with the fluting song of a blackbird. The evening was hot and thundery. Heat had been building all day. Victoria was clashing pots in the kitchen. It had been twelve hours since I'd sat on the blue chair in her courtyard trying to absorb the news about Brian, and slightly less since Luc had been bundled into the police car. Victoria's bag was repacked and back in the hall, topped with the sponge bag. She was off to Stonetown in Zanzibar in the morning, to photograph Arabic doors for the *Sunday Times*, but determined all the same to gather us together.

The burn of the whisky helped the ache in my throat. I'd held back tears all day; it had been possible to listen and examine patients, possible to answer phone calls and make house visits, but now the events of the last twenty-four hours came towards me like a wave: Nathan's assault, Brian's murder, Luc's section.

At coffee Roger had told me a patient said that Brian was

rich, he hid all his money in his house. Roger didn't believe that but most people were hiding something, he murmured as he stirred his coffee, it usually came out in the end. Betty put her hand on his shoulder as she collected the cups. He didn't mention Luc; the news of his section hadn't filtered through yet. When I looked at his details on the screen, I saw he'd transferred to Roger's list in early May although he hadn't been back to the surgery since that very first time.

The news of Brian's death spread like wildfire. People were scared, there'd been two killings now and the murderer was still at large. Brian's brutal death now twinned with Carol's was on the radio in the car and the television screens of the patients I visited. The streets were quiet as I drove home, but shock seemed to ripple in the air. The police were everywhere, going from house to house, their cars lined the streets. A helicopter hovered. Brian's house had been on the evening news, blue and white tape stretched across the door, police keeping guard.

Victoria put a fresh drink in front of me, the ice clinking in the glass among sprigs of mint. She sat on the arm of the sofa opposite in her spotty apron and pushed a strand of pink hair behind her ear.

'Abby phoned. It always amazes me how Ophelia and Blake discuss everything with her in the same room, no one in that house seems to see her at all. The police were talking to Ophelia after Luc had been taken away.' She stopped and looked at me.

'It's okay.' I sipped the drink. The alcohol seemed to seep into my bones, restoring me. 'You can tell me.'

'They're going to investigate links between Luc and the murders.'

It was very quiet apart from the blackbird. I replaced my glass on the table. It hadn't occurred to me they would think Luc could be involved, the idea was untenable.

196

'He was out of his mind with fear,' I told her. 'He didn't know what he was doing. How could anyone think that he had anything to do with the murders?'

But of course, that would be their very reason – I could see that, even as I was protesting. Psychotic terror, the police would note, they would be familiar with the things it could make you do. They'd see his illness, not the man behind it. They wouldn't know, as I did, that Luc was incapable of that kind of harm; that when he was becoming ill, he was more tender than ever.

'Abby says he was violent; I suppose they must have thought—' Victoria began slowly.

'Only because he was being restrained,' I said quickly. 'That's the very worst thing you can do in psychosis. They had him surrounded, he retaliated because he was terrified. It doesn't make him a murderer.'

'She told me they took a bloodstained shirt from his room.' She glanced at me. 'Don't worry, in a way that's good. When they analyse the blood they'll realize they have the wrong man.'

She was right: if there was blood on his shirt, it would have been his own. Their suspicions made no sense; Luc had never met Brian or Carol.

'. . . thought you told me this morning he'd been staying with you?' Victoria was continuing. 'Doesn't that rule it out?'

I got to my feet immediately. Luc wouldn't be able to give an account of his days, but I could. 'I'll go and tell them right now, they'll have to drop investigations immediately.'

This was more important than keeping our affair secret. I pulled my car keys from my bag and was at the door before I realized I wouldn't be able to help after all.

'It won't work. He left me late on Monday night or in the early hours of Tuesday morning. They think Brian was

197

killed on Wednesday.' I glanced around wildly as if the medicine mask or the little Buddha on the corner table could help me. 'I can't even lie and say he left later because Nathan came home on Wednesday, he'd know it wasn't true.' Tears stung; it must have been the strain of the day, the helplessness I felt. I wiped my eyes fiercely. 'It's easy for them to pin it onto Luc. He can't defend himself and there's nothing I can do for him.'

'There is, you must stay strong. You can do it, you're the strongest person I know.' She hugged me, her clasp was fierce. 'Now go and wash your face, it will make you feel better. The others will be here soon. I'll put some music on, take your time. We'll work something out. It will be okay, the truth will emerge, it always does.'

Her bathroom was painted a soft sage green and scented by bunches of lavender that hung from the ceiling by hooks. I washed my face as the cello chords of Saint-Saens' *Swan* drifted into the bathroom. My face looked deathly tired in the mirror. I had to hold my nerve somehow, Lizzie was coming, Nathan too. This nightmare would pass and justice would prevail. The killer would be found, it would turn out to be some cruel stranger that none of us knew about yet, one of those loners with a grudge against life who strike at random. I dried my face, brushed my hair and smeared dusty blue eyeshadow on my eyelids from a little pot by the basin. As I walked downstairs the warm scent of spiced meat and wine came towards me. In the kitchen, Victoria was slicing tomatoes for a salad. There was a new postcard on the mantelpiece, an aerial view of Central Park with blossom on the trees.

'How is she?'

'Holding her own. I'll be in Zanzibar for a week, then back here, on stand-by.'

'What can I do?'

'Nothing at all.' She shook her head smiling, most people would be fooled by that smile. 'That blue is perfect for you, it matches your eyes.' Then, as I picked up a tea towel, 'Don't you dare do a thing, I'm all organized.'

I leant against the door frame, watching her peel an avocado with expert hands. She couldn't talk about her mother yet, feeding others was her recourse, the way she dealt with sorrow. I wished, helplessly, for Luc, Luc at his best; he would take her hand and kiss her cheek, his warmth would be healing, it had healed me. But Luc was in a locked room, he would be cowed and confused, hungry though he wouldn't know it. Food might have been offered, but he would have thrown it at the walls, psychosis makes you do things like that. The staff could become impatient; he might be restrained. I shuddered although the air in the little kitchen was baking hot.

'Do you love him very much, darling?' Victoria was watching me as she scattered pine nuts over the salad.

When I was with him, he was everything in the way the sun is everything; if you put your face to the sun it heats your skin. The light is so bright you have to close your eyes and then it beats against your eyelids. You can't think about anything else, the warmth infiltrates your body and your mind like a drug. Was that love or madness? An illness like the one that had Luc in its grip? I nodded, it was easier than trying to explain.

'I'm pretty sure our Lizzie's in love,' Victoria whispered as Lizzie walked in. She smiled at us and leant her face sideways for a kiss, and, despite the terror and heartbreak of the day, the evening seemed to lift and brighten. Her cheek was as smooth and warm as a peach. Her hair was shining and swept into a little knot, her dark red dress flared loose from the low-cut bodice, she wore lipstick to match. Her eyes were made up with deep colours of brown and green.

My Lizzie, who never bothered about scent, now smelt deliciously of roses and cinnamon.

'You look beautiful,' I told her.

She gazed out at the garden and smiled, a small, secret smile.

'Sit next to me.'

'I need to walk,' she replied. 'My back aches, too much sitting.'

I walked around the room with her, looping her arm through mine. We hadn't walked like this for years and I wanted the moment to last forever.

'All well, my darling?'

She was still looking at the garden and didn't answer.

'Are you keeping safe? They haven't caught anyone yet, so—'

'I'm a big girl now, Mum.' She didn't want to talk about the killings, not this evening. I shouldn't have brought it up.

'So, how's the job?'

'Does it always have to be about work?' Her voice turned snappy, the mood had changed. She withdrew her arm and looked around the room, an exasperated glance that took in the table laid with Victoria's pretty coloured glasses and silver, the furniture, the garden through the windows. She shook her head and walked swiftly into the kitchen.

I could have bitten out my tongue. It was so obvious now, she was tired of my questions; she'd had enough of me, of these familiar rooms and doubtless of Salisbury. She wanted something different. Nathan had seen it before I had, he'd known months ago. I'd just made it worse. I always brought up her job, it was my way in, working from the outside towards the centre. The truth was I wanted to know about the man I'd seen in the library. There were so many questions in my mind that I couldn't easily ask: how long had she known him, what was he like? Was he kind? Did she love him? I couldn't hear what was being said in the kitchen, just laughter and the clash of plates. Thank God for Victoria.

I stood by the window looking at the rose petals that had been blown onto the grass, splashes of deep crimson, and the images arrived again: Brian's mutilated body in a gory puddle, a red stain seeping to the row of lambs that danced around the neck of Carol's jersey, the blood on Luc's terrified face.

I flinched at the touch on my elbow. Nathan had come in quietly and was staring down at me. It was as though I was encountering a stranger, a distant, watchful one. He stepped into the garden; Lizzie was glancing at us from the kitchen, I had no option but to follow. The mellow call of the blackbird had ended and swifts were swooping against the clouded sky with high, wild screams.

'I'm sorry about that patient of yours, what a terrible way to die.' He leant to give me a kiss. I turned my face away and the kiss landed in my hair, but he didn't seem to notice, he was looking at my face. 'How's Lizzie taking it?'

He was pretending nothing had happened between us. I had to swallow my outrage for now; I couldn't confront him about last night's assault, not while we were standing in Victoria's garden and she and Lizzie were near. It would have to wait until after the party, when we were back in our kitchen and facing each other across the table.

'We didn't talk about it,' I said. 'I'm not sure she's absorbed it yet.'

'Lizzie's good at putting on a front.' His eyes followed her as she moved about the room lighting candles for Victoria and a smile crept into his voice. 'Clever at hiding things, my daughter.'

I stared at him, surprised. 'What things?'

He looked up at the sky without answering, his eyes

tracking the swifts. I watched them as I waited and a few drops of warm rain fell on my face.

'I heard you went into the North Canonry earlier and saw Luc Lefevre was in trouble, were you able to help?' he asked, leaving my question floating between us, unanswered.

'How did you know?'

'Sarah told me. I think Oscar told her, I expect he was upset.' He continued to examine the birds, twisting and turning above us.

That was odd. Oscar was at school this morning when it happened, Ophelia had been glad that he'd missed it all. I'd always thought the Close was a good place for keeping secrets, the houses spaced apart, little worlds on their own. Luc's breakdown should have been a private family matter, but secrets have a way of leaking out.

Victoria called us in, the Denshams had arrived and it was suppertime. We stepped back into the room. I hadn't seen our other neighbours properly for weeks. I delivered Colin's medication from the surgery and sometimes left a shepherd's pie in their courtyard when I made one for us, it was Colin's favourite. Helen sat next to me with a sigh of relief and immediately began to talk about her grand-children in a continuous murmur that required no answer. The rain was clattering against the windows now, thunder rumbled. The storm was breaking at last and I remember being glad, we needed rain. The room felt safe, we were all together, secure against the outside world, although my heart was with Luc.

The tagine worked its way down the table, tender lamb scented with harissa and scattered with almonds. I stood to receive the pot, catching sight of our reflections in the large mirror that hung on the wall: Victoria leaning forward to explain tulip-planting to Colin, her hands shaping the size of the pit that had to be dug for each bulb. Helen was talking quietly next to me. If the scene in the mirror could be captured, anyone looking at it would see an image of friends coming together, talking and listening. They'd imagine content. The tension wouldn't be obvious unless they saw the tightness in my jaw. They might wonder as I did at Lizzie's furtive expression as she whispered to Nathan, they might notice the way he glanced at me, then away as if he had something to hide. Steam was condensing on the surface of the mirror, the scene with its secrets was becoming obscure. I served Helen and myself and sat down again.

I could get through this, it wasn't too difficult. I could get through this evening and tomorrow as well, and the day after that. The murderer would be caught and Luc would be freed. I wouldn't see him again but I mustn't think like that or I'd go mad. I would concentrate on being everything I was at the beginning of the year, a mother, a doctor, a wife at least in name. I would stay within the boundaries. I wouldn't look back.

I was still making those promises to myself when the doorbell rang. Helen dropped her fork on her plate, the little crash sounded loud in the silence. A ring on the bell in the evenings usually meant a late delivery or a wrong one, a pizza intended for someone in the Close before the gates were locked for the night. I'm not sure why we all stopped talking.

Victoria disappeared to open the door. It was difficult to hear what she was saying, she was talking very quietly, which should have alerted me. In a crisis Victoria always lowers her voice. When she returned, her eyes flashed a warning to me, a second before a bulky middle-aged policeman came into the room, followed by a younger policewoman, their navy uniform at odds with the room and its treasures. Their faces were wet with rain and strangely expressionless, their arms spread out a little as though to prevent an attempt at escape.

203

Several voices chimed at once: Nathan politely asking what they were doing while Helen's confused exclamations were drowned by Colin loudly demanding to know what the hell was going on, and, cutting across these, the calm voice of the policewoman as she stepped forward. Her smooth face was serious, the dark brows drawn.

'Dr Goodchild, I am arresting you on suspicion that you were an accessory in the murder of Brian Alder. You do not have to say anything but it may harm your defence if you do not mention when questioned something you may later rely on in court. Anything you do say may be given in evidence.'

I thought at first she was pretending, an actress employed to play an elaborate joke. The words were exactly like the ones they use in television dramas. I couldn't take it seriously even as she produced a pair of handcuffs, even as the cold steel enclosed my wrists. Lizzie must have thought it was unreal as well, she was looking at the policewoman then back at me, bewilderment on her face, as if she too believed this was a scene in a play but one she couldn't understand. I wanted to tell her not to worry. I stepped towards her but the policeman was in the way. He announced to the room that I was being taken into custody at Melksham police station, there being no facilities in Salisbury these days. No one answered. Nathan was silent, pale with shock, Colin began shouting. I tried to tell him to be quiet, that this wasn't worth a fuss, the police would realize their mistake as soon as I got to the station, but there wasn't time. I was being led or pushed towards the door. Victoria was the only one who was thinking clearly. She picked up her sponge bag and tucked it under my arm as I went out.

'Don't worry,' she whispered. 'A stupid mistake, bloody typical. It'll be okay.'

The last thing I remember, the image which has lasted the

longest, was Lizzie, not her face but her body. As I was hustled through the courtyard, I glanced back into the lit hallway. She was leaning against the wall as if to ease her aching back. Her loose dress outlined her abdomen revealing a small but definite bump; it wouldn't be obvious to anyone else but I was a doctor as well as her mother. My slim daughter was at the start of the second trimester of pregnancy.

Chapter 27

It was a new day, but Inspector Wainwright was tired, ninety hours is a long time. His shoulders were bent now, his eyes bloodshot; he might, like me, be finding it difficult to sleep. He would be aware, as I was, that in a few hours he had to charge me or let me go on bail. The tension in the room was sharper, I could smell it. He spoke more quietly and that made it worse, more menacing.

He took the photographs from the envelope again and set them out as he had done the day before; the images of Luc and me making love lay on the table between us, beautiful and incriminating.

'I told you yesterday I hadn't seen these before.' I stared at him, hoping he could tell that I was being truthful, though I knew how easy it was to be mistaken. I'd been wrong so many times. I'd doubted Brian and trusted my husband but Brian had been harmless whereas Nathan had assaulted me. I hadn't seen that Luc was ill. If I couldn't see into the minds of people I knew, how would the inspector see into mine?

'A set of these was found in Brian Alder's flat.' Inspector Wainwright continued as if I hadn't spoken. 'He took them, presumably on his phone though that is now missing. We believe he printed out two sets, one we found in his flat and the other he posted to you last Monday first class. It isn't hard to conjecture his motive – most blackmail is for financial gain, and Brian Alder had lost his job. He needed cash. The photos must have arrived on the Tuesday; you would have informed Luc immediately and he subsequently killed Brian within hours.'

'That isn't true.' Is this how people were trapped? By conjecture and supposition?

He continued as if I hadn't spoken. 'Let's look at the facts. Together.' His tone was gentler now as though talking to a child. 'We know you and Luc Lefevre were having an affair. You have now admitted as much, and of course, we have the photographic evidence in front of us. We also know that you were being threatened by Brian.'

'That's not true either. He didn't threaten me at any stage.'

'He confessed to following you.'

Who told him that? Nathan? Luc?

'That does not constitute a threat,' Judy snapped. She was tired too, growing impatient. Her face was paler today, her eyes ringed with shadow. She might have been up late preparing for today. The other concerns of her life might have crowded in, catching up with her; things she had put off until she couldn't put them off any more, like listening to her children or making time for her husband, enduring sex she didn't want.

'I put it to you,' Inspector Wainwright ignored Judy but maintained his friendly tone, 'that these photos were of great concern for you and the accused.'

'Don't answer that.' Judy glanced at me and shook her head.

'When you saw those photographs,' Wainwright nodded at the images in front of him, 'the matter would have become urgent, you would have wanted Brian silenced. Your reputations were at stake.'

'I didn't even look inside the envelope.' He can't have been listening to anything I'd said. 'I meant to, at work, but I ran out of time. I had no idea they existed until yesterday.'

I knew it sounded unlikely or, at the least, very careless. His glance was ironic, even amused. He didn't believe me, but he didn't understand how busy a doctor's day could be. He had no idea how tasks crowded into every minute competing for space: surgeries and scripts, emergencies, phone calls, letters of referral, meetings and visits. An average day passes in coping with crises; when it's finally over, the work bag is dropped in the kitchen, the bottle of wine opened and the contents of the bag left until the following morning.

Judy leant forward. 'The photos themselves do not provide evidence of motivation to murder, if that's what you are implying. There was no blackmail note.'

'There doesn't need to be; there was a printed slip with Brian Alder's name on it accompanying the photographs. It is obvious Dr Goodchild would have perceived him to be extremely dangerous, as would Luc Lefevre when she told him.'

'There is not one shred of evidence that either even saw the photos.'

'Brian Alder was obsessed with Dr Goodchild.' Inspector Wainwright changed tack as any sailor would, he was heading for port and the wind was behind him. 'It must have been disconcerting for her, even frightening. Members of her practice were certainly concerned.'

'They weren't.' I stared at him, surprised. 'He came to see me often, but no one ever speculated—'

'Carol White discussed Brian Alder's obsession for you with Dr Morris more than once; although, as he told us, the threat wasn't perceived by Dr Morris to be significant, which was a pity.'

Carol tried to take my part? The stab of regret was acute; another mind I'd misread, another mistake to add to my pile of mistakes.

He swept on. 'Mrs White herself had received a photograph from Mr Alder or purporting to be; it was identical to the one we found in Luc Lefevre's room and taken at an earlier date from those already in your possession; it showed you together with Luc in an outside place and was also somewhat incriminating.' He glanced at me impassively. 'She was heading towards your home, presumably to warn you of the existence of said photograph, when she was murdered. Whoever murdered her failed to remove all the evidence, leaving the envelope and one torn photograph behind.'

He pushed another photo towards me. The edge had been ripped, as if someone had attempted to pull it from the envelope but then ran out of time or been distracted. In the photo, Luc's face was against mine, my eyes were closed, there were tears on my cheeks. A different setting, the light was brighter, we were outside somewhere, but the background was a blur of different colours, it was impossible to see where we were.

The envelope it came from was on the table. Carol's name was on the front in blue font; it had been in her husband's hands as he waited for her in the surgery. When she saw what it contained, she must have come to warn me, meeting her killer on the way. I felt sick with guilt.

'Carol's husband Keith was holding that envelope,' I said slowly. 'That was the last time I saw her, he must know something.'

'We have spoken at length to Keith White. All he can tell

us is that the envelope had been delivered that afternoon. He has no idea who by, or where the photograph was taken. I was hoping you might be able to tell us that.' The inspector paused for my reply, but I had nothing to tell him. I had no idea.

Judy had had enough, she sat upright and lifted her chin, impatience sharpening her tone. 'You have shown us several photographs, hoping to extract a confession from my client, but photographs do not constitute proof of a crime. Your ploy hasn't worked because she isn't guilty.' She drew breath but she hadn't finished. 'There is probably no evidence even to tie the accused to the crime.'

'But there is.' Wainwright nodded calmly. 'When the forensic team attended the North Canonry, after Luc Lefevre was removed, they took a bloodstained shirt from his bedroom; it was found to have blood of the same group as that of Brian Alder. We await DNA studies. Other evidence has subsequently come to light, of a potentially incriminating nature which I am not at liberty to disclose.'

Other evidence? Was he implying it had something to do with me? With Luc?

Judy wasn't to be deflected. 'What you conjecture from a blood group is one thing, but you can't pin Carol's murder on my client or indeed Luc Lefevre. How on earth would Luc have known Carol had been sent any photographs?'

'I told you, he had been sent the same one. We found it in his room.' The inspector produced another envelope from his bag, a white one this time. He pulled out an identical photograph, our faces together in bright light, the same blur of colours in the background, and something else that he pushed towards me. A typewritten note encased in a clear cellophane folder. Two words:

'*Carol knows.*'

'The friction between Carol and Dr Goodchild was

common knowledge,' DI Wainwright continued. 'Something we were able to pick up when we talked to Dr Morris. Dr Goodchild would have shared the conflict with her lover. Brian Alder, a frequent visitor to the practice, would have picked up on it too. Brian must have thought Carol White would be an ally. He would have hoped that sharing the knowledge of the affair with Carol, and letting Luc know he had, would keep him safe from potential harm. He couldn't have known that meant she would be killed.'

The sequence of events he was proposing would be almost impossible; Luc would have got back from France at some point in the evening. He would have had to see the photo and read the note, find Carol, track her, stab her and leave her for dead where she would be discovered in the shrubbery in the early hours of the next day, the same day in which he would later come to see me. I closed my eyes. I couldn't hold this in my mind, even for a second. It made no sense, but that wouldn't matter to the inspector. When I opened my eyes, he was watching me closely. He put his hands on the table with the slapping noise of meat being laid on a butcher's counter.

'You are tired and clearly confused, although the case is very simple.' He looked at Judy. His voice became impersonal if weary, the voice of someone laying out the facts for the final time. 'Brian Alder was stalking Dr Goodchild, causing considerable distress. This would have been shared with her lover, whom we know without doubt to be Luc Lefevre, a vulnerable man with a history of mental illness. It is not hard to conjecture Luc would have been affected by this. When Luc subsequently looked at the photograph Brian had sent him, together with the information that Carol White knew about the affair, a response would have been triggered in his unstable mind. He knew how much Mrs White upset his lover, everyone did, and now he had evidence that she knew about the affair. Luc's worsening psychosis would have made him dangerously unpredictable and this would have been exploited by Dr Goodchild.' He glanced at me then back at Judy. 'The joint decision was taken that Luc should murder Carol. At some point during the five days that followed this, and probably on the Tuesday, Luc would have received the further information from Dr Goodchild of the existence of, ah . . . more intimate photos that Brian Alder had sent in the post; as a result, the latter was also brutally murdered.'

'Your whole bizarre accusation is based on speculation.' Judy's tone was contemptuous. 'There is no weapon.'

'The skin was damaged in exactly the same way in both victims.'

'Meaning?'

'It is clear the murderer used a serrated knife on both occasions, meaning the murderer was the same person; he also took a trophy each time. The police have been searching Luc Lefevre and Dr Goodchild's homes for the weapon. As I say, we have now uncovered more evidence.'

I found myself trying to remember the last time I'd seen our bread knife which was kept in the knife block at home. Luc had borrowed knives, but he had put them back – or had he?

I had to stop thinking like this, stop my thoughts sliding down the grooves the inspector had carved on purpose to lead me into his trap.

'My client played no part in either of these murders, neither deliberately nor accidentally.' Judy's voice was quiet, the kind of quiet that compels everyone to listen. 'Everything you mention concerning my client is anecdotal. You have no evidence of her participation in any of this. I apply for release with immediate effect.'

'She can leave in the morning,' DI Wainwright pronounced ponderously. He didn't seem to mind that he had failed to trap me after all, or failed so far. He'd been skilful, I recognized that, but if his intention had been to jerk a confession from me he should have chosen someone else; doctors are trained to keep secrets, it's one of the first things we learn.

Judy squeezed my shoulder, her eyes were lowered, hiding triumph. 'A short night that's all, you'll have bail by the morning.'

DI Wainwright left, his face calm. There was something he wasn't telling me which worried me, something that might be dangerous.

Sleep wasn't possible, the room was stuffy. I was sweating, the sheet was wet and wrinkled beneath my back. There was no window to open, no sky to look at. As the hours ticked by, I began to play the game of what if; what if I hadn't returned the notes to the practice that night in February and gone home instead. Luc would have been seen by Debbie, not me. I might still have gone to Ophelia's party; we could have chatted, Luc and I, but there would have been no reason to accompany him down the garden that night, he wouldn't have texted the invitation to his house in France. I would never have stayed with him. I might have come across him sometimes, walking in the Close, his wife by his side. We might have stopped to chat, Nathan and I, Luc and Ophelia. I might have been struck by his looks or unsettled by his warmth, but by the time I'd reached home and switched the kettle on, I'd have forgotten about him. He would be with his family now or maybe in France, not locked in a room, accused of the horrific murders of my supposed enemies. I'd have a job and a husband who trusted me. Undistracted, I might have been closer to my daughter; she would have told me about her love affair with the young man in the library, she would have shared the news of her pregnancy, the most basic exchange between a daughter and her mother. In the remaining hours that hurt swelled until it filled the room with beating wings.

Judy arrived the next day. Bail had been granted though it could be reversed at any time; it took a while to go through the conditions. I had to stay at home or very near it. I couldn't contact the practice or witnesses and I had to report to the police. I had to surrender my passport. I agreed to it all, I just wanted to go home. I was desperate to see Lizzie.

Chapter 28

Nathan was waiting outside in the car park at Melksham police station, leaning against the car. He walked swiftly towards me when I emerged, at the same time that a group of journalists hurried forwards, phones aloft.

The shouting began:

'Hi, doc, can you tell us when you first met Luc Lefevre?'

'Hey, Rachel, did you forget there are rules against seducing a patient?'

'So, did you ask your lover to commit murder?'

A phone was thrust into my face by a sweating man in a tight suit. A small woman with a ginger ponytail was taking photos with a grim look of determination on her face, others pushed behind them. I turned my head from the forest of phones and the shouted questions as Nathan bundled me into the car and then drove quickly out of the car park, the wheels screeching around the corner. His mouth was set in a tight line.

'Jesus, Nathan. How did they know I was getting out today?'

'They didn't, they've probably been lying in wait for days. They wait for me outside the house too. They've waylaid Lizzie. The newspapers are full of it. It's been on the national news. What the hell did you expect?'

I hadn't expected anything, not like this. I'd been focusing on Wainwright's questions, on Luc and on Lizzie. I'd forgotten about the outside world, the need for salacious detail.

'How's Lizzie?'

'Hiding.'

'Is she okay?'

'Yup.'

'Have you talked to her?'

He braked sharply, he had driven the car too close to the van in front. His hands tightened on the wheel. 'Can the questions wait until we are at least in Salisbury? I'm very tired, not sleeping that well.'

His thoughts must churn at night as they did for me, perhaps he stayed awake for hours like I did, and that was all my fault. I closed my eyes. At least our daughter was all right. The car was warm, Nathan began to drive more smoothly and, though I tried to resist, I felt myself sinking deeply into sleep.

I woke with a gasp as the car slowed at a light; we were already by the bridge on the Wilton road leading into Salisbury. The cathedral spire was visible beyond the playing fields and the roofs of the town. I must have slept for nearly an hour. I sat up in the seat, Nathan was glancing at me.

'I saw the photos of you and Luc.' He looked back at the road, his voice was very quiet.

I wished he hadn't been confronted by those images. Once seen there would be no unseeing, they could play in his mind for years. Nathan's face was calm; if it hadn't been for the way his hands gripped the wheel, we might have been on a normal shopping trip.

'Who showed them to you?'

'I found them. They were in your medical bag.'

'When was that?'

'The night of your arrest. Earlier that evening, the police found the same photos of you and Luc at Brian's place, they came round to confront you but we were having supper at Victoria's. They simply broke into ours and, after that, they came to arrest you. The house looked like a crime scene when I got back. Your medical bag was wide open, they left a couple of photos inside – probably by mistake, unless they meant me to find out.'

I imagined the moment; reeling from my arrest, Nathan would have said goodnight to Victoria and entered our home to find papers strewn, books pulled out of bookcases and, in the middle of it all, my open bag, the photos of Luc and I making love.

'I put the envelope in my bag but I had no idea the photos were inside. I'm sorry you had to see them.'

'Would you have told me about Luc if you hadn't been arrested?' He sounded curious and bitter at the same time.

'Luc and I are finished, Nathan. It's over, I promise.' I hadn't answered his question but he let that go.

'What conclusions did they come to back there?' His question was abrupt.

'The detective inspector thinks Luc killed Carol and then Brian to destroy evidence of our affair. They acknowledge he was ill but say I encouraged him because they were both, supposedly, my enemies.'

My words sounded unreal even as I said them. There were people everywhere, streaming in and out of Boots, WHSmiths and the pound shop. A woman bent to her crying child, a group of teenagers strolled across the road, each intent on a phone. Nathan slammed on the brakes as an old man strolled out in front of the car, oblivious to danger, pushing

219

his bike and smiling to himself. He wore bicycle clips around the ankles of his yellow trousers. None of these people would ever be accused of murder or of being an accessory to murder. I'd crossed a divide as transparent and impenetrable as the windscreen in front of me.

'They let you go, they can't really think that.' His voice was flat.

'I'm on bail, not free to go anywhere.'

'If they had hard evidence, they would have kept you in, accessory to murder is a serious charge.'

'They probably think it's a matter of time.'

'What do they have on Luc?'

'One of his shirts had blood on it, of the same group as Brian's. He was psychotic, which in their mind makes him guilty.'

I stopped talking, the words were taking me deeper into a place I wanted to step back from; a place that didn't exist. Psychotic people can do terrible things out of fear and desperation but real violence is very rare. Luc wouldn't have killed Carol or Brian, no matter how ill he was, no matter how scared. I knew it in my heart; I had to cling to that.

'Tell me more about Lizzie.' I turned to him, trying to escape my thoughts.

'What exactly do you want to know?'

'Something exciting has happened for her, well, exciting and worrying. I'm longing to talk to her. Has she told you?'

'She doesn't want you to contact her.'

I hadn't cried in my cell, I mustn't start now. There were too many losses to grieve; if I began to weep, I might never stop. Luc was seriously ill and falsely accused. Carol had died a brutal death and so had Brian. My husband had changed into a stranger and now my daughter had withdrawn from me completely.

We drove slowly through the Close. The cathedral looked

formidable, an impassive cliff of stone. I didn't glance at the North Canonry as we passed, conscious Nathan would notice the slightest turn of my head. As we drew up outside our house, I caught a flicker of curtains at the Denshams' upper window and a glimpse of Colin's face disappearing from view. I understood. People would look at me differently now, friends would thin out and disappear. There were a couple of cars outside the house and two men got out, their phones pointing at us; voices shouted my name and Luc's. Nathan ushered me in quickly and locked the door. The house smelt different – a flowery scent that took me back to Ophelia's party all those months ago – and in the kitchen I saw why. There were freesias on the kitchen table in an unfamiliar tube of glass.

I gestured at the flowers, trying to smile. 'They remind me of Ophelia.'

'Why would you say that?' Nathan glanced at them then back at me, his mouth tightening. I had stupidly reminded him of Ophelia's housewarming party, the first time he'd met Luc, a memory he didn't need.

'Oh, I don't know.' I mustn't mention the white flowers banked behind her that night, the scent we'd inhaled or the mass of people in the hall. Luc had emerged from the crowd during the evening and had borne me away. I cast about for something else, something pleasant without a dangerous trail of memory. 'Ophelia came to the surgery with Oscar the other day. She smelt of freesias.' I watched his mouth relax. 'She even looks like them, tall, pale, very beautiful.'

'I hadn't thought of that.' He smiled and a memory slanted across the kitchen of the way he'd stared at her at the party, the way she'd charmed him. The freesias could be homage, however unconscious. He turned away to make cups of tea. We sat opposite each other across the table and I wondered if he was thinking of the last time we had been together in the house and how he'd assaulted me in our bed.

'Nathan—'

'What happens now?' He put a cup of tea in front of me, but his tone was impatient.

I was the guilty one today, not him; the conversation I'd planned would have to wait a while.

'I wasn't told. I expect they will gather all the evidence they can, then I'll be recalled.'

'They've already got your laptop and stacks of papers from your desk.'

'They'll find nothing, there's nothing to find.'

'They found the photos.'

'That doesn't incriminate me in murder.'

A small spasm crossed his face and was gone, it was as though he was controlling pain or anger. He got up and began to put things away from the dishwasher. The phone started to ring but we both ignored it.

'You believe me, don't you, Nathan?'

'Do you need to ask?' He replaced the mugs onto their hooks on the dresser, put the plates into the cupboard and wiped the draining board before turning to face me. 'For what it's worth, I can't think you had anything to do with the murders, but I believe Luc is guilty, though it's obvious he was ill at the time. It's your misfortune you were ever caught up in his life.'

It was the other way around; it was Luc's misfortune he met me. He'd lost his health and his freedom. Love and guilt had caused the stress that had precipitated his illness; he would always be safer without me.

'This arrived yesterday.' Nathan fetched a slim white envelope from the dresser, put it in front of me and sat down again. I tore it open.

The medical practitioners' tribunal had suspended my licence to practise with immediate effect. I had known this would come, but as I looked at the words, they sank through my mind like stones through water without leaving a trace. I couldn't grasp them at all.

'I've been suspended,' I said, folding the paper into smaller and smaller squares. 'Though it's not clear to me why they've done that.'

Nathan stared at me. 'Not clear?'

'They don't say if I've been suspended because I had a relationship with a patient or because I encouraged him to murder the receptionist and another patient.' It sounded like a joke; I began to laugh.

'Lizzie's pregnant.' His voice sliced across the laughter.

I stopped laughing. 'I know.'

'How do you feel about that?'

'Happy.' It was true, I felt the seeds of happiness arrive as I spoke. A child would change her life, and mine. I hadn't allowed myself to feel joy in that featureless cell, but back home it was different. I could imagine a baby in a high chair in the kitchen or in a pram in the garden. I would hold Lizzie's child in my arms. I smiled properly for the first time in days. 'I wish she'd told us, though. I'd have thought she'd have shared something like this as soon as she knew.'

'She told me.' The complacency was barely detectable.

'When?'

'Weeks ago.'

I looked down at the tea, there was a milky ring on the surface, it was cold now. I'd have to throw it away and start afresh. It was stupid to mind, I should be pleased she talked to Nathan, that she was still in touch, if not with me.

'As regards the father . . .' He shrugged.

'Oh, I think I might have seen him.'

223

He looked up sharply, his whole face a question.

'At least, I presume it's him. I think he's a teacher, maybe a bit younger than her, it's hard to say. She doesn't know that I know, but I've seen them together in the library. He looks kind, she seemed happy and he was clearly besotted.'

Nathan shook his head. I wanted to tell him that an age gap was unimportant, but if I mentioned anything else about age it would take his mind back to Luc. He would become angry or withdrawn and I wanted to know more about Lizzie.

'I'll ring her.' I glanced across the kitchen to her photo on the windowsill.

'I doubt she'll pick up. She doesn't trust you, you've kept so many secrets from us.'

'I've no secrets left.' I mustn't take anything Nathan said to heart. He was hurt that's all, out to wound. 'What do you want to know?'

'Everything.' His voice was cool.

I told him the relationship had been circumstantial. I called it an affair and said it was time-of-life thing, a dip in hormones. I'd been lacking in confidence, that's all, a little lonely. It was a final throw of the dice. I was careful not to mention attraction, desire and sex. I didn't breathe a word about love. He bowed his head but his face had the same calm expression as it did when he listened to directions from the satnav in the car, as if he was absorbing information and making a plan.

Afterwards he got up and looked out through the kitchen window at the little courtyard. The magnolia blossom was over now, the flowers dead, the dried scraps of browning petals lying where they had fallen on the cobbles.

'What now?' he asked again.

'I told you, it's over.'

'So you're not going to meet up again?'

'Luc was ill the last time I saw him, he was terrified. I

told him I'd find him. I should keep my promise if only to say goodbye.'

Nathan shrugged but didn't reply.

'Do you know where they took him?' I asked.

'I haven't the remotest idea.'

'Surely his family have visited?'

'I gather Ophelia has been but I suggest you leave him alone.'

That hurt but I could hardly blame him for cruelty, he'd say I'd been far crueller to him.

'What do you want to happen now, with us?' I asked him.

'I'd like to go back to how it was before.' He sat down opposite me again, a hand on my wrist.

'I'm not sure if we can, exactly.'

'I am.' His grip was firm, just short of painful.

This was to be my punishment then. A pretence, a papering over. I was to act as if nothing had happened when we both knew everything had. I wasn't sure why this sounded so terrible; I'd been acting for months.

He went to bed. It took me a while to find my pyjamas, they weren't where I always left them in the airing cupboard but stuffed instead into the bottom of my chest of drawers where I must have put them, in a hurry, by mistake. I walked out of our room and up the next flight to the spare room next to Lizzie's. We hadn't redecorated in here; the same brown and yellow paper hung on the walls that dated from my parents' time, the same bed with dark wood headboard, the same little wardrobe. An empty bookcase was in the corner. The room felt unwelcoming, a little forlorn but I could bring books up here and all my clothes. I'd gradually make it my own. I undressed, put on the pyjamas and slipped between chilly sheets. I wouldn't mention my search to Nathan, it would be foolish to admit that my memory was becoming so unreliable I had been unable to find my own nightclothes. I would have to take the stand in court sometime soon and swear what I was going to say was the truth. If my memory was known to be faulty, who on earth would trust my word?

Chapter 29

June 2017

'It's bad timing but it won't be for more than a few days,' Nathan told me as he made two cups of coffee, he'd already had breakfast and cleared it away.

Simon had asked Nathan to accompany him to the headmasters' conference in Prague.

I'd only been back a week. I'd heard nothing about Luc and nothing about the trial. Lizzie hadn't been in touch. Nathan held my chin and kissed me slowly; his grip hurt, even his kisses seemed painful. He hadn't mentioned our new sleeping arrangements. There had been no opportunity for the talk I'd planned either, he was preoccupied, his career taking centre stage.

'It's an honour to be chosen,' he said, sounding cheerful for the first time in days.

His mood had improved; he thought the trip was confirmation of promotion. He was travelling to London for pre-conference meetings later today and then catching an early plane tomorrow morning. He'd got up early, he'd even cleaned the kitchen, there were roses on the table now, not freesias. They'd vanished after my return, like a mistake in a child's homework that he'd had to rub out.

'Roger said the police are going into the practice today,' I told him as I sipped my coffee. 'They'll look at everything I've done, all my cases.'

'You said you have nothing to worry about, so don't worry.' The curt logic of a busy schoolteacher, he might not have realized how dismissive he sounded. 'Keep busy.'

'I can't go further than the immediate neighbourhood while I'm on bail.'

He looked around the kitchen. 'Clean the house then.'

'I've done that already.'

'Do it again.' As if telling a pupil to rewrite an essay because the last one had been full of errors.

I watched him put his bag into the car and settle himself in. He was looking forward to this, he was wearing the grey tie in honour of the occasion, his eyes bright with anticipation that seemed almost sexual. It was clear he could hardly wait to get away. I wondered if Sarah would be there and if he'd now allow himself to sleep with her. I doubted he would – ambition, if nothing else, would stop him in his tracks; besides, Simon would be there. Nathan drove off without a backward glance. I turned to go in, there was a volley of clicks: a middle-aged man with dark glasses was standing by a car, his phone angled towards my face. I shut the door, feeling sick.

I began in the bedroom we'd shared, picking up Nathan's socks, dusting, hoovering, polishing the old wood of the chest of drawers and wardrobe until they shone. The room looked immaculate when I finished. It was his room now, not mine. I planned to take my clothes upstairs later that day. I was straightening the curtains when I saw Victoria picking flowers in her garden next door. She'd returned. I flung the window open.

'You're back!'

'Not for long.' She smiled up. She was wearing her coat, her hands full of sweet peas. 'These are for you. I was about to come round.'

'Wait right there.' I clattered down the stairs, hurried through the sitting room, stubbing my toe painfully on the chair that had been pulled from its usual place tucked close to my desk. I unlocked the back door, wrenched it open and hurried into the garden. She handed me the bunch of flowers over the fence.

'My favourites, thank you, Vee.' My eyes filled with tears.

'I'm sorry I was away just when you needed me. Are you okay?'

'Fine.' The default response, the one even dying patients give. The truth was it was so long since I'd been fine that I had no idea what that felt like any more. 'You couldn't have visited me anyway and it wasn't that long.' That was true, although it had felt endless.

'Come over right now, coffee's up.'

I went back through the house, leaving the flowers in the sink and closing our front door just as she opened hers. The same reporter got out of his car again, his phone clicking. Victoria pulled me inside her courtyard and slammed the door behind us. Close up her hair was greyer than before, she'd lost weight and looked tired; a bright bird shedding its plumage.

'You're thinner!' I hugged her.

'That's exactly the kind of news I like.'

'And Gladys?'

'She's not great. I'm flying to New York this afternoon. Things have deteriorated in the last few days and I need to be with her.'

'Ah, I'm so sorry.'

'Don't be, we've known this was coming for a while.' Her

eyes glistened as she surveyed me. 'You look gorgeous as usual, God knows how. What was it like?'

'A blank little cell, they're probably all the same.'

We went into her house and through to her sitting room; the last time I'd been here there'd been a storm outside and the police had blundered in. Today, the garden doors were open and the room was full of sunshine.

'Sit.' She patted her sofa, strewn with velvet cushions in jewel-bright colours. 'I'll get the coffee. I've an update.' She walked to the kitchen.

'Who from?'

'Abby,' she called back. 'She fetched me from the station this morning.'

She reappeared and put a warm mug into my hands, the nutty scent of coffee filled the room.

'Okay.' She glanced at me warningly. 'This is tough.'

'Tell me.'

'First up. Luc has been transferred to Broadmoor.'

I put the coffee down on the table. 'That's prison.'

She shook her head. 'A high-security psychiatric hospital.'

'Same thing.'

'Look at this.' She picked up a sheet from her desk and passed it to me; an aerial photo of red-brick Victorian buildings surrounded by modern blocks. She had printed it out to reassure me and it looked peaceful, but only in the way a factory looks peaceful from the outside, the noisy machinery is invisible. You couldn't see the fences in this shot, whether there were dogs or barbed wire or policemen manning the perimeter. You couldn't see inside to the corridors either, where the crying would echo against the walls. You certainly couldn't see into the rooms, but each would have a plastic mattress in the corner, there'd be no windows, the smell of urine would seep from the floor.

'The top psychiatrists in the country will be looking after

him,' Victoria told me. 'He'll be safe and cared for until the trial.'

Would he? There were pressures on the staff, cuts undermined care; fear came winging into the room right then.

'Do you know what the charges will be?'

'Abby heard Ophelia and Blake discussing them at breakfast yesterday.' Victoria put a hand on mine. 'They think he'll be charged with both murders.'

'That's ridiculous.' I should have known this was coming, it was exactly what Wainwright had said. 'He's psychotic and was sent some photos but that doesn't make him a murderer. There's no evidence.'

'You won't like this—'

'I know they found a bloodstained shirt in Luc's room but, even if the DNA is positive, that isn't enough. It could have been planted somehow—'

'It's worse, sweetie'

'Tell me.'

'They found the missing body parts in his car.'

'Body parts?' I stared at her, confused. Wasn't that an expression mechanics use about cars? And then realization filtered through: Carol's fingers, Brian's hand. Parts of human bodies, parts of people I'd known. I began to feel very sick.

'They were in a box in the boot of Luc's sports car.' Victoria's voice had become quieter still. 'Wrapped in cling film and hidden beneath sheets of architectural plans.'

In the silence that followed these words, birdsong came into the room, a pure run of melodic notes. Through the garden door I saw a thrush on the lawn, a beautiful flecked bird in the sunshine, his head held sideways, listening for worms. Victoria was still talking.

'. . . most likely a reduced sentence because he was so ill. Abby heard Blake say it would be manslaughter, diminished responsibility.'

231

'Luc didn't do it, Vee. He shouldn't serve any sentence at all. It wasn't him, no matter what they found in his car.'

'I know.' She gripped my hand more tightly. 'Of course I know.'

'If he's found guilty, what could happen?' I was surprised the words came out one after another in an ordered sequence, my thoughts were spinning with fear.

'Ophelia asked Blake the same question, he said seven to twelve years.'

There were grating notes in the thrush's song now mixed with the melody, a little run of harsher sounds and then the tune again, on repeat.

'The trial's a way off, they have to wait until he's well,' she continued. 'There'll be other evidence that will save him, you'll see. It's all speculation till then.'

But speculation can become truth and the truth gets twisted, no matter how long you wait. The wrong people get incarcerated, you read about it all the time. I looked back into the garden but the song had stopped and the thrush had disappeared. Twelve years within four walls, without birds and trees or the warmth of the sun; he wouldn't survive.

'You shouldn't be alone.' Victoria was watching me carefully. 'Should we call Nathan?'

I shook my head. 'He's in London tonight, then travelling to Prague for a conference tomorrow.'

'Abby said they've been talking about schools for Oscar in the States. California, she thinks.'

Ophelia was not the kind of woman to relinquish what was hers, she'd find a way to keep Luc near her if they moved back to America. She would organize his transfer to a similar institution over there. There must be many, she would manage it somehow. My throat constricted. I'd thought he'd come back to Salisbury after his release. We wouldn't be together, I knew that, but we would have walked the same streets and breathed the same air. If he chose France, I'd be able to visualize him painting by the window, chopping wood in the garden or sitting by the fire. On the other side of the world, I would be unable to picture him, his life would be lost to me forever.

Victoria picked up a brochure from the table in front of us, I hadn't noticed it until now. 'Abby found several copies of this on a desk, she brought one back for you.' She paused then handed it over as if reluctantly fulfilling a duty.

It was thick and glossy, the writing was in English, French and German, produced by a prestigious estate agency with an international market. Blake had wasted no time. The house looked impossibly perfect. The pictures had been taken by a drone from angles that occluded the hole in the roof and the parts of the wall that were crumbling, you couldn't see the blistered paint on the shutters.

A highly desirable Provençal estate set in its own extensive grounds and coming to the market for the first time in two hundred and fifty years. Wide-ranging views to the Alpilles. Saint-Rémy-de-Provence nearby, rail links from Arles. Huge potential for modernization.

As I gazed at the images I could smell lavender, hear the doves calling and see the light playing on the olive trees.

'Luc's grandpa left him this house, it's been in his family for generations. It belongs to him.' My cheeks were hot. 'They can't do this.'

'They can if they have power of attorney, sweetheart. Money may be tight. Apparently Ophelia left for London this morning to see family lawyers.'

Perhaps no one would want it. Once buyers arrived, they would see that the images in the brochure weren't representative, they might think it needed too much work. People who wanted a house in the south of France were after a different kind of luxury, not a garden full of wildflowers or a tiny shower where a swallow nested. They'd want power showers, a hot tub and a swimming pool, all the things that Blake would have organized, but if money was needed now he would sell it as it was.

Victoria went to the kitchen, I followed her. She lifted the coffee pot off the stove and smiled, trying to cheer me up. 'You've heard Lizzie's news?'

I nodded. 'Nathan says she hasn't forgiven me yet.'

'She will.' Victoria poured a stream of coffee into a fresh mug and gave it to me. 'She might go to Nathan first, she was always Daddy's girl on the surface, but it's you she'll need.'

'Has she told you about the father?' I asked.

'Top secret apparently.'

'I glimpsed him by chance. Sweet-looking, a bit young.'

'Young is good.' Victoria nodded sagely, pouring herself a cup.

Luc's body came to mind then, the beauty and strength of it, the effortless stride, the confidence of his gaze. That would be different now, he would be constrained, his gaze would be inward, his mind in turmoil. My head began to throb. I took a mouthful of coffee but it burnt my tongue.

'Though personally speaking, old is better.' She smiled wryly. 'I wouldn't go back for anything.'

I knew exactly how she felt, I felt the same. All the uncertainties and doubts of youth, the questions you thought needed answering, the tidy choices you tried to make, long before you realised some questions don't have answers and nothing was ever tidy.

I clung to her when I left, she was going to nurse her mother through her final illness, it could be months before we met again. Once inside my house, I heard the back door banging in the wind. I'd forgotten to fasten it so I pulled it shut and bolted it. The rooms smelt different even after that

234

brief time away, scattered rose petals had blown in on the carpet. Nathan had usually deadheaded the roses by now, but he hadn't been in the garden once since my return.

My face looked older in the hall mirror, my hair lank, the skin more lined. I put the sweet peas in a vase and went upstairs to the bathroom. I let my clothes fall to the floor. I had lost weight; every spare inch of softness had gone. Once I would have been glad but now I didn't care. I stayed under the shower for a long time, massaging in shampoo then conditioner, the hot water pouring on my head mercifully driving out thought. I wanted to stay there for hours but a sudden crashing noise alerted me and I turned off the shower. I'd shut the back door so it had to be a window banging in the wind.

I stepped out of the shower, wrapped myself in a towel and walked into the bedroom then stopped dead.

The room had been overturned.

My heart began to pound as I took in the disorder. The carpet was hidden under a mass of clothes thrown about as if in anger. Tights tangled on the floor, bras tumbled among them, pants strewn. All the drawers had been yanked open. The wardrobe doors were gaping, my dresses and suits flung out, hangers broken. Fear rang in my head like an alarm. Someone must have come in while I'd been next door with Victoria, whoever it was must have escaped when I was in the shower.

Another crash came from downstairs, like a chair falling to the ground. I heard footsteps in the sitting room. The noise wasn't a window banging in the wind after all.

The intruder was still in the house.

Chapter 30

June 2017

I backed out of the room and ran into the bathroom, ramming the bolt across. It was a flimsy thing, a single metal bar that anyone strong could break in half. I fumbled for the phone in the pocket of the jeans I'd left on the floor when I showered. I jabbed the numbers in, asking for the police, hissing in a frantic whisper though I wanted to scream for help.

'There's an intruder in my house, he's downstairs. I can hear him.'

'Are you safe?'

'I'm in the bathroom, the door's locked but he could break in.' My mouth was dry, whispering was difficult.

'The address?'

The woman on the line repeated it back with unbearable slowness. She said something reassuring but I missed the words. All I could hear was the blood pulsing in my ears.

The images of Brian on the floor of his house seemed to splash themselves on the walls of the bathroom in vivid red. I looked at my hands, the wrists, the twisting veins, the bones beneath the flesh.

What would it feel like to have the skin cut into by a serrated knife? The muscles divided, tendons hacked through, the bones wrenched apart.

What noise would it make?

Vomit rose in my throat and I swallowed it down, retching would make too much noise. Sweat trickled down my back.

I phoned Nathan but he didn't pick up. My hands were shaking too much to text.

The intruder could be on the other side of the door. I strained to listen to his breathing, as he might be straining to listen to mine, but I heard nothing. He might be calculating whether he had time to break in and attack me before the police arrived.

Through the open window I heard a taxi chug to a halt, a door slam shut. Victoria was leaving for the station. I wanted to scream for help but she would come to my rescue without a second thought and straight into the path of danger. I stuffed my fingers in my mouth. The taxi drew away, the noise of its engine growing fainter.

Five minutes passed; ten.

I crouched, sweating, praying Lizzie wouldn't choose this moment to come round to share her news with me after all, throw open the door, call up the stairs, inadvertently bringing the intruder down to her. I began to text her with trembling fingers but at that moment I heard the outside door open with a crash, footsteps cross the courtyard, fists hammer at the door.

The police had arrived.

I opened the door of the bathroom inch by inch then, abandoning caution, ran down the stairs, stumbling at the bottom step, and unlocked the front door. A policewoman and policeman stood on the threshold, three others behind them. The woman was stocky with round cheeks and a wispy bun; she looked capable and kindly, like a farmer's wife in a children's storybook. I wanted to fling my arms around her. She stepped inside, her movements were slow, designed to calm. She made me a cup of tea while her colleagues checked the house. I was shaking, still wrapped in my towel; another female officer brought my dressing gown to me.

The questions came fast.

'Did you see him?'

I shook my head.

'Did he break any windows?'

'I left the back door open while I went next door to my neighbour's house. He must have walked straight in.'

'Anything missing?'

'I haven't had time to look. My underwear has been scattered all over the floor, there are clothes everywhere.'

'The panty drawer is always the first place thieves look.' The male policeman, young, smooth-faced, had just come back into the kitchen; there was a trace of amusement in his voice.

An officer walked around the house with me. The drawers of my desk were slightly open but I couldn't remember if they had been closed before. The papers on my desk might have been moved but nothing was missing. The hall cupboard was open, the boots tangled together on their side. Had they been like that before? In the kitchen the pantry door was ajar, I couldn't remember if I'd closed it or not. The officer was staring at me. I probably sounded crazy, I must look crazy too, with my tangled hair and pale face, a dressing gown, mid-morning. He must think me unusually forgetful, but terror can scramble your thoughts. I turned away from him, tightening the sash of my dressing gown. He was in his early twenties; he might not yet have experienced those icy moments of mind-altering fear as Carol and Brian must have done; terror would have driven them insane even as they died.

I told the policewoman about the man I'd seen in the garden, and the shape behind the curtain. The policewoman nodded, she asked if anyone else had seen him and I shook my head. I didn't mention that Luc had been there at that time, though she'd know about the affair. The whole of Salisbury must know and further afield than that. On Judy's advice, I'd avoided the news, the papers and social media. I'd slammed the door on every reporter.

The break-in was a significant development, the police-woman said, but she didn't elaborate. Hope jostled with fear; did that mean they thought, as I did, that the intruder could be the murderer? That Luc might be released? She didn't answer my questions but they took away the pants and a bra to check for the intruder's DNA.

I was advised to bolt the doors, not to leave the house and not to answer the door. A helicopter would be sent to search the area and they'd place a car at the end of the street. Their manner was courteous, a little wary, unlike the police who had arrested me. I went back to the bedroom and dressed quickly. Before I replaced the dressing gown on the hook I lifted down the leather satchel still in Nathan's bedroom; it felt soft, familiar, warm as if from the sun. I sat on the bed, opened the satchel and took the pictures out.

I needed the memories that seeped from the paper. With his paintings spread out in front of me, I could hear Luc, his deep voice, the way he said my name. After a while I slipped the papers back into the bag and took out the case, unwrap-ping the painting and laying it on the bed. This time the trees looked tortured, twisting as though in pain. The grass seemed flattened, as if a great wind was blowing, the red streaks on the ground were the crimson hue of blood. The mountains were split into cliffs. The landscape resonated with violence and drama.

I carefully folded the papers back around the painting,

wondering what kind of man the artist had been, what thoughts had possessed him. The fears that he'd painted were palpable. Perhaps he suffered from manic depression as well, the illness passing to Luc down the generations. I would never know. For now, all these pictures were mine, my secret comfort, a way of touching Luc. I replaced them in the case and then the satchel under the dressing gown where it disappeared from view as completely as the dressing gown itself had vanished for Nathan; after twenty-five years he had simply ceased to see it.

Nathan must have seen my missed call, his message pinged through on my phone as I rearranged the folds of the dressing gown.

Can't talk now, phone later.

I knew he was in meetings, what had I expected? He had no idea about the break-in, he would have phoned if he had, he would have been kinder. He would have offered to return though I wouldn't have agreed; his flight was in the morning and now there was nothing to be done. The police were at the end of the street but, all the same, I was alone. I wanted to speak to someone, a friend who would cheer me up. Victoria would be mid-flight by now. Blake would have been my second choice, he'd come to my rescue before. He would hug me and grin, sit on the kitchen table, pour me a glass of wine and make a joke, something ridiculous and irreverent, and I'd feel better. I might even persuade him to halt the sale of Luc's house, at least until Luc was better. Blake might be greedy, but he wasn't immoral. He'd listen, he'd wait. If Ophelia was with him, she wouldn't make any jokes, nor would she listen, her cool glance might linger over my face then move away.

But I couldn't talk to Blake and certainly not to Ophelia. I would never be able to talk to either of them again. In her eyes, and now doubtless his, I was evil, the bitch who had taken Luc from his family, upset him and caused the breakdown. If they thought him guilty of murder, that would be my fault too, my influence. Whatever the outcome, Blake and Ophelia would never forgive me.

I tidied the bedroom and then walked around the house, closing cupboard doors, picking up the chair that had fallen by my desk. After that, I sat at the sitting room window staring into the garden. The fence seemed impassable but it had been breached three times now. We needed security lights and an alarm, I should organize that immediately but, as the day wore away, I didn't move. I was terrified that if I stopped watching, I might miss the moment the intruder climbed back over the wall, perhaps bringing weapons this time.

I must have fallen asleep in the end because it was quite dark when I was woken by the phone ringing. We'd kept the one my parents used, the old-fashioned kind made of Bakelite – you couldn't see the caller's number but tonight it didn't matter. It had to be Nathan, returning my calls. I snatched up the receiver.

'At last. Can you talk?'

No response.

'Nathan?'

The voice that answered me was very cool. 'Ophelia here.'

Chapter 31

June 2017

'Oscar's sick.' There was a tremor in her voice, a slight one but I'm trained to pick up tiny indicators of stress. Ophelia was terrified.

'I'm sorry to hear that.' Keep calm, stay professional. Don't ask about Luc, don't even think about him. 'What kind of illness?'

'A cracking headache. He hurts all over. I thought it was flu but it's worse than that.'

He had announced his headaches in the waiting room with glowing pride, that beautiful, healthy boy; it might be something he was prone to, a childhood migraine, painful but not dangerous.

'The headaches are unlike anything he's had before.' It was as if she could read my mind.

'Has he a rash?'

'No.'

But people miss rashes all the time.

'Any vomiting?'

'Once.'

243

'Can he bend his neck?'

'He won't do anything I ask.'

'Have you called a doctor?'

'She refused to come. Blake got him drunk on vodka last night; when the doctor heard that, she put it down to a hangover. Now Blake's fucking disappeared.'

I hadn't heard her speaking like this before. 'Have you called an ambulance?'

'I phoned an hour ago but they haven't arrived. We'll be at the back of the line but they'd listen to you. You're a doctor, if you told them it was serious, they'd jump on it.'

Everything about this told me it was serious. Ophelia, remote, capable Ophelia, wouldn't be phoning me if it wasn't. Her husband's lover would be her last resort. I understood; if Lizzie was in trouble and her life was at risk, I'd try anything. I owed Luc's family, he'd want me to help.

'I'll come, but you need to know I was recently arrested, I'm only out on bail. I've also been suspended from practice. That means I'm not allowed to see or treat patients—'

'I know everything that's happened and I know what it means. Will you come?'

I wasn't sure how she knew about my suspension, perhaps everyone did. The media might have dissected my downfall in detail for all I knew. Oscar needed medical help and I was a doctor, that's all that mattered to her.

'Please hurry.' Her voice broke.

'I'm picking up my bag now. Try the ambulance again.'

It was midnight. The Close gates would be locked. I opened the front door quietly, bag in one hand, Close gate key in the other. A white police car glowed from the top of the road. The police were there to keep me safe, but under the terms of my bail, I was not supposed to contact potential witnesses and Ophelia would be counted as one. I had to be very careful. I kept to the wall, then unlocked the gate and slipped through. The Close was silent. I had to walk the length of the shrubbery, there was no other way. My hands slid with sweat on the handle of my bag. I could see lights in the North Canonry to the left across the Green but at any moment an arm could come round my neck, a knife slide through my ribs.

My skin stung with fear. I wanted to turn round but Oscar's smiling face was in front of me along with Luc's frightened one, as I had last seen him. I was doing this for both of them. I gripped the bag tightly, ready to swing it around if I was approached, and then I began to run, the bag bouncing against my legs, breath rasping in my throat. If there had been following footsteps, I wouldn't have heard them. I raced, gasping, across the wet grass on the Green, through a small white gate, across the road to the left and then the few yards to the North Canonry. The great wooden gates were open and I ran inside. Luc's red Mercedes had gone, it must have been taken by the police and would be with forensics now. There was just a black Aston Martin – Ophelia's or Blake's, I wasn't sure which.

I knocked at the door, still struggling for breath. Ophelia opened it immediately, she must have been waiting on the other side. She motioned me inside, her face white in the gloom. There were boxes in the hall behind her, large cardboard ones, the kind supplied by removal firms.

'Oscar's worse.' Her expression was unfathomable but her hands were clenched at her sides. 'I was in London today but Abby called me back. He's gone downhill since.'

I followed her upstairs and along a landing, past closed doors. I was stepping deep into her territory, though I had done that already of course. Guilt hovered in the shadows of doorways and in the recessed windows. She led me into a room at the end of a corridor; there was a bed by the window, heavy furniture against the walls, a bucket on the floor. The stench of vomit. A thin figure was visible under the covers in the dim bedside light, a fair head flat to the mattress.

Ophelia snapped on the overhead light. Oscar groaned, and she turned it off immediately.

His eyes were closed, his face the colour of clay. I slipped my fingers around his wrist, the skin was hot. I didn't need to time the pulse, it was galloping.

'Oscar, it's Dr Goodchild. Your mother has asked me to have a look at you because you're poorly.'

There was no answer.

'I need to examine your tummy if that's okay?'

A faint murmur. I pulled the duvet down, lifted his pyjama top and shone my torch onto the skin of his chest and abdomen; there was a small mark on the left side of the lower rib cage under his heart, like the touch of a red felt-tip, non-blanching on pressure.

I tried to flex his head, but he resisted with a guttural protest.

I beckoned Ophelia out of the room. 'You were right to call me. It's serious,' I nodded, giving her a few seconds. 'I'm afraid Oscar has meningitis.'

Her eyes widened in fear.

'This is what we are going to do.' It was straightforward, one of those emergencies that's taught to every student at the beginning of medical school. 'If you agree, I'll give him a shot of antibiotics but, because I've been suspended, I'll be acting illegally.'

She stared blankly at me. 'I don't have a choice.'

'So you agree?'

'Of course.'

'Is he allergic to penicillin?'

She shook her head.

I had to be very quick. I opened my bag and rattled through

246

the bottles inside, finding the Benzylpenicillin powder, in date, thank God.

'Phone for the ambulance again, tell them the GP has diagnosed meningitis. I'll speak to them if I need to.' I found a syringe and needle, withdrew sterile water from a small container, injected the contents into the powder, shook the bottle and withdrew the contents into the syringe, then changed the needle.

'I need to give you an injection of antibiotics,' I told Oscar. 'To help fight your infection.'

He didn't flinch as the needle pierced the side of his buttock, he was sinking deeper into unconsciousness.

Ophelia reappeared. 'They're on the way.'

'Give me a cool flannel, we need to bring the temperature down.'

She produced the flannel within seconds, and then we waited silently, one each side of the bed. The room was quiet. Ophelia seemed barely to be breathing, her gaze on Oscar's face. I kept my fingers on the pulse at his wrist and when he retched, turned his head rapidly. He groaned and vomited a stream of yellow bile on the pillow.

When the ambulance men arrived they were swift and gentle. Oscar moaned as he was transferred to the stretcher and Ophelia winced, there were fine beads of sweat on her forehead as if she was the one with the illness. I didn't tell her it was good that her son was moaning, that silence would have been more worrying.

Unusually they let us both into the ambulance. I had a pass, they said, because I was the GP, but they might have been feeling guilty for the delay – if they knew I was banned from practice they chose to ignore it. More blotches were appearing on Oscar's neck, another on his right eyelid. I was given a cannula which I inserted into his antecubital fossa, the veins on his hand having collapsed. I injected another bolus of penicillin, then attached a bag of saline, dripping it in fast. As I was slipping an oxygen mask over his head, the ambulance stopped. We had arrived at the hospital; time had ceased to exist. I'd even forgotten Ophelia was there. We scrambled out after the stretcher and didn't turn at the squeal of car brakes behind us, we were running to keep up. Oscar was wheeled to the infectious diseases ward and taken to a side room, we were shown the visitors' room by a young nurse. She promised someone would come back with news.

The room was warm and well-furnished. I'd been expecting plastic chairs against the wall, but the upholstered armchairs were deep and comfortable. Ophelia paced backward and forwards in front of the window, her slim profile cutting the darkness outside like a knife.

After half an hour, a doctor came in. The lumbar puncture had been straightforward. The cerebrospinal fluid was cloudy which indicated bacterial infection.

'It was extremely fortunate that Oscar had already been started on antibiotics.' The doctor looked at me and nodded, her round brown eyes were tired but warm with approval. Ophelia's glance in my direction was level, I read respect rather than gratitude. I was helper now as well as enemy.

The nurse reappeared. Ophelia was invited to see Oscar and she motioned for me to follow her. In the darkened side room, his narrow chest and the twin points of his pelvis jutted against the sheet. There was a new red blotch on the fingers that curled on the bed clothes. Ophelia knelt by the bed and touched his head. Her face was drained of expression as she gazed at her son, the oxygen mask in place; a thin child who could have belonged to anyone.

Back in the visitors' room, the pacing began again, back and forth as her face grew paler. After five minutes I took her arm.

'Sit, Ophelia.' I guided her to a chair and turned off the

harsh light, the room sinking into restful darkness lit only by the light from the corridor.

'It happened so fast.' Her voice was hoarse. 'I felt so help-less.' She was breathing rapidly, her control slipping.

'Tell me a story.' It was something my mother asked me to do when I couldn't sleep as a child; it used to help Lizzie as well when she was worried– the effort involved seemed to block anxiety.

'What about?' Her voice was still rough with fear, but she sounded faintly intrigued.

'Anything you like, your childhood maybe.' It would have been cocooned in wealth, a happy time of ponies and picnics, yachts and skiing holidays, comforting to recall.

'We had nothing except each other.' She spoke after a long silence; her voice had quietened. 'We were reared in a trailer park in the Midwest, my father was a drunk. Our mother walked out when I was two, Blake was eight.'

I listened, hiding surprise.

'As soon as he judged us old enough, Dad left us for weeks at a time. I didn't care, I had my brother. I adored him. He was good-looking even then, better than everyone at sport, lessons, making friends.'

She glanced at the no-smoking notice on the wall by the coffee machine and took a pack of cigarettes from her pocket, tapped one out, lit it with a small gold lighter, inhaled and leant back.

'Walking to town, we'd pass the houses where folk with more money lived. I'd look through the gates at the gardens, toys on the grass, bikes flung down, things we didn't have. If anyone smiled at me from the door, Blake would pull me away. Possessive.' She glanced at me. 'Still is.'

Blake, possessive? His dimpled face appeared before me; it was difficult to align that word with the carefree man I knew.

'He began stealing at school, small stuff at first, things like markers, maybe sneakers and then a bike. He wanted what his classmates had, he thought things gave you power. No one suspected him, he looked so cute. He was part of a gang at fourteen. He got hold of a gun, God knows where. He was gambling by then and needed money. There were fights in the park, an armed robbery. A woman was shot.'

'Blake was involved?'

'Involved? He was in charge.'

'You mean he actually killed someone?'

She shrugged. She didn't know, at least not for certain. The doctor put her head around the door, her hair had come loose, there were dark marks under her eyes but she was smiling.

'He's stable; you can see him now. The antibiotics are getting to work, it's early days but he's no worse and that's encouraging.'

Ophelia uncurled from the chair, stubbed out her cigarette and stood; her face was wet with tears although you wouldn't have known by her expression that she was feeling anything at all. She followed the doctor and this time she went alone. I watched through the windows as the countryside emerged from the shadows, the trees and meadows, the chalk hills in the distance shrouded in darkness but becoming clearer.

Chapter 32

June 2017

Ophelia returned, stooped for her coat. 'We should go now.' Her expression had changed, the muscles of that beautiful face were more relaxed. 'Let's walk home.'

It felt good to step into fresh air, even at four thirty in the morning. We walked along the road that led between the fields to the town in the valley below, still wrapped in low-lying mist. The cathedral spire emerged clear of the surrounding fog, a tall needle pointing to the heavens, as sharply defined as it must have appeared hundreds of years ago, when people had to turn to the church in sickness; prayers not antibiotics. There were no vaccines then, no intravenous drugs.

'Oscar wasn't vaccinated against meningitis; this is all his fault.' It was as though she had read my thoughts, but the venom in her tone was startling.

'He's a boy, Ophelia. He doesn't know any better.'

'Blake's fault, not Oscar's. Blake didn't want Oscar to have any inoculations. He persuaded him against them, he said they were harmful, but it's to do with power, his power over me and Oscar.' Her feet were pacing fast, I had to hurry to keep up.

Memories began to surface in my mind: Ophelia tipping into Blake as he held her on the doorstep when Luc was sectioned, the tightness of his grip on her arm at the house-warming party, the way he'd talked about power.

The first lorries started to thunder past us along the road. We were walking in step, faces lowered, and she said nothing more. After fifteen minutes we passed by the walls of the Close, those thick grey walls that were supposed to keep the inhabitants safe, a place of ancient privilege, a long way from a trailer park in Midwest America.

She unlocked the wooden doorway set in the high street gate then relocked it behind us.

The Cathedral towered in front of us, dominating the sleeping houses and the shadowy Green.

'He fucked me when I was thirteen.' Her words were very clear in the silent surroundings. It was hard to believe that this self-possessed woman had faced the worst kind of violence as a child, almost impossible that Blake would have been capable of that.

'Jesus, how terrible. I'm sorry, Ophelia.'

'Don't be. It wasn't rape.'

'I thought you said—'

'There are many different kinds of love, you must know that. A brother's for his sister, a sister's for her brother.'

We were walking fast, the facts coming too rapidly to make sense. I was out of my depth.

Ophelia glanced at me. 'I would have done anything he asked.'

We passed the statue of the weeping woman, Elisabeth Frink's grief-stricken Madonna, walking away from the cathedral, her shoulders raised in barely supressed anguish.

'I was fourteen when I fell pregnant. We ran away.'

'My God, Ophelia. What about your father? Surely he came after you?'

'He was run over soon after we left, crossing the road. Drunk, apparently. An accident, it was in the papers. We didn't care, not one bit. By then we'd hitched to California and hired a tent in a cheap trailer park. Marilyn ran the park; she fell for him. Women do.'

As I had done; even Lizzie had warmed to him once.

'Blake fucked Marilyn instead of me. It was a relief, I'd had enough. He'd become controlling. When Oscar arrived, Marilyn looked after him. I went to school and Blake learnt about property from her. We were a family of sorts, though Blake's never told Oscar he's his son. He's terrified Oscar would hate him. It all worked for a surprisingly long time.' Her voice was unemotional, as though it was all so far in the past, it no longer felt real to her.

We were back at the North Canonry now. She opened the door and we went through the dark hall to the kitchen at the far end of the house. There were plates smeared with ketchup and a bottle of vodka on its side on the draining board. Scattered orange rinds, an opened pot of jam. Oscar's mess probably, but I couldn't see Ophelia or Blake clearing it up, no wonder they needed Abby. Luc must have kept order – the house in France had been simple but tidy and clean.

Ophelia took two cups from the shelf, the thin china was exquisitely painted with hummingbirds in brilliant colours, French-looking. She made coffee and then tipped whisky into two tumblers, pushing aside plates to put them down. She sat opposite me and lit a cigarette.

She began talking again, the words pouring out in a stream, like a river when the barrier breaks, bearing its load of unwholesome debris with it. She must have held this story back for years; worry and sleeplessness had loosened her hold and, almost by chance, I was her recipient.

'After four years, things started to go missing in the trailer park, things like money and guns. A man was killed, a notorious criminal who supplied arms, no one found the culprit but they didn't look very hard. The police were probably pleased; the victim had been a troublemaker. Blake was drinking heavily, gambling again, getting into debt. I didn't know if he organized the murder but it wouldn't surprise me, he has a deeply vicious streak.' She sounded calm but it must have been a terrifying time.

'I'd had enough. I took Oscar and got out. We went travelling in Europe. We didn't have much money but at least we were free. I met Luc on a beach in the south of France three years ago. His grandfather had just died; he was in the midst of a breakdown. We rescued each other.'

Ophelia got up and leant against the window, sipping whisky and looking at the cathedral, but she might have been seeing the Mediterranean instead, stretching blue and unbroken for miles in front of her. I could imagine her sitting next to Luc, her hand on his knee, plans coalescing in her head.

'We stayed with Luc in that wrecked house of his. Oscar adored him. Then Blake turned up, he never let me out of his sight for long. He decided Luc should marry me; he liked the idea of a proper family and he could smell money. He even arranged our wedding. Luc's father was thrilled.'

Luc had told me she'd proposed before Blake came, but the details were irrelevant; he couldn't have withstood the combined will of three people.

'Afterwards we came back to Luc's apartment to live in London. Blake had wanted a fresh start and it turned out to be easier than he'd thought for us to get residence here. I was married to Luc by then, and we had an English grandmother on my father's side which meant Blake got in on an ancestry ticket plus some false documents about Canadian citizenship. He weaselled his way into Luc's architecture firm as a property restorer.'

The room was still shadowy. The kitchen was in the north-east part of the house which made sense, it had been built at a time when there were no fridges. The sun wouldn't reach this side of the house until much later. Although it was mid-June I felt chilled. Ophelia hadn't mentioned love once.

'It was fine for a couple of years but, once he saved enough money, Blake started gambling again and drinking hard.' She stubbed out her cigarette and lit another immediately. 'The debts ballooned. There was a break-in down the road within the year, an armed robbery, someone was shot though the culprit wasn't found, again. Blake is extremely clever at covering his traces, good-looking men with charm aren't usually the first suspects in a murder case. He probably used blackmail. It's what he did with me, threatening to implicate me if ever I was tempted to shop him. He warned me he'd hurt Oscar, though I never believed he would be capable of that until now.'

Her voice had become emotional; she'd told me about her childhood as if it belonged to someone else but what she was relating now was deeply personal. I watched her tapping ash on a plate. She may not have loved Luc but I began to understand that he must have been a lifeline in a terrifying world.

'That's when I found this house.' She glanced round the kitchen. 'Blake fell in love with it as I knew he would, along with the Close, the cathedral and the school. Quintessential England. He wanted it all for Oscar. Luc didn't care, the only place he loves is that house in France.'

The house phone rang and we both jolted. Ophelia dropped her cigarette and stepped on it. She gripped the receiver tightly.

'Yes?'

I could hear a voice talking slowly, seriously.

'Thank you.' Ophelia's voice was different, lighter, happier. She replaced the receiver and walked back to the window.

'Oscar's out of danger.' Her face had relaxed, her eyes shone. The sun was coming up and from the kitchen window we could see that the tip of the spire was a rosy pink, the last traces of the early mist evaporating.

'Blake had it all at last; a family, this amazing house filled with things he'd taken from Luc's place in France. I thought that would be it, that finally he'd stop. I had no idea he was just getting started. Everything fell into place better than he could have dreamt. He had you to thank for that.'

'Me?'

She sat down opposite me again and lit a third cigarette. Her expression was inscrutable. 'Luc fell for you, Blake watched it happen and I watched Blake.'

'Blake watched us?'

'Once you told him Brian had trailed you, Blake followed you as well. He wanted you to think it was Brian all the time, so you'd tell Luc. Crazy Luc who loved you; who better to blame for a murder?'

'Luc's not a murderer.' My face was hot, my heart beating hard.

'Of course he's not. He was set up. Blake killed Brian.'

'That can't be true.' That gruesome murder, the mutilation, it wasn't possible. 'You're exhausted, Ophelia; you can't be thinking straight. You should sleep.'

'He deliberately made the killing look like the work of someone insane, the better to implicate Luc.' She laughed, a bitter, short sound. 'It worked.'

She didn't sound tired at all, she sounded calm and utterly sure of what she was saying. I began to feel extremely sick.

'That's why he attacked Carol in the way he did.' She nodded calmly. 'Although to be honest, he didn't expect her to die.'

Those random stab wounds, the fingers he cut off. My eyes filled with tears.

'I don't expect you come across men like my brother very often in this pretty little town.' She stared at me expressionlessly. 'Blake is capable of acts of cruelty you could not imagine. He killed the puppy I was given as a child; I won't tell you how. He likes inflicting pain, it makes him feel powerful.'

Blake had told me that Brian wanted power, that everyone did; he must have been talking about himself all the time.

'But why choose Carol and Brian, what harm had they done him?'

'You'd told him they were your enemies.'

'Carol and Brian weren't my enemies, he knew that.'

'Let's say he banked on people knowing they caused you problems and sure enough that filtered through to the police. It wouldn't be hard for them to conclude a psychotic lover might feel he had to protect you.'

Blake had been right; that's exactly what DI Wainwright had thought.

'It helped that Blake soaked a shirt of Luc's in Brian's blood and left it in Luc's bedroom, the police found that pretty quickly.' She glanced at me, narrow-eyed. 'Blake put the victims' body parts in Luc's car. He knew the police would conclude that only someone truly deranged would do that.'

'What possible reason would he have for doing this to Luc?'

'Take your pick.' She stubbed out her cigarette in a pool of jam. 'Blake is insanely jealous; he hadn't thought of that when he engineered my marriage. He miscalculated how he'd feel, and now he wants me back. He craves the little family we used to be before Luc came along. He can't bear that Oscar loves Luc like a father.'

She lit yet another cigarette, her fourth. It seemed as if chain-smoking was the only way she could get through her terrible story.

'On top of that he needs cash for his gambling debts, a divorce wouldn't give him enough. If Luc is incapacitated, Blake gains access to everything Luc owns through me: the house in France and the flat in London, the architectural company.' She turned her head away, her voice became very quiet, the voice of a frightened girl. 'It's more than that, though; he gets off on destroying people. That's what has terrified me for years.'

I looked outside; if I craned my neck, I could see people hurrying to work along the road, normal people who would spend a day at work and then return to their families. I thought of Luc, crouched in an empty room, being injected with tranquillizers, rendered helpless. His days had been robbed of normality, and then another thought crashed in on top of that one. Luc's illness had been convenient, far too convenient.

'How could Blake have known Luc would become ill and unable to defend himself?'

'Because he made it happen.' Ophelia nodded calmly as if she had been expecting the question. 'If anyone can manipulate illness, it's my brother.' She smiled a bitter smile. 'When Oscar's headache began last night, I searched for paracetamol. We'd run out so I went to Blake's flat at the top of the house. He keeps it locked but I have a master key. I've never dared use it, but Blake was out, and Oscar was desperate. I didn't find any paracetamol, but I found something else, a packet of citalopram on the tray by his kettle, almost empty. He'd been feeding it to Luc.'

I stared at her in disbelief. 'You can't know that.'

'I'm as certain as it's possible to be. Blake and Luc drink

tea together every morning to discuss plans for the day, they've done so since they met. I know my brother; I know the kind of choices that make sense to him.'

'How would he even know citalopram could make Luc manic?'

'We all knew. When he got the prescription, I read out the leaflet. It said that you shouldn't take citalopram if you have a history of manic depression. I remember the exact moment; we were still in London. It was breakfast time. Oscar had gone to school, but Blake and Luc were both there. Luc was feeling less depressed by then; you'd helped him over the worst. When he heard the contraindications, he decided he wouldn't take citalopram. Blake pocketed the box in a flash. I remember he grinned and said they might come in useful. I'm convinced beyond doubt he's been slipping them into Luc's tea until Luc reached a tipping point and things unfurled from there.'

That made sickening sense. 'Luc said the name was familiar, so I trusted he'd taken them before.'

'I was prescribed them once way back, that's probably why.' She shrugged. 'It's not your fault – if it hadn't been citalopram, Blake would have found something else. He saw Luc's breakdown before the wedding, he knew how helpless he was. He got power of attorney then and there and he's been waiting for his chance ever since. I told you he was smart. Cruel, violent, and very smart.' She glanced at the clock on the wall, a beautiful thing of polished wood with carved sunflowers round the edge. Luc's too, probably.

'I have to leave.' She got up, draining her glass of whisky.

'Where are you going?'

'To the police, as I should have done years ago.' The jaw jutted in her pale face. 'Then to the States.'

'But what about Oscar?'

'He's out of danger. If I stay, I could lose him. Blake's

259

clever, he'd turn the tables on me like he's threatened to several times already. I'd end up in jail and he'd take my son.' She collected her cigarettes and lighter. 'I have people here who will bring him to me.'

A choice that seemed swift but would have been carefully calculated. She must have made many over the years, pushing emotions aside, focusing on survival.

'Will the police believe what you'll tell them about Blake?'

She smiled. 'I've prepared for this moment for years. I've kept a scrapbook of newspaper clippings from the States and from London, the unsolved crimes that match with everywhere we've lived. Thanks to me, we moved fast and kept ahead of the police, but the records I have are incriminating. I've recorded every drunken boast. I took his laptop and his diary yesterday when I was in his room. I've got his toothbrush and comb, they'll find the same DNA on the victims if they look hard enough. There's enough evidence to land him in jail for the rest of his life.' Then her face hardened. 'I've been scared for years, frightened into silence about what he could do to me or Oscar. The difference is that this time, Oscar could have died.'

She left the room. I stood motionless, gazing through the window at the cathedral in the sun, not daring to rejoice that Luc might yet be freed. So much was yet to happen, I mustn't tempt fate.

Ophelia reappeared a few minutes later with a rucksack and a bulging laptop case over her shoulder. She was right, she was prepared.

'I'll drop you back at your house,' she said as I got up.

'Is that all you need?' I asked her.

'It's never been about things for me.'

She was rattling the car keys as she walked out past the packing boxes, past the rooms with the books, the globe and the art on the walls. She didn't glance at them once.

260

'Where will you go in the States?' Once in the car, I put on the seat belt and turned towards her.

'Don't worry, I'll find somewhere safe before Oscar joins me.'

'You'll be on your own apart from your son, how will that feel?' If it hadn't been for me, Luc would still be by her side.

Pity flickered briefly in her eyes. Doctors are hard-wired to detect emotions even if they can't understand them. I had slept with her husband but somehow she was sorry for me; it didn't make sense. Ophelia was a complicated woman, she'd had to be, to survive. There would be things about her that I'd never understand.

'We'll cope.' She didn't say anything else as she drove round to De Vaux Place. The police car had disappeared, maybe it had been stationed on the street for one night only, or perhaps the driver had gone for breakfast.

Ophelia stopped the car outside the house, then turned to me. 'Could you visit Oscar in hospital for me?'

'Of course.' I undid my seat belt.

She put a cool hand on my arm. 'One small thing more. Luc said he gave you some paintings as a thank-you present.'

For a moment I was surprised Luc had told her, but he must have thought the gift sounded innocent enough, a present from a grateful patient.

'Oscar needs something to remember his stepfather by,' she continued evenly, her eyes on mine as she spoke. 'I'd like those paintings for him. Luc would agree if he knew we were leaving, he loves Oscar.'

There were other words beneath these spoken ones. I had slept with her husband; she hadn't mentioned that at all. Giving her son his work was the least I could do. It would be a wrench, more than she knew. I felt Luc through those paintings, the only part of him that was left to me, but Oscar was his stepson and Oscar loved Luc too. I nodded.

'Could you leave them in his hospital locker? And Rachel, could you include that old picture Luc inherited? The one his great-great-grandpa painted? Oscar loves the colours, he always has. It's worthless but Luc wanted to keep it in the family and Oscar's his family. The only thing Luc wants is you. I'll step aside.' She nodded.

So that was it, her bargain and her blessing. Luc loved that painting. Ophelia must have guessed he'd trusted me with it but I could see that to her, it wouldn't seem much to ask.

'I'll go and see Oscar as soon as I'm allowed.'

'With those paintings?'

I nodded; it was partly true.

'Thank you.' She started the car but her face was still turned towards me. 'I'm off to the police now. Blake might come to see you. He's clever, he might have worked out that I've told you about him. Call the police if he arrives, he's a very dangerous man. Don't let him in, don't believe a word he says.'

She drew back and looked at me for the final time, a clear-eyed, unsmiling look.

'Good luck and take care of yourself, Rachel.'

I didn't tell her I wasn't going back to Luc, that I'd caused him enough harm and that, when freed, he'd be better off without me. I got out and turned to say something, goodbye or good luck, but she'd started the car and drove away without another glance.

I unlocked the door and went into the house. I was exhausted. Lack of sleep had caught up with me. Pepper was sleeping in his basket; Lizzie must have dropped him round earlier this morning before work while I was out. I put my phone to charge and then kicked off my shoes. I'd sleep, then call round to see her at lunchtime, tell her about Blake before the news got out. She'd liked him; she would be disbelieving at first then shocked, maybe hurt. I went upstairs slowly and into the bedroom to take my dressing gown off the hook and go on up to the spare room but I didn't get that far.

Blake was sitting in the chair by the bed.

Chapter 33

'At last. My favourite doctor.' He smiled but it wasn't his usual grin, it didn't reach his eyes. He had a glass in his hands, it looked like the brandy Nathan saved for Christmas.

'What are you doing here?' My heart was hammering so loudly he could surely hear.

'I wanted to see you.' He continued to smile as if offering me the chance to collude in the fantasy that this was a social visit.

'How did you get in?' I sat on the edge of the bed, trying to return the smile, to sound mildly curious, as if it was unsurprising to find him upstairs in the house that I'd left locked.

'Your sweet daughter unlocked the door for me.' He sipped from the glass.

Fear gripped my heart. 'Is she okay?'

'She's fine. She's gone home to pack.'

'Pack?'

'She deserves a little vacation.'

Could Blake be the friend Nathan told me Lizzie had

265

planned a holiday with? Had this been organized a while back? Why choose my daughter? I felt in my pocket for my phone before I remembered I'd left it downstairs on a charger.

'So you are the heroine of the hour.' The discussion about Lizzie seemed to have ended. If I could slip downstairs, even for a second, I could grab my phone and warn her he was dangerous, charming but deadly dangerous.

'How am I a heroine?'

'I was coming home last night when an ambulance came screaming out of the North Canonry. I thought my sister might have done herself an injury. She's tried to, before now. I followed it to the hospital and waited in the car park.'

Those brakes squealing behind us; we hadn't had time to turn round or we might have seen Blake staring at us through the windscreen of his car.

'When I saw Oscar coming out of the ambulance on the stretcher, well . . .' He looked down, the smile had gone. 'The hours passed slowly. When you both left, I checked with admissions then visited the ward. I said I was related, which is true of course.'

'Of course.' It must have been difficult under the circumstances to pretend to be the uncle and not the father, he would have wanted to proclaim his true identity.

'The doctor was helpful. I gather you started him on penicillin and that probably saved his life. Thank you.' He meant it; a shadow crossed his face, masked today with a fuzz of stubble. 'I love that kid more than anything else in the world.'

'I'm tired, Blake. I've been up all night.' If I could persuade him to leave before he incriminated himself, I could phone Lizzie, warn her, then phone the police.

'I'll go, but first I need the painting.'

'What painting?'

He smiled. 'The one in the satchel that I saw Luc give you.'

'Satchel?' My bewilderment was genuine; how could he possibly know about the satchel?

Blake sat back in the chair making himself comfortable, but he was watching me closely as if interested in the impact his words would make.

'Back in May, I tried to make an appointment with you in your surgery. I wanted to slip in a few questions, find out what you knew. Luc had seen you as a patient and I'd watched you both at Ophelia's party. Something was bubbling, the chemistry was obvious. I thought even then it might be something I could use. I pretended I was ill to see if I could trick something out of you, but your receptionist said you were in France for a medical conference.' He smiled. 'I knew Luc was in France, I was visiting him the very next day. I guessed you'd be together so I caught an early train to Arles planning to slip into the garden and take photos of you both, useful for blackmail if it came to it. I was standing in line for an ice cream on the platform when I saw the two of you walk by. It wasn't that much of a surprise; you'd timed your departure ahead of my arrival, how were you to know I'd caught an earlier train?' He leant forward, his eyes narrowed. 'I got the pictures I wanted but I was surprised to see him give you the satchel with my favourite painting inside.'

It came back in a heartbeat: the tears, the satchel on my sunburnt shoulder, the approaching train. Blake must have been inches away taking photos on his phone.

'What makes you think that the satchel contained any paintings?'

'Because I watched Ophelia put the painting in that satchel. Hell, I even bought the safe to keep it in.'

'Luc has a roomful of paintings. I'm sure he would give you any you asked for. I've promised Ophelia the ones in the satchel, she wants them for Oscar.'

267

He threw back his head and laughed, 'Oh Rachel, Ophelia doesn't want them for Oscar, she just wants one, for herself.' He put his head to one side and his expression darkened. 'The trouble is, so do I.'

'Surely his wife and son have first rights to his work? Can we discuss this later?' I couldn't quite believe in this new Blake. The old one must be there somewhere, if only I could reach him he would be kind. 'I need to sleep. I'm exhausted, it's been a long night.'

'Ophelia must have warned you against me.' His voice was colder now; my appeal hadn't worked. The other Blake had disappeared, if he'd ever existed at all. 'She probably spun you her favourite story, the one she threatens me with. Blake, the wicked criminal who impregnated his sister at a tender age.'

He must have seen a flicker in my face because he laughed. 'I knew it. I don't suppose she mentioned Oscar's real dad, a fellow art student at Berkeley?'

'She didn't go to Berkeley.' A flush was sweeping up from my chest, anger burning. 'I know the whole story – your mother died, your father was a drunk. You made her pregnant then you ran away together.'

'Our parents are highly successful art historians.' His gaze was level, his tone very calm. 'I'm Oscar's uncle not his father. I adore my sister but I draw the line at incest. Ophelia was a grade A student at Berkeley studying history of art, and got pregnant by a boy in her third year, a fellow called Dan. A nice enough guy but it didn't work out. She's mid-thirties not mid-twenties but her looks fooled you, they fool everyone.'

He was right. I had been fooled by Ophelia's looks. It was possible I'd been taken in by the incest story as well, but I believed in her fear; with Blake sitting so close, I felt fearful too.

268

'I'm not his father but I'm far closer to Oscar than Dan or Luc ever were,' Blake continued as if staking a claim. 'I looked after him while she worked in a gallery, hunting down art for the super-rich, hunting down a wealthy husband at the same time.'

'If she was after wealth why would she choose Luc? I know you want his house but he's not one of the super-rich—'

'I'm itching to have that house, but you're wrong. Luc is a hundred million dollars rich.'

'That's ridiculous.' I would have laughed if I hadn't felt so frightened.

'When Ophelia first saw the painting hanging on the wall in that dingy kitchen in the south of France, she knew at once that it was priceless, but, clever girl that she is, she didn't let on.'

'That picture was painted by his great-great-grandfather, an amateur artist.'

'That picture is a Van Gogh.'

In the silence I heard the cathedral bell sound the hour, and a door nearby open and close, Helen going shopping. Blake's anxiety about Oscar must have taken a toll, he had overstepped all reason.

'We are both exhausted, Blake. Overwrought. This is a mistake—'

'My sister doesn't make mistakes. She knows her artists inside out. Van Gogh was generous. He gave his works to everyone, including his psychiatrist who lived next door to the asylum in Saint-Rémy, a doctor who was also an artist. It's not hard to imagine the bond between them. Van Gogh would have felt better in that hospital, fed and rested. The paintings he did there were some of his best. He would have been grateful to the people who looked after him.'

He nodded as if to himself, this was a story he'd worked out very carefully.

'He rewarded his doctor with a painting rather than the usual sketches he gave away. The doctor hung it above the kitchen sink where he could see it every day. He might have told the family he'd painted it himself, or perhaps that's the conclusion they drew. Van Gogh wasn't famous then and, once the doctor died, no one knew any better. It was simply a picture hanging on the wall that became a picture the doctor had painted himself. And there it stayed through the years growing dusty, though luckily in a dim spot where the light was poor. The house passed down the generations, the family were reclusive like Luc, there weren't many visitors.' Then he laughed. 'Until Ophelia arrived. She couldn't believe her eyes. She didn't utter a word but made sure it was wrapped and stored safely. Luc was bemused at the fuss, but he liked the picture, so he went along with it. He had no idea.'

Was that true though? Luc had asked me to keep it safe, he'd stared at it in wonder. 'The essence of Vincent' he'd whispered the night he came to my house. He might have known its provenance all along and simply decided to keep it hanging where he could enjoy it, safe in the knowledge no one would recognize it, at least not until Ophelia walked into his kitchen.

Blake was continuing. 'Why else do you think she proposed marriage? The poor guy didn't stand a chance.'

He was watching my face and must have seen the dismay because he chuckled. 'It may sound mercenary to you, but think about it. It worked out quite well for Luc. Ophelia runs things for him, she transformed the house in the Close.'

But Luc didn't need Ophelia to run things, he didn't care about things. He hadn't wanted the house in the Close. He was after something more simple, he told me that himself: an empty room, a sheet of paper. Trees and mountains and sky.

Blake was still talking. '. . . waited a very decent interval postnuptials so no one would join the dots, then I was given the code of the safe and dispatched to France to nick the painting. Ophelia and I had planned to leave for the States together after that, only I was just too late.' He looked at me, his eyes glinting. 'When I saw you with the satchel in the station, I hopped back on the very next train, texting my excuses to Luc. We needed a different strategy. I started following you as soon as I returned to Salisbury. At that point I wanted to see if you'd lead me to the painting. I wasn't sure you'd keep the satchel at home. I thought you'd worry about Nathan discovering a gift from Luc.'

I stared at Blake. Ophelia had told me he'd started following me once he knew that Brian had done so, but that was wrong. Blake had started much earlier than that. Ophelia had misled me. She didn't want me to know they were after the Van Gogh; she hadn't mentioned it once. The lies she told and the secrets she kept would be irrelevant against the prize she was still hoping to win.

'So it was you who followed me by the shrubbery and in the street,' I said slowly. I should have known. Blake's stalking had been much worse than Brian's, far more frightening.

Blake nodded calmly. 'And after you told me about Brian in the pub that day, I stepped it up. I knew you'd think it was him, still stalking you.'

I felt very sick, I had played into his hands, unwittingly supplying him with useful victims, while all the time he was coming closer to me.

'It was you in our garden under the tree,' I whispered. 'You were watching me and Luc together.' It hadn't been my imagination or a detaching retina. Blake had been crouching outside in the dark, taking photo after photo as we lay on the sofa making love.

'Shameless behaviour.' He grinned. It was unclear whether

he was referring to us or the fact he had been spying, but he was evidently amused.

'It must have been you who went through my stuff while I was in the shower.'

'That was easy, you left the back door wide open.'

'How did you get over the wall?'

'A rope ladder. I've done that kind of thing many times.'

He tapped his fingers on the arm of the chair as he glanced around the room. 'I have to hand it to you though, I've looked in every drawer and cupboard for that painting. I've been through the whole damn house. Where the hell, could it be?'

The answer was simple. He'd only had to look behind the door he must have opened many times. If I'd known he'd come searching, I'd have found a more sophisticated place, or given it to Victoria to hide, but perhaps that's why the doctor hung the picture in plain view all those years ago. He knew people don't look carefully at what's in front of them.

'I need to go through this room as a policeman would, but you've disturbed my search every time.' He shook his head with mock ruefulness as his eyes roamed the room.

He'd have the time for an uninterrupted hunt now. He wasn't used to the dressing gown as Nathan was, used to ignoring it for so long that he'd stopped seeing it. An uninterrupted search with fresh eyes would soon uncover what he was looking for. I had to distract him before he looked any further; there were other questions to ask and he seemed to like that, I guessed it gave him a sense of power.

'Those photos you took—'

'You have to admit they were good if rather explicit.' The dimples were so deep they were filled with shadow.

'When did you plant them at Brian's house?'

He stared at me silently, smiling a little as he waited for

me to work it out. It was obvious really, it didn't take long. It must have been the night he murdered Brian who would have let him in gladly, having met him at the pub with me. Blake left the photos behind when he'd finished with Brian, before shutting the door on the blood-spattered room, the lifeless body lying on the floor.

Blake was still smiling. 'I had the feeling those photos of you both might have shocked our Carol so I sent her the one I took at Arles instead.'

'Having planted an identical set in Luc's room with a note to incriminate him.'

He didn't answer, he was too clever for that, but all the same, the corners of his mouth turned up as if he couldn't help registering pride; disgust welled.

'Was it necessary to inflict such agony on two innocent people?'

He wet his lips with his tongue, his eyes glowed. I felt sick. I'd been so wrong, so blind. I'd thought Brian was creepy but he had simply been lonely; the man in front of me was evil. He had murdered his victims for pleasure as well as greed though a hundred million dollars would probably justify any vile crime in his eyes.

'And you fed Luc the citalopram.'

Blake's eyes narrowed, the smile faded. That was careless of me, I'd gone too far. Now he would know Ophelia had been in his room, he might guess she'd gone to the police.

I got up from the bed and walked out of the room, casually, as if I'd just remembered something. I'd entice him from the room and make my escape. I was still fit from my jogging, I'd outrun him. I grabbed the phone from the kitchen and had made it to the outer door when his arm came round my neck. Blake was fit too; I'd miscalculated how fast he could move.

'There's no point in protecting Ophelia,' he panted. 'It

273

was she who masterminded the whole thing.' He pulled me back across the courtyard and into the house, dragging me into the kitchen. 'You need to tell me where the painting is right now. I'm seeing Lizzie soon. We both want her to stay as well as possible.'

So that was why he had been so willing to tell me everything: he had my daughter, the best bargaining chip in the world. He knew I'd keep quiet, that I'd give him anything he wanted just to keep her safe.

'Tell me where the fuck it is, Rachel.' His voice was cold now, the voice of someone who didn't care what he did as long as he got what he wanted.

'Why Lizzie?' My voice was hoarse; his grip was tightening.

'I took to her. She's a rebel like me and now there's a bonus, you'll tell me what I need to know. You won't breathe a word to a soul, not if you love her as much as I think you do.'

She's taken already, I wanted to say but my trachea was being crushed. She's happy, she has a boyfriend, there's a baby coming. Leave her alone. But it was becoming difficult to breathe as his arm tightened round my throat. Blackness crept in around the edges of my vision.

'Tell me,' he snarled in my ear.

Several things happened at once: darkness occluded my vision completely, there was a thundering on the door followed by a splintering crash and my phone began to ring.

Chapter 34

The echoes took a while to settle once everyone had left. The barking of police dogs, Pepper's shrill yapping, Blake's vicious swearing, sounds that echoed on in the kitchen as though they had a life of their own. There were quieter voices that lingered beneath those, mine and the policewoman's. Her approach had been different from DI Wainwright's, she was respectful, gentle, apologetic.

I told them what Ophelia had told me: that Blake had wanted Luc's estate. I told them about his debts, his jealousy, the stalking and the citalopram. By inducing Luc's psychosis, Blake had been able to pin the murders he had himself committed onto his brother-in-law, Blake's method of getting his rival out of the way, while taking everything he had. I didn't tell them about the Van Gogh. Ophelia wouldn't have mentioned it and nor would Blake, both would have known they'd have been charged with attempting to steal a priceless work of art. I'd promised Luc I would keep it safe. If I told the police that I had a Van Gogh in my possession they would take it for the trial; any proof of the original gift to his great-great-grandfather might not now exist, Luc might never get it back.

The policewoman told me he was recovering with rest and medication. She hinted that in the light of the developments, all charges against him would be dropped as soon as possible.

I declined to go to hospital to be checked over. My throat felt bruised, but I wanted less attention, not more. I needed peace. Nathan was on his way back home, but he would be a few hours yet.

I went upstairs when everyone had gone, took the case from the bag and unwrapped the picture, laying it on the bed. The work of the most famous artist in the world at the height of his powers, and I hadn't recognized it for what it was.

The last time I had looked at this painting I had seen fear; Van Gogh's fear of his madness filtered through my own terror. Today I saw the way the wind moved the branches, as if free from restraint, the way the sun came through the leaves. There was a rough brown fence by the side of the olives and running beside that a yellow line I hadn't noticed before. I'd been too close. When I stood back, the line became a path that led through the trees and up towards the luminous mountains and clouds, towards space and freedom. I imagined Van Gogh with his head back, absorbing the marvellous light, breathing it in. Healing properties, Luc had said.

The cathedral bell striking eleven brought me back, I needed to see Lizzie. Blake's story about the planned holiday and their relationship must have been his clumsy attempt to blackmail me. She could have no idea of his plans, no concept of his crimes, I wanted to tell her before she heard the news. I packed the painting away in the satchel and hung it on the hook behind the door in the spare room this time. It would be near me when I slept. I draped my dressing gown over it again. It belonged to Luc and I had to keep it safe until I worked out how to give it back.

I walked to the library or rather half walked, half ran – it felt urgent, though I wasn't sure why. I was breathless by the time I arrived. The boyfriend was at a desk, none of his students were around today. He seemed familiar already, with his mop of dark hair, the length of him folded into a chair. He was reading but Lizzie was nowhere in sight. I walked over but he didn't look up.

'Hello there.' It seemed strange that I didn't yet know his name.

He glanced up, one hand keeping his place in the book.

'You know my daughter, Lizzie.'

He shook his head, looking blank, as if he'd never heard the name. Was he shy? Embarrassed?

'Lizzie, who works here.' No need to be coy, I wanted to add, I know she's carrying your child, my grandchild. I couldn't help smiling, it was still so new, so astounding.

He peered at me with lifted eyebrows, close up his cheeks had the pockmarks of acne.

'Lizzie Goodchild,' I said, the charade was becoming irritating. 'She has long dark hair, I've seen you together—'

'Oh, the librarian.' His face cleared. 'How can I help?'

'Where is she?'

'She was here earlier.' He glanced around the library. 'She must have left.'

'When?'

'The staff would know.' His eyes drifted down to his book.

'I thought you two were, well, friends.'

'Is that what she said?' He glanced up again, pleased.

I'd made a mistake, another one. I had seen what I wanted to, not what was there, and then drawn the wrong conclusions. Lizzie was happy but this man wasn't the reason, nor would he be the father of her baby.

The woman behind the desk looked like a young Miss Honey in *Matilda* or how I imagined Miss Honey might look. Milky skin, a thin fall of pale hair, a gentle enquiring smile.

I smiled back, though it was an effort. I could feel my lips trembling. 'I'm Lizzie's mother.'

'Oh that's lucky, I can give you this.'

She reached down behind the counter and produced a cloth bag with pictures of books printed on it; there were shoes inside, a notebook I'd given Lizzie when she started the job, still with its paper band around it, a mug from home.

'They were in such a hurry for the plane, she must have forgotten.' She handed the bag to me but I must have looked very blank because she laughed. 'Lizzie and her sister-in-law, well, future sister-in-law. Such a lovely girl, all that thick blonde hair.' And then she laughed again, a tinkling sound that might become irritating if you heard it too often. 'I'm sure I'm not giving any secrets away; you'd know of course her brother's the baby's father.' She pushed her hair behind her ears and her smile became wistful. 'I can't help being envious of Lizzie though you mustn't tell her. I've always wanted to go to California.'

I'd believed almost everything Ophelia had said – well, some of it was true. She could be flying to the States to escape her brother, but she'd neglected to tell me she was taking my daughter with her and that Blake was the father of Lizzie's child.

I had to hold the edge of the desk while images flashed through my mind like photographs speeding by on a reel: Lizzie's face when she met Blake at Ophelia's party, her pretty clothes and new make-up, the fury when she saw me put a hand on his sleeve. He must have been the mystery man Victoria had seen in the car. When Ophelia told Lizzie the truth about her brother's crimes, as she surely must have done, Lizzie would have been devastated.

'When did they leave, exactly?'

'Lizzie came in to say goodbye, oh, about four hours ago now. Her friend arrived soon after that to pick her up, they were driving straight to the airport. Off they went, laughing and chatting.'

I ran with the bag in my hands, my feet thudding on the pavement, but I didn't need to go all the way; the for-sale notice outside Lizzie's flat was obvious from the end of the street. They were probably in the air already. The direct flight to Los Angeles took Victoria all night two years ago but it must be quicker now.

Laughing and chatting; that was something to hold to.

When Nathan returned from the conference, he wasn't as surprised as I'd thought he would be, not nearly as upset. He listened calmly as I told him what had happened.

Lizzie wouldn't have wanted Blake, he said, not once she knew about his past. Ophelia would have told her the truth about him, as soon as she knew Lizzie was pregnant; as the baby's future aunt, she would have felt responsible. Ophelia was being kind, Nathan said, acting for the best. She had offered our daughter another chance to escape and Lizzie would have jumped at it. It was a dream come true, and like all dreams it would come to an end. Lizzie would return once she'd had her child, Nathan was sure she would.

I listened in silence, recognizing all those things my daughter had felt, her longing for freedom and adventure; how could I not? I'd longed for them too. I'd had my own dreams, doomed as they were but Lizzie had pulled far away from me now, opening up old wounds. The wrench had been so sudden, it felt as if some living part of me had been roughly torn away.

My eyelids were swollen with crying but Nathan was philosophical. He said it was a matter of time. He seemed relaxed about it but my heart was breaking.

I couldn't tell Nathan about the Van Gogh, not yet, not ever. It wasn't my secret to share. The risks were too great, the news might leak out, he might hand it over to the police. No one had known about the painting until Ophelia had arrived and no one need know now. It was safest that way. I'd return it as soon as I could.

Judy and DI Wainwright came round, sparing me the journey to the police station in Melksham. We sat in the sitting room, Judy next to me on the sofa, DI Wainwright wedged into the opposite chair. He didn't apologize but his awkwardness was palpable and he kept it brief. Blake's guilt was not in doubt. He had been apprehended in an incriminating act of violence against me. Ophelia's tapes helped, along with her scrapbook with the cuttings and the hard drive of his laptop which revealed his search history on the effects of citalopram and how to perform amputations. Wainwright suspected the murder weapon had been discarded in the river though it hadn't yet been found, but Blake's DNA had been recovered from the degraded material in the boot of Luc's car. That's what they were now, Carol's fingers and Brian's hand: degraded material to be retained for study then returned to the next of kin or disposed of. Grief and regret mounted. I wanted, more than anything, to say I was sorry to both of them.

DI Wainwright stood up. There were ends to tie up and Blake's historic crimes to pursue, but they had their man. He had waited for confirmation from the Crown Prosecution Service and could now reveal that my bail was dropped. I was free. His handshake was surprisingly weak for such a large man, but Judy gave me a warm hug, and then they were gone.

Oscar was sitting up in bed on the ward when I arrived a week later. He looked thin but better and smiled at me, though I doubted he remembered the night of his admission. The couple by his bed were mid-seventies, maybe older, both dressed in soft camel coats, with the kind of looks that defy age and speak of wealth and maintenance. They had tans and dazzling smiles.

The woman stood up, she was tall, with blue eyes and grey-blonde hair scooped back. Thick gold bangles slid down her arm as she grasped my hands tightly in hers. She smelt of freesias too.

'Ophelia said you'd come by. She had to fly to the States on urgent business as you probably know.' She smiled. 'We are taking our grandson back with us when he's better.'

The woman's grip was like a vice, her rings bit into my fingers. I freed my hands.

'Where do you live?'

'Chicago my dear. My husband's professor of art at the university there.'

I stared at her suntanned face; so Blake's version of his and Ophelia's parentage had been the correct one. Ophelia must have known I'd find that out when I came to see Oscar, but she wouldn't have minded, not if she got what she wanted.

'Oscar will be fine, my dear.' Close up there were deep frown lines between her eyes, filled with foundation. She patted my hand. 'He'll probably stay with his father until Ophelia joins us. Dan will be thrilled, he always used to share Oscar's care.'

The art student from Berkeley was a responsible father after all; proof, if I still needed it, that Ophelia had lied about Oscar's origins as smoothly as she had lied about her own. She must have hoped the story of incest would stir my pity so I'd give her the painting she asked for, it had also been another blow to strike against her brother. She and Blake had both played with the truth like a game of chess and Ophelia had won, or thought she had.

'She asked me to deliver some paintings for Oscar,' I told her.

The woman's eyes lit up like sapphires. 'Ah yes, dear, she said you'd drop them by. Give them to Ted to keep safe for the journey, would you? Now? There's a good girl.'

Did she speak like this to her children? Hold their hands so tightly? Tell them what to do? No wonder Ophelia had wanted out, no wonder she told lies. It was harder to see why Blake had committed his crimes, but a skilled psychiatrist might pick it apart: stifling parental control or its opposite, affluent neglect, sibling rivalry gone rogue, aberrant DNA. It could take years to diagnose and longer to treat.

'So the pictures, my dear. For Oscar.' Impatience disguised in a glittering smile.

'I've sealed them up.' I handed the parcel to her husband. 'Against the light; best not to take off the wrapping until you arrive.'

That way they wouldn't discover the Van Gogh wasn't among the paintings I'd sealed in the package until it was far too late to do anything about it. At least Oscar would enjoy his stepfather's pictures, I'd wrapped up eight of them instead.

'Of course not.' Ted's voice was deep and gravelly. 'I wouldn't dream of tampering. I'll let Ophelia open it.'

Did they envisage dizzying wealth? Or were they more philanthropic? A gift to the Metropolitan Museum of Art perhaps, ensuring lasting gratitude and fame. I tried to picture the dismay on their faces when the package was opened but it was too difficult to dislodge their gleaming satisfaction, even in my imagination.

'Say hi to my stepdad for me,' Oscar whispered when I left. 'Please thank him for me.' He grinned at me, a mischievous look borrowed straight from his uncle.

Chapter 35

October 2017

Nathan was due to go in half an hour.

Months of preparation had come down to this moment. His visa, the work permit and updated passport were ready on the table. So much packing, so much rooting in drawers for clothes, so much searching through the house for missing papers and books and, now, so little time. He still wasn't ready. I was making Marmite sandwiches for him, his favourite, he wouldn't have time to stop for lunch. I searched in the cupboard for the Thermos flask remembering after a few minutes that I'd left it on the train weeks ago.

I'd missed the Salisbury stop on the way back from Broadmoor and had to catch another train home from Exeter, leaving the Thermos on the seat in the rush. I was unable to think clearly. The day had not gone as I'd hoped. I'd waited till mid-July, four weeks after Luc's admission. He'd been cleared of the crimes by then and I'd thought the visiting rules would have been relaxed.

The receptionist for Luc's ward at Broadmoor was far younger than me, an attractive woman in her twenties with curly dark hair and freckles. By the time I'd negotiated the extensive security to reach her office, separated from the building housing Luc by a path and some grass, I was tired. I didn't mind that she spoke slowly as if to a child but even then, the facts took a few moments to sink in.

'Luc Lefevre is not allowed visitors other than family members at the moment.' Something about the way she enunciated each word reminded me of Carol.

'Might I be allowed to see him next week then or the week after that?'

'He is being transferred tomorrow.' She didn't bother to disguise the note of triumph in her voice.

'Where?'

She smiled a little scornfully and returned to her screen.

'Can you give this to him, then? It's urgent.' I put Luc's case on the counter. It had passed X-ray scrutiny and the woman gave it a cursory glance; if I told her it contained a priceless painting from one of the world's greatest artists, her expression would have changed from boredom to incredulity. She would have snatched it up, made urgent phone calls and then hurried to put it in an official safe. As it was, she dumped the case on the floor and continued to type, glancing at me with irritation.

'I'll wait here until it's been delivered to him,' I told her.

After an hour she gave in, summoning a porter to the desk. A tall young man with dreadlocks appeared and tucked the case under his arm. I followed him outside.

'Would you give to him personally? Only it's important, it has sentimental value.'

He nodded, his grin was friendly; it seemed a long time since anyone had smiled so openly at me. It was all I could do not to weep.

'Could you come back and let me know what he says? Please?'

He glanced into the office, then winked at me.

I waited in the sunshine. My heart was beating fast with the hope that Luc might appear side by side with the porter, hurrying to greet me. He might look thin and pale by now. I tried to prepare myself for his expression: smiling or possibly confused, perhaps blank-faced or even frowning. After fifteen minutes the young man appeared alone, jogging towards me effortlessly. How stupid I'd been. Luc wouldn't be allowed out, the whole point of this place was security.

'Did you give him the case?'

'Sure did.'

'Did he say anything?'

'Just thanks.'

'Nothing else?'

'Nope.'

'What did he look like?'

'Normal, I guess.' He grinned again and jogged away from me towards another building.

Normal. That was something to take away with me, to turn over in my mind in the sleepless hours and be grateful for. The journey back was exhausting but everything I did now was exhausting. At home I looked at the few remaining paintings of Luc's, touched them, breathed them in, then sealed them up in layers of black paper and taped bubble wrap as carefully as I had the Van Gogh itself. They were as precious to me, they had to last me a lifetime. I'd replaced the package in the satchel, and it had vanished behind the dressing gown on the back of the spare room door.

I wrapped the sandwiches in foil and put them on the hall table.

'The train goes in twenty-five minutes,' I called upstairs.

'Nearly ready,' he sounded cheerful. 'Just looking for a travel bag.'

He hadn't sorted that yet? My meticulous husband could still surprise me; he had surprised me already. He'd been a different man for weeks, much happier. The promised promotion was slowly approaching but he wanted the chance of adventure first. The headmaster had sanctioned a sabbatical at the Bishop's School near San Diego in southern California, a private secondary school where the curriculum was progressive. Nathan was to bring his experience back to his new role.

He hadn't made a fuss about our separate bedrooms, sex seemed to be the last thing on his mind. We talked about Lizzie, although he didn't seem as heartbroken as I was. He listened carefully whenever I tried to make sense of what had happened.

'We weren't present when she needed us.'

'We were much too present,' he replied. 'You must see that, we submerged her.'

You submerged her, that was what he meant, and I nodded. I was ready to accept any blame, guilt floated on the surface of my life like a plant with tendrils, attaching itself to everything.

We began to go for walks again, Nathan planned them, long walks over the chalk downs and along the Nadder Valley, following the river, listening to the birds. Once we saw a kingfisher. He insisted on cooking the meals. The flirtation with Sarah was a thing of the past; when we met her, they chatted calmly, old friends, nothing more. Perhaps I'd been mistaken.

Roger offered me my job again. It seemed the medical practice tribunal had decided that since I'd seen Luc just once as a doctor, and as he hadn't been vulnerable at the point our relationship started three months later, my licence could be restored. It was up to Roger to decide if he wanted me back.

'We miss you, Rachel.' Roger had taken off his glasses, polished them and put them back on. 'It's not the same without you, come back half time if you like. We could up your salary.'

But it was as though I had divided my life with a pair of sharp scissors, before and after Luc, before and after work. The cuts seemed absolute.

'I'll think about it.' I'd thought about it already, but Roger hated absolutes. He liked to embellish the truth with hope, which was why his patients adored him. I knew he understood what I really meant. 'In the meantime, maybe that money could go towards funding a psychotherapist,' I suggested. 'It might save time in the long run.' And lives, though I didn't mention that, lives like Liam's.

'I've been thinking about psychotherapy funnily enough, writing letters.' He gestured towards a pile of paper on his desk, knocking others on the floor. 'Betty prompted me. Someone's coming in next week for an interview.'

I wished I could have told Lizzie.

'I want something to carry my passport and ticket in, my work for the journey, all those sorts of things.' Nathan jumped down the stairs two at a time like an excited boy and hurried past me in the hall.

We'd seen a photo that Lizzie had sent Victoria, our big-bellied daughter in a pool under a blue sky, palm trees in the background. It was bittersweet, I wanted to be with her so badly. I wondered whereabouts they were in California; it was an outside possibility Nathan might run into them, in a shopping mall or at a leisure centre somewhere, maybe on a beach.

He planned to send for me as soon as he could.

'I can see us staying out there,' he said, nodding thoughtfully. 'I could hand in my notice at the Cathedral School if it came to it, but one of us should stay here for now, in case she comes back.'

I agreed. I was tired. The only decisions that I seemed able to make were negative ones. The truth was, unless Nathan found Lizzie, which seemed unlikely, I didn't want to join him. I was looking forward to his departure, I longed to be left in peace. He seemed to watch me all the time and I didn't want to leave my home. I didn't want to leave Victoria either, although she was still in New York and I hadn't seen her for weeks.

'Why not use your briefcase? It's in the sitting room by your desk.'

'Hands-free would be better. Something over my shoulder so I can delve for my passport more easily.'

'Take a rucksack then, my blue one if you want. It's in the chest with the maps.'

'I worry things could get taken out behind my back in a rucksack.' He came into the hall, took a gulp of my coffee, glanced at his watch. 'Jesus, I'm running out of time.' He started up the stairs then stopped short, as you might if you'd had an afterthought. 'How about that leather bag?'

'What leather bag?'

I knew of course, I knew immediately. I sat down on the bottom step, my heart beating strangely. I felt dizzy.

'The one you brought back from France,' he continued cheerfully, staring down at me. 'You know, after that conference in Paris. You were wearing it over your shoulder when I collected you from the station.'

'Ah, that one.' But it hadn't been over my shoulder, it had been deep in my case, hidden between layers of clothes, so that he wouldn't see it. 'I'm surprised you remember.'

'It struck me as good quality at the time; it would be exactly the right size with a nice wide strap.'

So that's what he'd been looking for these last weeks,

searching in the drawers and cupboards, under the beds, that's why he'd watched my every move. He must have been shown the image of the satchel along with one of the painting itself. How stupid I'd been.

'Where is it, Rach?'

Blake would have sent Ophelia the image of the satchel even as he watched Luc settle it on my shoulder in Arles station, months ago. She would have got to work immediately. She'd had scarcely three days but, if you looked like Ophelia, if you possessed her determination and intelligence, you wouldn't need long. Nathan would have been flattered, a fruit ripe for picking, and now the truth tumbled down around me, like apples from a tree in a storm: it was Ophelia who had left her lighter in the car, her freesias in my kitchen and her scent on the sheets. She'd bought him the tie. He must have known about my affair with Luc by the time I returned from France; he'd begun his own with Ophelia by then but I'd transgressed first. I had to be punished, hence the assault.

Nathan had always liked treasure hunts. He would have started searching for the satchel as soon as I'd returned but he neglected to put things back, forgetting I grew up in the house and I knew it off by heart. He'd shifted a kitchen chair to reach the top of the cupboard and moved the one by my desk to look through my papers. He'd searched in the airing cupboard, removing my pyjamas while he did so, putting them back in a different place by mistake. Blake must have lost patience with Nathan's cautious searching, hence the break in, the yanking open of cupboards, the scattering of clothes and later the confrontation in the bedroom, that threat of blackmail.

Neither my husband's stealth nor Blake's intrusions had worked; this was Nathan's last chance, his and Ophelia's. He had worked hard for this moment for a long time, building

289

my trust, all those walks, all those meals. Now it was pay-off time. His heart must be beating in his mouth.

'Rachel? It's getting late.'

Sex with a new partner would have been overwhelming, I could have told him that. He hadn't gone to see his mother; Ada had been right all along. Ophelia and Blake hadn't gone to France together either. Ophelia would have planned some luxury break with my husband instead to seal his commitment. He would have been as unaware as she was, I had to believe, that Blake was about to murder Carol and would go on to murder Brian.

When her parents gave Ophelia the paintings to unwrap, her disappointment must have stung more than theirs, but she had Nathan as her back-up plan. Women like Ophelia always have a back-up plan and hers had been my husband.

'Rachel?'

'It's on the back of the spare room door, under my dressing gown.'

I could hear his feet pounding up two flights of stairs, there was a hush and then a jubilant cry tinged with relief. 'Got it!'

That fractured plate was in fragments now, the pieces lay scattered on the floor at my feet.

'There's a sealed package in there,' I called up. If I didn't mention that he'd think it odd. 'Could you take it out and leave it on the chest of drawers?'

'Sure,' he shouted back. The lie was immediate and convincing as so many of his lies had been; I had swallowed them all until now.

He appeared seconds later, his hair sticking up, flushed with triumph, the satchel over his shoulder.

'Thanks baby; this is perfect.'

Baby. That new, American endearment again – but it wouldn't be new to Nathan of course, he had picked it up from Ophelia. He took me in his arms. He would have checked the package in the satchel, maybe even held it in his hands, but he was in a rush, there wouldn't have been time to examine the contents: too much tape, too many layers of bubble wrap and black paper. He would assume he had the Van Gogh; after all, it was in the very place he'd been told it would be. He couldn't have any idea I'd returned it to Luc weeks ago or that the package in the satchel contained the last of Luc's paintings and nothing else. For now, as far as he knew, the contents of the leather bag on his shoulder represented a dream come true and I knew how he must feel. We'd all invested in dreams, Blake and Ophelia, Luc and I, Lizzie and now Nathan.

'I'll phone you when I get there.' He hadn't noticed I was trembling; this was, after all, the very end of our marriage. He was braver than I had been, he was going after a new life in a way I hadn't dared. He wasn't really a criminal, he'd just got carried away by someone cleverer than he was, who knew exactly what she was doing. He picked up his case, in a hurry now, gambling on getting away before I realized he hadn't left the package on the chest of drawers as I'd asked.

'If you happen to bump into Lizzie . . .'

His gaze didn't quite meet mine. 'Realistically, baby, it's not going to happen any time soon. California is a big place.' He glanced at his watch. 'It's late, let's go.'

He'd be seeing her tomorrow or the day after that, at the latest. The flicker of pity I'd seen in Ophelia's eyes made sense now: she had stolen my husband and was about to take my daughter too. I was the one who would be left on my own, not her.

I put my hand on Nathan's arm and spoke very clearly; this was important. 'When you do, give her my dearest love. Tell her to come back as soon as she can.'

I dropped him at the station five minutes before the train

was due and he hurried to the entrance, the satchel bouncing against his hip. I waited for him to turn around and wave, but he didn't. He didn't phone the next day or the day after that, or anytime in the following weeks.

He had gone.

Chapter 36

November 2017

After clarity, darkness, although it's supposed to be the other way around.

The days passed, one after another, slow drops falling into dark water. I understood what had happened. The reasons behind each decision seemed simple enough: for Lizzie it had been the promise of a new life, for Nathan, the same. Blake wanted money and, for all three of them, there had been Ophelia, the glittering prize. I would think about each one of them in turn as I walked with Pepper in the cold evenings by the cathedral, looking at them each in turn in the way one examines stones on the beach for their colours when the tide goes out, though after a while they lose their lustre, resisting discovery.

I understood completely but my heart didn't.

I had entered a new landscape, it was quiet, lonely. The loss of Luc. The absence of Lizzie. The death of Carol and Brian. The end of my marriage, the end of my career.

I understood about Luc's layers of ash now. I understood what Liam and Brian had endured. Too late, I understood exactly how they'd felt. The grey stillness, the lack of meaning, the effort involved in getting up in the morning. The exhaustion. Sometimes the sound of a child crying in my dreams woke me in the middle of the night, unsure if it was the memory of Lizzie as a baby or the thought of my grandchild, due in two months' time. I had to tread down the panic of not being able to reach Lizzie in time should she need me. Nathan and Ophelia were looking after her now and I tried not to mind, but the days when I did were exhausting.

Luc had disappeared. I had no idea where he was and no way of finding out. My lawyer didn't know and nor did Abby. I imagined him in his house in France, painting in that room of paintings, maybe taking architectural commissions when he needed money. The Van Gogh would be in the vault of a bank. I kept images of him in my mind, as carefully as I had the painting, his face in certain lights, his voice, his walk, his hands. I dreaded the time when they would fade; I doubted he would have kept any of me. I had belonged to a stage in his life of unravelling. He had been ill when he met me, ill when we parted. I might even be part of a nightmare that he would block from his thoughts. He hadn't tried to contact me, no one would want to relive a nightmare.

The neat cut I thought I'd made between my working life and my present one began to spring further apart like skin that's been sutured under tension and gives way. The wound fails to heal and widens, becoming messy. I missed the desk in my office that had been mine in the way nothing else had been, the mornings when you never knew who would come through the door and what might unfold, the whispered confidences. The way Roger pushed his glasses up and smiled his reassuring smile, his kindness. I missed Carol and her certainties. I missed the sense of purpose that had powered my days, but all the same I didn't have the energy to go back. I didn't have the energy to finish my sentences.

Victoria hardly had time to phone, her mother was dying. When she did, we talked about her life, her family. Not mine, there was nothing to say.

In the mirror I was a thin stranger, my eyes looked blank. As the season deepened, winter closed over my head like a river, not the tumbling mass of water I'd longed for as a child, but a quiet deep silence. It's easy to sink from sight if you want to, even in a small town, even in a small part of that small town. I'd become one of those figures I'd seen about the cathedral walls, hurrying against the cold, leading a dog, going home to a silent house, the empty cup from breakfast, the empty bed. At last I understood why people had clung close to the cathedral; it was for the comfort of familiarity, the grey stone unchanging in a changing world. Endurance in the face of time.

Chapter 37

February 2018

The fluting song of a blackbird startled me on a day when the sky was blue for the first time. I saw geese winging east above the spire and a week or so after that the almond tree in the garden sent out delicate pink petals. I began to sketch, small things, not landscapes, but pebbles, buds, Pepper sleeping.

Blake's trial was another step forward. I was in court, but it turned out I wasn't needed. His guilt was undisputed. His luck had run out; in the stand he seemed smaller, fatter, he had shaved his head. The painting wasn't mentioned once. I returned home to find Laura Chambers had left a bunch of daffodils by the door and a note, she was feeling stronger. It had been over a year since Liam's death. We began to go for walks together.

Two weeks after that, a message arrived from Ophelia's phone.

She sends love.

A picture of a baby, a perfect little girl, just a few weeks old, with a feathering of fair hair. I carried it in my pocket for a week then had the picture printed out. I put it in a frame on the kitchen windowsill alongside the one of Nathan and me with Lizzie; if she came back she would see it as soon as she walked in. The hope was painful.

When I met Sarah by chance in the town it transpired Nathan had resigned from the Cathedral School soon after his arrival in the States, he was hoping to make his job at the Bishop's School in California permanent. I took that to mean Ophelia had forgiven him the loss of the Van Gogh; I found I was glad for him.

In March, Laura and I went together to the National Gallery, we needed the colours. Van Gogh's *Sunflowers* were the first thing I saw, the only thing. Oranges and green in thick layers of shining paint, I could have warmed my hands by them.

'Loneliness,' Laura whispered. 'Each one is so separate from all the others.'

'Endurance,' I whispered back. 'Look at the strength, the undefeated way he painted them.' I'd seen the wrinkled petals and the dark seed heads but I hadn't noticed how fierce, how full of life they were. Hope shining in ochre and emerald. Luc had told me they were beautiful and finally I saw that for myself.

A month later Victoria came through the arrivals at Heathrow, a tall gaunt figure, wrapped in cashmere.

'Vee, you haven't been eating a thing.'

'Christ. The doctor complex, still. Where's the bloody car?'

I put the thinness down to stress and grief. I understood, how could I not? And then I heard the cough through the walls and in the garden, much worse than before. I made an appointment with her doctor and went with her.

'Do you smoke?' A severe young GP, younger than Lizzie.

Victoria looked bored so I nodded.

'Family history?'

I nodded again.

She organized an X-ray and while we waited for the appointment to discuss the results, a postman came with a heavy package, registered post. The postmark was illegible, the parcel thick and flat, cushioned. Tax documents? The photos from the police, returned? Something from Lizzie?

But it was none of those things. It was the Van Gogh painting.

Chapter 38

April 2018

Victoria arranged it all: flights, car, hotel.

The X-ray had not been normal, the cancer was small, a little shadow by the hilum of her left lung.

'Tiny then,' Victoria said scornfully when the GP put the X-ray on the screen. 'It hardly counts.'

I gripped her hand as much for my comfort as hers, we both knew how much it counted.

She complied with chemotherapy but, in the gap between sessions, she wanted to go away. She needed a companion for her trip to the Camargue for *National Geographic*, she was much too tired to carry everything. She had booked a hotel in Saint-Rémy de Provence. When we came back, she would complete the therapy.

'So, you have to come with me.' She smiled her dazzling Victoria smile.

'He hasn't been in touch, Vee; don't make me.'

'A Van Gogh painting is being in touch.'

Laura took Pepper for me. It was raining when I and Victoria arrived in Marseilles. The taxi delivered us to the hotel. It was on the outskirts of Saint-Rémy and conveniently placed, but we were cold, the rooms were built for summer and April was cool that year. The floors were marble, the walls thin; the concierge gave me more blankets and I heaped them onto Victoria's bed.

We explored the circular streets of Saint-Rémy, the house where Nostradamus was born, one of many on a back street. The Musée Estrine was exhibiting a collection of Van Gogh's work, paintings that had been done while he was at Saint-Paul-de-Mausole; the wheat field at the back of the hospital, the olive trees and mountains were so like the ones in the painting he gave to Luc's great-great-grandfather I couldn't move away. How had I not recognized it? How hadn't Luc?

Or had he? He might have chosen not to lay the burden of its origin on me but I still didn't know for certain. I would probably never know.

I looked for him in the streets that we walked through and the cafes we entered, wondering if I would see him, a tall figure, thinner now with longer hair, a deeper glow to his skin. I imagined him sketching in a corner while a cup of coffee cooled in front of him, preoccupied, content. And then I imagined him in Paris with friends. Or somewhere else completely, a different home, a different life with a different woman. I put off going to the house to return the painting until nearly the end of the week.

At lunchtime on Thursday we were on a restaurant terrace surrounded by potted lemon trees. The air was citrus sharp. Victoria leant her chin on her hand. Her head was tightly encased in a scarf, which gave her cheeks a carved appearance; she was more beautiful than ever.

'I've a couple of things to tell you, sweetie. Now's the time.'

I looked up from my plate of mussels steaming in their

fragrant broth. I felt cold with fear, but she was smiling.

'Look.' She pushed her phone over the table. 'It arrived today.'

Texts with photographs of photos don't work very well. I looked at the screen in the light, but the image was bleached out. Then, tilted towards the shadow, I saw a girl with a baby held close. A long shawl.

'Lizzie?' Tears stinging. Lizzie and her baby.

'Look again.'

I tipped the phone further into the shadow and then I saw that the girl was myself, holding Lizzie in her christening robe.

'It arrived today.' Victoria was smiling. 'There's a message if you scroll down, just a few words.'

Tell Mum I get it now.

I stared at the screen for a long time, warmth beginning to infiltrate every part of me; so the wound had started to heal from the base. We sat together in peaceful silence, there were no words for how I felt. The waiter took away my bowl of mussels and brought hot coffee. After a while Victoria put her cup down and sighed.

'It turns out I'm busy tomorrow. I've booked a taxi to Saintes-Maries-de-la-Mer; I'm planning to photograph the wild horses and the church.' She stretched out her legs in the sun. 'On my own.'

'You'll need someone to carry your cameras. I thought that was why you asked me to come.'

'The driver will help me.'

'You'll need a companion.'

'I'll need complete silence.' She smiled.

'You have no idea how silent I can be.'

She leant across the table and took my hand. 'Courage.'

I walked to the house in the early morning, the parcel under my arm, it wasn't far. Past Glanum and up the road towards Saint-Paul-de-Mausole, large posters of Van Gogh's paintings lining the drive. We had driven this way, Luc and I, but I'd missed them then, I hadn't been looking. The road was the same past the hospital, with each turn I remembered the heat in the car, Luc's hands on the wheel and Coco on my lap, how convinced I'd been I was making a mistake.

As I turned down the path in the green gold shade, it was as though I was turning back time. I thought my heart would burst from beating but as I rounded the last corner I saw the green truck was missing. The relief was intense, I wouldn't have to meet him, wouldn't have to sense the change in how he felt.

The garden looked as it had when I saw it last, grass, wildflowers and trees. At first glance the house seemed the same then I noticed the shutters had been painted and mended, the roof was now intact. The door was slightly ajar. I knocked and waited but no one came so I pushed it open. There was a jug of flowers on the table, a covered dish of butter. New china in the cupboard, a pretty blue. The embers in the fireplace were still warm. The chair had been repaired, the horsehair tucked inside, you could see the neat stitching in the leather. There were rolls of paper stacked against the wall.

I'd told him I'd find him, and I'd kept my promise, because he was here in the warm embers, the chair, the rolls of paper. The jug of flowers and the china. It was clear his life had mended, and he was happy, working. He didn't need me. I put the package on the table. He would know I'd come, that I had done what I said I would do. That was enough, it was probably better like this.

On my way back I stopped at the gates of Saint-Paul-de-Mausole where the first story began; the story that lay between the Dutch painter and the trees and the mountains, the light and the colours that took his heart and soul. I went in. From the window of the little room that was furnished as his, I could see the burning sun, the red of the grass, the blue of the trees, the yellow of the sky, the same yellow that Luc had shown me. I stayed until the tourists around me had gone, looking at the mountains, thinking about the man who painted them, what had been in his heart of loneliness, endurance and hope. He had been sane here, madness was a burden he had shouldered but treatment had given him freedom at least for a while. He had given his transcendent gifts to the world who didn't want them then, and it had cost him his life. Luc had taken his life back, that would be my consolation.

When I turned to go, Luc was there in the doorway, waiting.

Epilogue

'Are you hungry, little Ada?'

The blue eyes are dark with thought. Her hands, her hair and her knees are splashed with orange paint. Her fair curls bounce as she nods, there is a pretty shell necklace around her neck. She is almost one and a half years old.

'Luc is going to cook some fish.' I don't call him uncle, though as her father's ex-brother-in-law that's who he is. Lizzie will explain one day.

Ada looks at her orange fingers and her knees then quietly tips forward into my chest, her arms around my neck. I stand slowly, the warm weight pulling my back. I don't care that this means sciatica, because this is one of those moments I wait for in the winter, like the moment when Lizzie gets off the train in Arles with Ada and I can hold them both and breathe them in. Happiness, like my hand in Luc's. Luc. Those are the things that complete my life, along with the sky in any season, the birds, the sea, the fire in winter. Happiness that I'd never thought possible.

Lizzie looks up, her back against the cherry tree, one finger keeping her place in her book. She smiles then looks down again, absorbed. She needs this space, she is busy with her teaching job, busy with Ada.

It wasn't easy but Victoria helped; one of the things I owe her, one of the countless things. She listened to Lizzie on the phone, she encouraged her to answer my emails and, later, to talk to me. She arranged for counselling on Zoom for both of us. I learnt things, hard things; Lizzie thought I'd ignored her as a child then tried to control her as an adult. She'd had to leave, though she hadn't gone as far away as I'd thought, or at least not for as long. She returned to London with Ada when her visa expired after six months and bought a tiny flat from the proceeds of the sale of the Salisbury one, then looked for a job. It took a year for us to meet in person but I didn't mind the wait, it was my second chance.

She hasn't told me everything. There are things I may never know, about her time with Blake in Salisbury or her thoughts concerning Ophelia. I know Ophelia and Nathan took good care of her when she lived with them in California, she had the best obstetric care money could buy. I'll always be grateful for that.

Luc has lit the barbecue. I walk round the garden with Ada in my arms. When we reach the graves in the shade of the pine tree she wriggles to get down. She squats on the ground to choose a fir cone, putting it on the smaller stone.

'Coco will love that. She was brave and friendly, like you.'

Ada is too young to really understand but she nods seriously. She turns to the larger stone, runs her orange fingers over the V, bends to smell the flowers. There are always fresh flowers on Victoria's grave, in the deep colours she loved.

'We borrow our bodies for such a little while, darling. Don't be sad,' she'd whispered. 'I've loved living near you.'

She had touched my face with trembling fingers, an effort. 'Take me with you.'

Van Gogh's colours paint the landscape around her grave, the afternoon sky is yellow. The mountains glitter. As the day ages, the glare softens and mauve shadows emerge. The light becomes pink and orange. The sky deepens from rose to crimson at the horizon.

We sit round the table in the garden, Luc, me, Lizzie and Ada. We will swim later and later still the darkness will creep over the garden, the cicadas will quieten. Stars will emerge and eventually the pale grey of the tombstones will be visible only by moonlight. As we sleep the view through our window will be reflected in the painting that hangs above our bed: trees and mountains and sky.

Acknowledgements

Thank you to my two extraordinary Harper Collins publishing editors on both sides of the Atlantic: Rachel Kahan of William Morrow and Phoebe Morgan of HarperFiction: your perception, wisdom and encouragement have meant the world. I feel very lucky to be working in tandem with such brilliant women.

To my agents Eve White and Ludo Cinelli thank you for the years of hard work, support and friendship.

Rhian Morgan, copy editor, whose painstaking approach made all the difference.

Nick Shaw Police Constable (retired) Advisor on all police and legal matters, I'm so grateful as always for your generous input.

Tricia Wastvedt. MA tutor, mentor and friend; you've taught me everything about storytelling. Thank you for your readings of *The Patient* and our conversations.

Warm thanks to Tanya Attapatu, Victoria Finlay, Emma Geen, Susan Jordan, Sophie McGovern, Mimi Thebo,

Vanessa Vaughan, Hadiza Isma El-Rufai; fellow writing group members. Ten years and counting.

To my husband Steve Gill and our children, Martha, Mary, Henry, Tommy and Johny. Thank you.